DEEP DARK RIVER

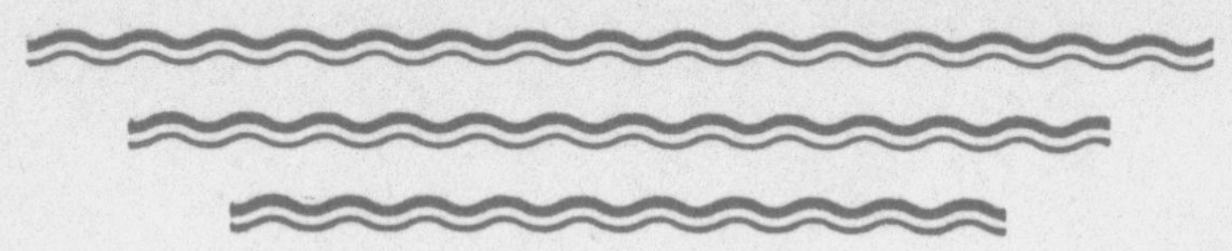

ROBERT RYLEE

DEEP DARK RIVER

FARRAR & RINEHART
INCORPORATED
ON MURRAY HILL NEW YORK

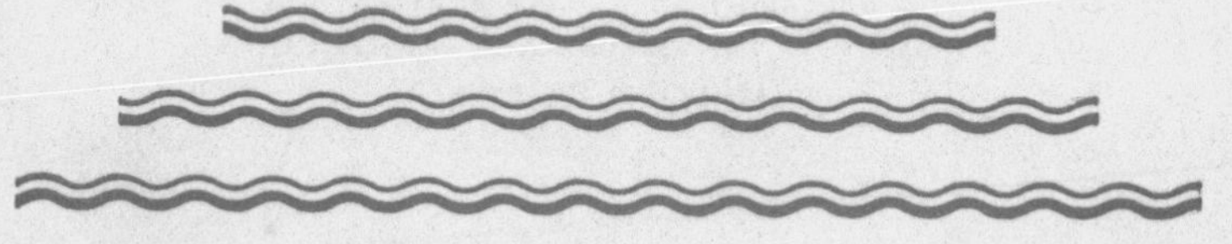

PART I

I

SHE is a woman of medium height and build. She wears a plain, dark blue dress with straight severe lines and a black straw hat of narrow brim, set somewhat back on her head, showing a high ridged forehead. A mass of dark brown hair frames an olive-skinned face and dark, somber, determined eyes. Her cheek bones and the two outer edges of the chin are prominent and there are heavy lines sloping down beside the nose to the corners of the mouth. Her hands are white and bony, and she holds in one of them a packet of papers. Walking from the door to the car that stands at the curb, she seems preoccupied; it almost seems that her lips move, as though she were carrying on an imaginary conversation. There is a certain manner in her walk and an arrangement of the features of her face that suggest a southern European. But it is not decided enough; one might be mistaken. It is an intelligent face with depth, vitality and the strength of sadness. There is latent force in it that might become bitterly aggressive or sharply sarcastic. It might easily warm into glowing sympathy. A touch of the mystic in it somewhere, a shadow of the unpredictable.

This woman is probably between thirty and thirty-five; certainly not less. Only by a miracle could a younger woman's face be so mature; more broken perhaps, but not so developed and intelligent.

The street is unpaved and arching trees hold it shadowed

as the car moves slowly away from the house. At the end of the street the car turns to the left and goes around the courthouse, a massive, gray stone structure, sprawling among the brittle-leafed oaks. The woman turns her head instinctively toward the building, but she seems to be looking into it and not at it.

After driving several blocks further past the stores and the hotel, she reaches her destination. It is a two-story brick building. Gold letters on the plate glass windows of the first floor say: Farmers and Merchants Bank. The room within is vacant, and there are dust and spider webs across the bars of the teller's window, and trash lies on the floor. The entrance to the room is cut across the corner of the building, and on the door one reads, in a diamond-shaped label,

MEMBER FEDERAL RESERVE SYSTEM
CAPITAL: $250,000.00
SURPLUS AND UNDIVIDED PROFITS: $50,000.00

The double door is locked.

The woman peers in through the door but does not stop. She goes around to the side of the building to the entrance to the second floor and climbs the steep wooden stairway.

The long hallway widens at one end where there is a large, full-bellied wood stove. The woman stops at the first door, which reads, Mary Winston, Attorney at Law. There are six other doorways opening off the hall.

An old negro porter said, "How is you dis mawnin, Miss Winstun?"

"Just fine, Uncle Moly, and how are you?"

"Yas'm, nicely, thank you."

"You didn't get your shot at the bank much too soon, Moly."

"What you mean?" He cocked his head on one side, apprehensively.

"I mean a sparrow wouldn't find much down there now."

"Ain't it de truf? Yas'm, but I done served my time an I wouldn't tetch nothin no more didn't blong to me. You knows dat."

"Well, you better not. I can tell you that. You'd never get off so easy again."

The porter half turned away, then grinned and chuckled to himself.

"What on earth's the matter, Moly?" She was puzzled.

"You know, Miss Winstun, an I don't mean nothin, but hit jes strikes me funny. In the gentlemin's offices I goes in an cleans an cleans, an befo lunch time dey is all littered up an has tobacco juice all over de floors worse'n a hog pen; an I cleans yore office an I goes back de next mawnin an it ain't never dirtied up."

"All right now, Uncle Moly; you have your little joke on me. Maybe I don't have many clients. But just you wait. You'll want me to do something for you sometime, and I won't forget about this."

"Miss Winstun, you knows I don't mean to say nothin to hurt yore feelins. You done been a fine lawyer. I hears folks say dat. You was only jokin. I can see dat. You is Moly's fren. Moly done know."

The woman turned the key in the lock and entered the waiting room to her office. It was a dingy little room, hardly lighted by the blackened windows. A few old law books were stacked on a table and there was a roll top desk, in one corner, and two straight-back chairs. The walls had once been painted cream color but were now a dirty brown.

She went on to her private office and sat down at a long table on which papers and folders were arranged in neat piles. She took off her hat and laid it on one corner of the table. Then she picked up a pencil and sat with it in her hand, gazing vacantly at the wall before her. After a moment, she roused from her revery and began to read over the papers she had brought with her.

Someone knocked at the outer door.

She called, "Just come in here, please."

A negro man came to the door and stood holding his hat.

"Good morning, Uncle. Did you want to see me?"

"Yes ma'am. Is you de lady lawyer?"

"Yes. I'm Miss Winston. What was it you wanted to see me about? Just come on in here."

"Well, I tell you, ma'am, I come to see you bout my cow."

"Is your cow sick? What's the trouble about your cow?"

"Well, not sick. Leastways I hopes not. I don't know. I wants you to help me git mah cow back."

"You'd better shut that door. Now you can sit down in that chair over there."

"You remembers a boy name Gotley, Walter Gotley?"

"Yes."

"Well, he done tole me how you hope him git his bonus money an I done hear de Red Cross speak bout you. You know de ladies at de Red Cross?"

"Yes. What did you say your name is?"

"Allen."

"Allen what?"

"Allen Southwick."

She wrote the name on the back of an envelope.

"I done think maybe you could git mah cow back."

"All right. You tell me about it and then I'll tell you if I can help you any."

"You likely knows de gentleman what's took de cow cause he's a lawyer here in Claksvul too, Mister Cawell."

"Yes, I know Mr. Caldwell. I can't believe he'd take your cow, not unless you owed him money."

"Well, dat's jest hit. He done say I owed him money. But, ma'am, hit's de truf, me an de other boys, we did tell him we'd try to raise a little money when pickin time come but I didn't never tell him he could have de cow. Charity, dat's mah wife, wouldn't part wid dat cow no more'n nothin. No, ma'am, she wouldn't. An you knows cullud people ain't none of 'em got no money dis time a year nohow. An he greed to hit an we greed on both sides an we left hit dat way. An then last week he come out an looked roun de place an he say, 'Allen, tell you what, I jes take de cow on count'; an I tole him hit waren't in de greement an how I needs de cow fer us an de chillen, an I tole him I'd jes give him a few pullets, how would dat do. An hit didn't suit him an he went off. Den de same evenin he waited twell I was gone an he come back wid a truck an showed Charity a paper, an she can't read nohow, an tole her I'd done signed de paper fer him to take de cow. An cose she left him have hit. When I went to see him bout hit, he tole me he'd done sposed of de cow an talked pretty rough an made me go on off. So I brung it up to Mister Dancy."

"What Mr. Dancy is that?"

"Mister Lucius Dancy out nawth o' Lisbon. I is on his place."

"Yes, I know him, too. Go on."

"Well, I brung hit up to him an he jes riled up all over. He say he git mah cow back shore nuff. An he gits in he car an come off to up here but when he git back, he done cooled down a heap. He say he don't think he better take no hand in it cause he don't rightly know jes how de greement was an all an he can't ford to make no hard feelins wid Mister Cawell, cause Mister Cawell a bad man to deal wid anyhow. So I didn't know what to do an I was boun I'd git mah cow back. I talked hit roun some an Walter tells me bout de bonus money, cose I'd done heard bout dat long time ago, an he say, 'Dey is one pus'n kin git de cow back an she's dat lady lawyer in Claksvul.' "

The woman smiled. "Now you haven't told me what you were owing money to Mr. Caldwell for in the first place. You said you and the other boys. What did you mean by that?"

"I was goin to git to hit. They is one or two more cullud people besides me, cose I is his brother, what was feelin like he hadn't done nothin an we fixed to git him a lawyer to git him off. An we tole Mister Cawell how we didn't have no money jest den but we'd git him some at pickin time. He says he'd look into it an he's done gone already and talked to Mose bout hit. But Mose, he say, he don't think Mister Cawell botherin hissef bout it much nohow."

"Who is Mose and what does he want a lawyer for? Is he in jail or what?"

"Yes'm, Mose, he mah brother, an he shore am in jail. Dey

got him fer murder, an Mose say dey goin to hang him fer shore or try to anyhow."

And slowly and in his own time Allen told what he knew of the murder, what Mose had told him and what he had learned from the other negroes on the plantation.

Mary said, "I am very sorry to hear about your brother. But if the story is as you say it is, I don't see how he could possibly be convicted. And I am sorry Mr. Caldwell took your cow. But since he has it, I question the advisability of your taking any action against him. I might be able to help you recover your cow, but it would not be the thing to do at this time, not while Mr. Caldwell is defending your brother. Do you see what I mean? I believe it would be better just to forget about it for the time being."

"Yes'm, I sees how you means. Only I thought maybe you could git Mose off yosef. Then you could git me mah cow too. Mister Cawell ain't got no notion botherin much bout Mose. Mose done studied hit out hissef, lak I tole you."

"But Mose has already entered into the case with Mr. Caldwell. It's not a matter about which I have anything to say."

"Yes'm, but he's a mind to drap Mister Cawell. He ain't got no claim on Mose. I done tole you bout us not bein able to raise no money. But we'd try to pay you a little in de fall if you'd help Mose. He goin to hang effn somebody don't help him. An Mose ain't nobody to help hissef none. Mose done been a good preacher an a good worker but he can't do nothin fer hissef, he done been all de time tied up."

"Does Mose ask me to defend him?"

"Yes'm, he do. He'd shore be bliged to you too."

"All right, Allen. I'll do my best for Mose, if I find everything just as you say. It was a mistake for you to go to Mr. Caldwell in the first place, but of course you can't be blamed for that. I can not say that I always agree with the way Mr. Caldwell does things. But the thing for you to do, if you really want me to defend Mose, is to go to Mr. Caldwell and tell him you have decided to get another lawyer. You must do that."

"Yes'm."

"I'll do what I can about the cow. But you want to understand in the first place that Mr. Caldwell hasn't got your cow at all. He's too smart for that. He's sold or killed that cow days ago. But maybe we can get him to pay for it."

"Yes'm, cause I shore needs the cow."

"Now about Mose. It's not the sort of case I want at all. You know that. But I hate to refuse to help him. He is really in a desperate situation. But I'd rather you'd think it over a little more. A day or two longer won't make any difference. You talk to Mose about it again, talk to your people and then you come back to see me if you decide you want me to defend him. If I don't hear from you again, I'll know you made some other plans and that will be all right."

In the early afternoon of that same day Allen came back with a note for Mary.

"I done talked it wid Mose agin and he done writ you a letter." He handed her the note.

It was penciled on a piece of brown wrapping paper. "I makes Miss Winsun my lawer abot the shoten. Mose Southwick."

Mary read the note carefully.

"You and your brother have decided you really want to do this?"

"Yes'm, we sholy does, if you'll do hit. Mose done say he know you do the best fer him."

"All right then, Allen, you tell Mose I'll do it. First thing, I'll see Mr. Caldwell about the cow, but not until you have had time to see him yourself to tell him what you've decided to do. Then I'll have a talk with Mose and the District Attorney. You come back in a day or two, and I'll let you know if I've been able to do anything about the cow."

"Yes'm, I'll see Mister Cawell. I'll be back. I'll be comin back to see Mose too." He bowed his way out of the office as from a holy place.

Later that afternoon, as Mary was leaving, she turned at the door and looked at the black letters across the glass of the door, remembering what Uncle Moly had said and what Allen had said. Moly had but echoed Clarksville through his own good nature. Allen had echoed Mississippi; and what else she did not know.

She walked down into the dirty street and was a contrast to it, walking erect and firm with quiet determination. This town was not hers, and yet it was too; she was part of it and lived in it because she loved it even as she hated it. Mississippi's town was hers; her father had given her that right. And again she knew that now she had set herself against it more strongly than ever.

PART II

I

IT HARDLY seems possible that nature herself will leave any permanent record of the journeyings of Mose Southwick, though there might be found some minor entry in the scribblings of a contemporary economist or local newsgatherer in the parish. In the general history of the times, such things as he suffered are trifling events from whatever angle observed, unless indeed the experience of having journeyed along a like road might cause someone to observe them from the point of view of Mose himself.

It so happened that a certain gravel pit in North Louisiana became exhausted (or perhaps the gravel market suffered from over-supply or under-consumption). However that was, a means of gaining subsistence was cut off from the diggers and shovelers, and Mose of necessity put off for the moment a universal view of the world and turned to the particular regard, the trivial, bread-and-butter regard. For, if a man is hungry, he inevitably regards particular things with great concern. It is only when his paunch is successfully filled and his roof is turning rain that his greatest happiness is extended into the realm of universals.

Perhaps, in briefest terms, men consider the greatest happiness as the attainment of some star, unseen and barely imaginable. One has said that, properly guided, a well-chosen team of black and white horses may reach this star. But this seems a too simple solution.

Mose was, then, a man who had looked beyond the realm of common things. By day he dug and shoveled in an energetic and faithful fashion, so that among the other negroes in the pit he was counted a good hand. But in the back of his mind there lurked an activity of far greater importance to him. Though not yet ordained, Mose had heard the call of God and longed to turn his collar hind-side-to and preach the inspired and chosen word. Under the kindly tutelage of Brother Vincent he had learned to read and write with fair ability, this instruction being given in return for an exactly calculated tenth of Mose's earnings duly deposited in the collection box each week. Evenings and Sundays Mose spent in the cultivation of this calling and of late had risen to the post of Senior Deacon, so that during sermon or prayer when he pronounced a well-intoned and emphatic "Amen," the brothers and sisters nodded assent and remembered that truth had been in circulation that day. The scriptures he could now decipher, at least orthographically speaking, with fair accuracy.

Sometimes, both in the interest of conserving his own strength and of instructing the neophyte, Brother Vincent himself took the Amen Corner at Wednesday evening prayer meeting and permitted Mose to speak the word from the pulpit.

Not an unpleasing figure he made, his craft-competent, powerful hands nervously and rhythmically cradling the holy book, his body swaying across the creaky platform. "My frens, I have heared the Lawd God speak to me." And Sister Benneson responded, "Hear dat man talk, hear him talk."

In the warm tangible twilight a smoky oil lantern suspended from the ceiling of the unpainted meeting house cast shadows into the corners where blue dirt daubers droned in restrained flight. Odors of cut pine came in the windows to mingle with unorthodox perfumes and body smells. But here Christianity flourished in its true form and original spirit. For one felt here the word as the Galilean spoke it, a word to a defeated and submissive people, promising to the patient and long-suffering an eventual reward.

Tall and black, with shoulders rounded and head drooped forward, Mose seemed to look out and up at his God in the attitude of some domestic fowl about to take flight. His long arms hung in front of his body in the easy position of a relaxed wrestler; his graceful, rail-like body accentuated his height. His kinky hair was close cut leaving a good stretch of shining forehead. "I have heared the Lawd God speak to me." You would not have doubted it; the earnest simplicity of his speech contained no guile. Doubtless he had, in one way or another, heard a divine voice. Surely no judge could rightly deny his allegation; let truth go with him as far as it may.

And Mose had had no particular reason to be inquiring or skeptical. Born into the travails of his race, he had accepted them and had turned into himself for a means to express the passionate warmth of his heart. For he was a steady and kindly individual, reasonable in action and expression, with that sureness of execution natural to people who are moving toward a desired consummation without any undue let along the way.

He came into the world in a shack beside the railroad tracks in a Texas city, where the position of the negro is possibly less wretched than across the Mississippi. He moved as a manual laborer from Texas into Louisiana and finally came to rest as a worker in the gravel pit. He thrust his shovel into the earth, loosed the gravel and sent it up over his shoulder into the waiting wagon. He kept his body clothed and received his just portion of pone, greens and sow belly with occasional fried fish and chitterlings as the seasons brought these delicacies to the market.

"Weary, weary, Lawd, this child am weary," he chants in mournful voice, and the shovel swings up into the air, heavy laden; "All day long I'se weary, Lawd," and the shovel is grinding at the earth again. But in mind Mose is living with the heroes of another age. "And Moses, he say, you lef my people go way from here." Mose is standing there himself, and great Pharaoh trembles; then the first born is dead, and he is beating a path across the wilderness. "Weary, weary, Lawd, this child am weary; all day long I'se weary, Lawd." But his spirit is fresh and hopeful.

When Sister Benneson flung herself about on her bench in an occasional ecstasy of religious fervor and the tumult spread among the faithful, Brother Vincent was interested to observe that the infection had no great hold on Mose. He maintained always a calm that seemed to provoke by contrast a more than usual response from the congregation. Consequently they came to like Mose as a preacher, and the old mammies, as they nodded over their snuff sticks, remarked, "Brother Southwick am shorely a right upstandin man. Don't ricollict I ever hear nobody preach better. An he do sing 'til you can feel the glory tetch your haid; that he do."

Though Mose had not been blessed with riches, he also had escaped their responsibilities. It had not been difficult for him to earn a living; he performed a daily task and received life's necessary goods in return. So the path of ideas through his head was quite likely to be in straight and simple lines. The necessity for the fine balancings and qualifyings that begins to appear along with logic and other collaterals of the educated, to the end of utterly sterilizing progressive thought, had not come to Mose. Not that this made his conclusions any more truthful or valuable, but for and in Mose they were an integration. He had a way of life and a view of life, that he could have related in a coherent fashion.

When the foreman at the pit said, "Mose, I'm sorry, but I've got to lay you off; you're a good nigger, but the pit's shut down," Mose said, "Yes, sir," and went his swinging way into the town.

He found Brother Vincent at the Superior Café, indulging in mock-cherry pie and coffee.

"They have shet down the pit," Mose said.

Brother Vincent wiped coffee from his chin. "You don't say? Shore 'nough? Well, Mose, the Lawd's hand is on the lamb and the Lawd will lay his hand on you too." Brother Vincent looked sad. His fees for tuition were endangered. As a minor cleric Mose had been unusual.

"I been thinkin," Mose said, "maybe I could be ordained now. I feels like I'm ready. Maybe the Lawd laid me by jest so's I could take up his work." And he leaned forward and looked at his senior with a solemn, inquisitive but laughing gleam in his eyes.

Brother Vincent wiped his mouth on his sleeve and showed some real concern. He was not always sure he really trusted Mose. As an apprentice Mose was not a competitor, but with a frock he would be another matter entirely.

"They's somethin in what you says, Mose; indeed they is, but the ways o' the Lawd ain't the ways of man. An when the Lawd do somethin, it ain't allus jest what it look like it is. You see it's this-a-way. Maybe the Lawd's ready fer you to take up his work and maybe he ain't. Maybe the Lawd want you to have some more trainin. Maybe the Lawd decide old Vincent done done you all the good he kin. Maybe he want you to travel round a little and find where they's work need doin more'n here in Biddyvul. I reckon the Lawd want to try you, Mose. Tha's jest it. The Lawd want to try you." Brother Vincent brightened considerably. When he had begun this discourse, he had not been sure where it would land, but it seemed to have turned out quite well.

Mose had not exactly followed this neat piece of divination, but he rolled his eyes in appreciation and murmured, "Uh huh."

Brother Vincent was too good a strategist not to follow up his advance. "An another thing, Mose, these is right hard times an they's goin to git a heap harder. I hears the white folks say things is shakin loose all round. You knows that yoresef, Mose. Up North they's been courtin the devil fer a long time. They's been gittin too high an mighty, an the Lawd's goin to humble 'em and bring 'em to they knees agin. It's the punishment o' the Lawd; tha's what it is. It's hard enough fer one preacher to git a libin in this town, let alone two. Ain't all white folks as liberal in the Lawd's work as you is, let alone cullud folks. But the Lawd'll reward you; he'll lay a mantle o' glory on you."

Mose caressed his skull with his lean, tapering fingers. "I knows that, Brother Vincent. But what is I goin to do?"

"Well," came Brother Vincent's next effort, "you got folks, ain't you, Mose? Why don't you go stay wid your folks?"

"My mammy an pappy's dead," Mose said. "An my sister Milly's husband don't like me nohow. But I got a brother what farms in Missippi. I ain't never tried farmin much, but maybe I'd do right well at it."

"Now that's a right good idea. If you goes and farms a while, it's more'n likely you can find you a church up there. Them Missippi cullud folks ain't very God-fearin. I reckon the Lawd would like for you to carry the word up there, Mose. But don't you be a fallin to bad ways." Brother Vincent accepted this as a decision made and dismissed. Mose would leave the local market for religion undisturbed.

And so Mose, as though guided by the hand of God, prepared himself to visit his brother, Allen Southwick, with a view to locating in or near his brother's domicile as a farmer. Removal from Bideauxville was not a matter of great difficulty; his belongings, including his Bible, could be tied into a small bundle.

Just before daybreak on a morning several days later Mose arrived at the river and walked along the bank under the great elms to the mooring post of the ferry that comes over from Ventura. The sky was just beginning to gray, a time to turn a man's thoughts inward, and Mose was troubled. Those past few days of walking and hitching rides on trucks, sleeping in open fields and being chased by dogs, had not been easily fitted into his philosophy. He liked an orderly existence and, lacking Brother Vincent's reassurances of God's assisting hand, he looked less calmly on the immediate future.

The river lay troubled and writhing before him. Muddy,

dark, uncommunicative, it flowed like some great despair, carrying driftwood of uncertain origin and destiny, agitated by whirlpools that sucked themselves into gaping mouths. Unbeaten through the centuries, it flowed on, a constant threat to the surrounding miles of black, fertile land, over which it sometimes spread itself in a mighty destructive rush; blasphemous, unsympathetic, crying to man of his own weakness and pitiful efforts. Unordered and blind, it followed no course; with the unpredictable fury of a beast it would flee its channel and cut a new course, leaving a chain of blue-green, cypress-guarded lakes like giant footprints to show where it had formerly been; a river built on sand.

To Mose it was as though he had come to the sea, beyond which lay an unknown and unfriendly land where he must find his fate. And at his feet this mourning, surging flood seemed somehow to speak of the transiency and final obliteration of all things. This was not the Jordan nor yet the sea of Galilee. It would have taken Brother Vincent's ablest discourse to have persuaded Mose, in his present frame of mind, that Jesus could have stilled this river. This was not water to be walked upon.

The ferry landing on the other side was hidden in an inlet behind a wooded island, so Mose searched in vain for the boat, the sight of which would have temporarily comforted him.

It began to grow perceptibly lighter. Smoke curled from the chimney of a cabin on the other side of the river. Then, not a dozen feet away, a rabbit hopped into view and whirled off into the underbrush when it saw Mose. A white heron swung out over the river like some lonely and graceful messenger. From a near-by shanty came the sounds of a creaking windlass and the clattering of pots and pans and the slamming of doors. Out of the mystery of night emerged a heated day. Mose shifted a greasy, worn black felt hat and scratched his crinkled hair. He rubbed his eyes and began a vain search through his pockets to see if any biscuit remained from the day before.

An old negro man, bent into a semi-circle with age, rocked up the road and sat down on a log by the landing. He grinned at Mose: "Mawnin."

"Good mawnin, uncle," Mose said. "What time that ferry boat git here?"

The old man giggled across his frayed gums. "Ain't no tellin that. Shore ain't. Sometimes it git here fore now. Sometimes it don't come a tall. But it'll be here fore long now. See that smoke?"

Behind the island a finger of agitated smoke seemed to move along the line of tree tops. A full, deep-toned note from the whistle further confirmed the presence of the boat.

Now a battered Ford and people on foot came to the landing. They watched the white river steamer creep out from behind the island. It cut an oblique course down stream across the main channel and then beat its way back up the bank in the quieter water, making a course about triple the straight distance across.

"See a boat try to come straight across one mawnin," the old man said. "Got out a little piece and jest sot thar whuppin the water, and then the old river commence to push her down, and she beat it back. Takes a powerful boat to whup that channel."

With keen admiration Mose heard the great stern paddlewheel churning the water and watched the husky stevedores bundling baggage about the deck. Streaks of red light shone from the boiler room, giving the faces of near-by men a strange glow.

With a creaking of beams a landing was made and a gangplank lowered to the log-road. Passengers on foot, autos and trucks were put ashore and others taken on; ropes were loosed from the mooring post, orders shouted to the pilot house and the boat started on the return journey.

By now the sunlight was a green, hot glaze on the surface of the river. Rising waves of heat blurred the outline of objects on the shore. Standing aft, Mose watched a turkey-buzzard sailing on the distant sky, searching for the decay that might have been thrown up by the night. The bird began to circle lower and disappeared below the horizon. The boat was made fast under the levee, and Mose crossed over and descended into the town of Ventura.

II

MISSISSIPPI is a state without a myth.

General Grant once came and sat at Vicksburg and got a victory child out of starvation. There is still a society composed of the descendants of those men who bought bonds of the State of Mississippi before the Civil War. On occasion they meet and calculate the accumulated principal and interest and draw up resolutions, but Mississippi sends them not even a magnolia blossom. And she never will; she can not.

Set in a pine grove in the red hills near Moss Mound there is a square white house, simple in design and structure. With pleasing dignity it looks down the broad pasture across the muddy creek to the woods beyond. A hundred yards to the side of the house there is the brick-walled burying ground of the family that originally built the house. There were two deaths of men in the family between 1860 and 1865. The terminal date of several stones is that of the great yellow fever epidemic that swept the hills in the latter part of the nineteenth century. On the back porch of the house a shiftless lad will show you a dark stain on the floor, the blood of the last of that family, shot down in feud-battle. The place is now let to tenant farmers. A white-haired woman, barefoot and toothless, with sagging, sapped breasts, cooks a stew of tomatoes and corn meal for her brood of jaundiced children who will swarm in at noon from the fields, an illiterate, stupid lot whose bearing has left the veins of her limbs purple and swollen.

Rains fall in the sandy hills in the north, and the creeks carry the water down across the broad delta plain to the river. Often in winter they overflow the country, to leave it later cold and sodden. Only in summer when the cotton blooms is there any evidence of natural vitality and energy. Midsummer comes soon; the plants are too large to be worked, and the crop is laid by. The land swells and burns under a full sun like some sickened tropical flower. The bolls burst, and the negroes sing down the rows, draping the cotton sacks over their shoulders like cowls. These are the few weeks of feverish activity when the crop is harvested in the fall. If it is sold at a good price, the negroes are robbed and excessive commitments are made in the sudden vision of wealth. If the price is low, as it usually is, cruelly high land taxes are left unpaid and the ever-present mortgage interest lapses. There is no diversion; one waits through the dull gray winter for another spring. Periodically, as a protest against the forced inactivity, there is a murder or a lynching, which affords a temporary relief from the monotony and an expression to the morbid passion of the people.

When the pantry is all too bare in the winter, the farmers will talk of planting more corn and sorghum next year and raising more cattle and hogs, but when spring comes, they plant cotton until it covers the black land like a white shroud, to be plucked away, leaving tough brown stalks to sway in the wind. The priests of all the professions devise nostrums, but the Thebans knew better than this thousands of years ago.

And yet,—miles of black clinging earth under the cotton

rows, with brushing lanes of green leaves and pink and white fragile blossoms; silent moccasins in the stagnant bayous; negroes in their cabins, chanting against the night, haunting memory even to man's last day; cypresses, the loveliest and stateliest of trees, never quite achieving the bloom of other living things, dark and rough, mysterious as the faces of old and bitter men, with tops thrust against the heavens and roots sunk in the slimy ooze of the swamp. Against the distant sky the repulsive vulture becomes beautiful and graceful. The summer's consuming heat, rising off the cane brakes, stills the very insects into a dull trance. The gray winter days are a cold sadness, when the smoke from the chimney tops lies heavy upon the ground.

Such a land does not have poets and songs. Its people are likely to see it as those women see the world who sit intently at their windows, tapping on the glass, calling softly to men who pass in the streets without. And so some of them have seen it, but they have not seen all. For no man can quite blot out the face of nature. He may drive his furrows deep and far into the earth and may breed all manner of strange things from her broad, hard flanks, but eventually his grasp weakens on the plow handle, and wind and rain will level the nice rows he has made; the vines will creep out from the woods into the fields; the summers and winters will continue in their endless rotation, absorbing his dust and preserving it.

III

VENTURA, the town to which Mose had come, lies upon the heart of the river plain. It is not different from a score of delta towns. There is a red brick court house, an empty stone watering trough, unused for many years, and a square of brick store buildings, none over two stories in height. Tin awnings cover the sidewalks. There is a hotel, where greasy food of a sort and brackish coffee are served, advertised as "Cooking—Southern Style." Up the side streets, leading off the square, are frame and corrugated iron buildings, feed stores, garages and stables. Beyond these are a hundred or so frame dwellings. A railroad track comes down the center of the town; the whites live on one side and the negroes on the other. When a white man crosses the tracks after dusk, he pulls his hat low and keeps in the shadows.

In recent years some of the streets have been paved, but from the others the dust still rises in clouds to settle over the town, graying the chinaberry trees and the thin, untended lawns. It is a desolation of dull tones, without any touch of beauty or aspiration.

Mose gave little notice to the architecture of Ventura. He came directly down the main street past the court house, continued beyond the depot and crossed over into niggertown to where a sign on a low building proclaimed, "Hot Cat Fish—For Colored."

He sat at a long bench in front of a counter. Before him,

tacked on the wall, was a rotogravure print of Christ with the crown of thorns and a bleeding heart, this being flanked by colored comics from the Sunday newspapers.

A mulatto girl clad in a tight calico dress brought him his coffee, fried salt pork, biscuits and molasses. The meat was rank and the sorghum strong, but Mose liked them all the better for it.

"Them is good victuals," Mose said.

"Course they is," the girl agreed. "Ain't I cook 'em myself?" She was sweeping the litter of the previous day from the floor but paused to look at Mose critically. "Maybe you wants somethin to shore nough warm yoresef, and if you does, that's what I got. Boy, it'll burn yore guts."

Mose blinked and grinned at the girl. He was cautious by nature, but being at present homeless and lonely, he felt a touch of daring come over him. He had not had much experience with liquor; Brother Vincent had tied it up too closely with hell and damnation. It burned his throat besides.

"How much it cost?" Mose asked. "I means jest one good throw an these victuals."

The girl figured silently for a moment. "Give you one good slug an the breakfast, all for two bits."

Mose nodded assent, and the girl retired to the kitchen. He heard what sounded like a top being unscrewed from a Mason jar, and presently she returned with a china cup a third full of a clear liquid. Mose took a deep breath and drank. His throat seemed to close up completely. He coughed silently and beat on his chest with his fist. "Befo God, gal, tha's the devil's own water."

"Sure, hit's got power."

Mose leaned back to enjoy the comfortable warmth creeping over his body, cleaning the particles of food off his gums with deliberate thrusts of his long tongue.

"You is a stranger here, ain't you? You ain't come from Ventury?"

"No'm," Mose answered, "I comes from Lousiana. Jest got off the ferry dis mawnin. Lawdy, I was shorely skeered too. Out in de middle o' dat river dat boat didn't look like nothin at all; no, woman, it shorely didn't. Dat river could a busted dat boat to smithereens jest like I could bust a maypop in my hand. But the Lawd done guided my feet over, and I aims to keep 'em on de groun fer a right long spell."

"Why, boy, you don't know what you talkin bout; no, indeed. Dat river out dere now ain't nothin no more'n a big branch. You ought to see hit in flood time. I wouldn't walk under dat levee in flood time no more'n I'd ask the Lawd to strike me dead. You kin hear it roar plumb cross dis town. An you listen to what I'm tellin you. One of these days hit's goin to bust clear through dat levee, and then it's goin to be kingdom come in Ventury, shore nough."

Mose assented meekly, "Well, I guess dat's so. I guess it is now."

"You aim to stay here in Ventury?"

"No'm, I don't reckon so. I done lost my job. I'se gone and left Lousiana fer good, I guess. I'se goin up to Claksvul to where my brother's at to see kin I git a job up there."

"What your brother do?"

"He farms."

The girl spat vigorously on the floor. "Boy, that ain't nothin; tha's worse'n nothin. They ain't nothin in farmin fer white folks, an it's jest plain hell fer niggers. I has hear white folks say dat. I kept house wid a man on a farm once.

I didn't last no time. It like to busted my body in two. Dis here's hard enough fer me, but I gits along." She smiled and adjusted her dress.

"Yes'm," Mose said, "but a body is bliged to do somethin less he want to starve to death."

"You can have it if you wants it, but none o' farmin fer me."

Mose heard a rattling at the back door. The girl left the room, telling him, "You jest make yoursef at home whilst I see who's makin all dat fuss out there."

She was gone for some time, and Mose listened to the ensuing commotion in the kitchen. Apparently a white man and a negro had entered. The white man spoke of some chickens just hatched out and laughed loudly. Mose could smell the unmistakable odor of new whisky and concluded the restaurant business was a minor part of the activity of the girl's establishment.

When she returned, she explained, "Jest some mens come to leave me some groceries."

"Yes, I could tell dat," Mose said. "Now how much you say I owes you? Two bits?"

"Tha's right."

With complete lack of modesty and caution Mose pulled a small roll of bills from his pocket, his total wealth, and handed over a five dollar note. "Maybe you could change dat. I could use it."

The girl reached in a drawer under the counter and handed him his change. Then she placed two cups on the counter. "Jest you have one wid me befo you goes. Jest you an me; what you say? Ain't cost you nothin." She leaned over the counter, so that the top of her dress fell away from her body.

Mose took a good look, with the feigned unconcern of a connoisseur. "I done had a right smart already," he said. "I reckon maybe I ought to be gittin on up the road. I done got a heap further to go. How fur is it to Claksvul?"

"Aw hit ain't so fur. They'll be more passin later on. Course if you don't want it, tha's different. You jest got to say so."

Mose reflected a moment. The girl smiled full lipped at him and turned her head sideways. She held the jar poised to pour. "What you say, big boy?"

"Well, jest a small one. Maybe they will be more passin later on like you says."

The girl poured and pushed one cup over toward Mose. She lifted hers and looked across the top of it at him. "I hopes it don't burn you plumb down."

Mose was not posted in the etiquette of such occasions but he half lifted his cup with a solemn gesture. "Yes'm, I does too."

They drank.

"You takes dat like it was water," he said.

"Boy, if you'd drank as much o' dat stuff as I is, you would too."

Mose responded to this by delivering himself of long deep laughter, more to express his rising spirits than for any other reason. "I guess tha's so, I guess it is. I ain't what a body'ud call a drinkin man mysef."

"What you do befo you come over here?"

"I worked in a sand pit, an—" He hesitated, thinking his other occupation might not seem just in keeping. "I did other things besides. Mostly I jest worked in the pit. But they shet it down. I vized wid folks. Yes'm, I vized wid a heap o' folks an hit didn't seem they was nothin else to do but to come up on to Missippi. I has some business to tend to up at Claksvul an I reckon maybe I'll stay there an farm."

The girl came around and sat on the front side of the counter, resting her feet on the bench beside Mose, who looked with interest at the pink garters she had managed to have in full view just above her knees. "Maybe you'd like to stay here wid me. What you think bout dat? You an me could git on."

"No'm," Mose answered. "I couldn't do dat. I couldn't do you no good nohow. I ain't know nothin bout this here business. Course I ain't makin no jedgement; I jest tries to keep out o' trouble. Dis here ain't de Lawd's work. You knows dat. You ought to give dis here up. De Lawd'ud open de door wide to take you in. He'd retch his hand out to you."

The girl pulled her skirt down. "Liquor sets funny on your stomach, don't it? Give most mens a drink, an they'll have they hands on you befo it gits good settled in 'em."

"Yes'm, I guess as how that's so."

"You say you was goin up to Claksvul. Was that hit?"

"Yes'm. It ain't jest at Claksvul; it's up that way. I ain't never been there."

"Jest you wait here a minute." The girl went to the back door and called, "Callie, oh, Callie." She had a powerful, resonant voice. "Oh, Callie, where's you at?"

A negro girl came from a near-by shanty.

"Where Shorty?"

"I don't know, mama. I ain't see him."

"Well, git on down town an find him. An tell him to come on home. Tell him I wants to see him."

She returned to Mose. "I done sont for Shorty. He been sayin for a week he goin to have to go up to Leander. Tha's part way to Claksvul. He'll take you that fur wid him. Now you come on out an wait in the kitchen 'til he git here."

Mose followed her into the back room and sat, as he was directed, on the edge of the bed, while the girl gathered the dirty dishes in a large pan on the stove. There was a strong smell of cheap perfume in the room, and Mose sniffed. He did not exactly dislike it, for he preferred things to smell and taste strong, but it was strange to him.

On nails along the wall clothing was hung; soiled clothing lay across the bed and on the floor. In one corner of the room were several half-gallon and quart jars of white whisky. A double-barreled shotgun lay on a shelf beside the door. There was a dresser with cracked white paint; to the mirror was pasted a yellowed photograph of the girl and a man.

"Callie, she yo' gal?"

"Yes, she mine. But she ain't no count. She too triflin to be no good. I use to whup her, but it didn't make her no better. She ain't stay here much no more. She's gittin a pretty big gal now. She got her a man, I think, but she don't say nothin to me bout it. I don't ask her neither. I don't like to mess in the chile's business."

"Hit's the way wid chillen. You brings 'em up an they goes off an leaves you."

During the interval until Shorty appeared Mose waited in the kitchen with the girl. Twice a customer appeared and purchased a bottle of whisky. Mose was astonished to find himself so little concerned at being in the midst of this unlawful traffic. It was merely a new phase of life that he had not observed hitherto, and he was curious. He questioned the girl about the source of the liquor and the profit. She was vague in her answers but let him understand that hers was a protected monopoly in niggertown, guarded by a certain white man connected with the local sheriff's office. She merely acted as agent and got part of the profits for herself and was not molested in her business.

"An dis man Shorty you done sont after, he your husband?"

"Well, he is an he ain't. He is more'n anybody else. He has a intrust in dis here place."

Mose did understand this situation very well. It was a problem he and Brother Vincent had discussed at length. A woman's security and the possibility of a high morality among women were two things that men, both black and white, seemed to consider as infringements on their native rights. At least it seemed so to Mose.

"He treat you good?"

"He treat me pretty good." She paused for a moment. "Boy, jest what the hell difference that make to you anyway? You the most buttin-in nigger I see fer a long time."

Mose did not reply to this, and the girl continued nervously with her dishwashing.

Presently a noisy Ford touring car came to a halt in the back yard, and Callie and Shorty got out. Callie called, "Here Shorty, mama," and went lazily off across the lot.

Shorty had been well named. He seemed to have been sawed off somewhere. A withered leg gave him a shuffling walk that added to his stumpy appearance.

He clambered up the steps and thrust his head against the

screen door. "Belle, jest what the devil you mean sendin Callie after me? I has a mind to take a round out o' you." He saw Mose sitting on the bed, quietly observing him, and paused. The girl did not wait for him to enter the room but went out herself some distance from the house and talked to him in a low voice that Mose was unable to hear.

Shorty came back and stuck his head in the door. "Belle tell me you goin up to Claksvul."

"Tha's right; I'se goin to Lisbon; tha's right at Claksvul. But I don't want to put you out none."

"You ain't puttin me out none. Come on an git in, an I'll take you as fur as Leander. That'll save you some."

Belle and Shorty got in the front seat and motioned Mose to the back. The car sputtered and heaved and finally got under way. Mose felt a certain tension in Shorty's attitude toward him and concluded it was because Belle's Samaritan act did not appeal to Shorty.

They drove slowly out of the town and took the road north. They had to cross a dilapidated wooden bridge over the bottoms at the edge of town. It trembled under the weight of the car, and Mose took a tight hold on the seat. From there a mile or so of narrow concrete extended to the county line, where the gravel road began. Passing cars made it necessary for Shorty to edge off the concrete at frequent intervals. The heavy dust behind each car was stifling. As Shorty was not a skillful driver, it promised to be a rough trip. But Mose was used to springless wagons and he thought it a pleasant mode of travel.

Now they were out in the country under a full June sun. It was late morning and hot. The highway paralleled the railroad track, laid on an embankment too high to see over.

But on the right were the broad fields of cotton with woods beyond. Here and there a cypress swamp held out against the progress of civilization. The cabins of the negro laborers squatted picturesquely against the earth.

Mose studied the scene eagerly. Some place like this was to be his home. Soon he would be in those fields himself. He felt a strong desire to be at his work and was sorry it was so late in the year. At best now he must harvest another's crop. Many months would pass before he could break ground for his own planting. Belle's warning was soon forgotten. Already these were his people. Children standing on the porches of cabins waved to the passing car, and Mose lifted his arm in return, the gesture having for him the significance of a benediction.

They came to a place where the road widened in front of a country store. Shorty stopped the car and bought some gasoline.

"How fur is it from here to Leander?" Mose asked.

"Tain't so fur. Tain't so fur," Shorty replied, laughing. Mose failed to understand the laughter but inquired no more. They took up the journey again, continuing for about two miles to where a dirt crossroad led to the east.

Shorty slowed the car and turned off.

"Where we goin?" Mose asked in sudden alarm.

"Jest you wait an see," Shorty shouted across his shoulder. "Dis here a short cut."

The road became a narrow twin-rut that skirted a woods dense with undergrowth. On the left high green corn was so close Mose was tempted to reach out his hand to brush the graceful blades. The road twisted frequently following the uneven line of the field, so that the highway was soon lost from view.

They reached a small branch or stream overhung with leaning trees and trumpet vines. Shorty switched off the engine. He got out and shuffled toward the bank down which the ruts made an irregular track to the bed of the stream.

"They ought to be a bridge over dis branch. I'm goin to have a good look fore I tries to git across. These here branches has quicksand in 'em."

Mose felt that, being sound of limb, he should assist and got out too. He walked quickly ahead intending to try the bed of the stream himself. As he passed, he noticed Shorty dropped his right hand to his back pocket, but it did not seem important at the time. Only later he remembered it. As he got just in front of Shorty, he heard a scream from Belle that was suddenly cut short by a dull, soggy blow on the base of his head. He could no longer see; his consciousness seemed jumbled and whirling and then collapsed; the world became black.

IV

When Mose regained consciousness, he was lying in the thick weeds on the creek bank. The heat was consuming his body, and his head throbbed with pain. He felt in his pockets, knowing beforehand that he would find nothing. The futility of pursuit and the injustice of his situation overwhelmed his self-possession, and he lay for some moments sobbing audibly, beating the earth with his clenched fist. "Sweet Jesus, sweet Jesus," he murmured, "that dirty, stinkin nigger."

On one of the branches of a great gum tree a gray, slender mockingbird was working over a minor symphony. Mose struggled to his feet, gathering great clods of earth into his hands, and charged toward the tree, hurling the clods. The bird fluttered and flew away, leaving Mose trembling under the tree. "I show you. Set dere an holler at me. I'll bust you wide open."

He walked down into the creek and drank the muddy water and bathed his face and head. He brushed the dirt off his clothes and clambered up the bank into the road and walked slowly back toward the highway, hunched forward, shuffling and muttering to himself. But Mose did not have the proper energy to maintain the passion of anger and before he had gone very far, he was humming quietly to himself. But it was a sadder and a wiser tune. For perhaps the first time Mose was becoming aware that the conflict of life is not always fraught with results of an immediately calculable value.

Mose had no intention of returning to Ventura. He knew the chance of recovering his stolen money was small, and the pleasure of revenge, which might take much time and was assuredly a dangerous enterprise, seemed of less importance than his present objective. Revenge is to many people a religion that exacts endless and wearying sacrifices, often leaving the worshiper broken and unsatisfied. Mose rejected it on simple, practical grounds.

When he turned into the highway and started north again, he tucked the entire unpleasant episode back in an unused corner of his head. If this then was the way of life, he resolved to experience it with what fortitude he might be able to command.

Mile by mile he proceeded until at the end of the second day he reached the little town of Lisbon, which is situated some eight miles west of Clarksville and half as far again to the river. It is a dreary little collection of walls that house the commerce and family life of a farming community. It has the appearance of being neglected and forgotten, having none of that dignity that some villages have retained that have built up a traditional life for themselves long after the front rush of civilization has deposited them and swept on ahead. The little buildings stand like snuff-rotted stumps of teeth, the fences are loose and falling, the board walks decayed until walking on them is a perilous adventure for the barefooted children. And just a little distance away the cotton fields begin, and further, there against the sky, the great warm breathing forest is waiting, patient and alive. In the distance, through a break in the trees, rises the long ridge of the levee, like the grass-encrusted remains of an ancient battlement, suggesting the great beating artery of the land, against which it is raised.

Poking about among the shanties of the negroes, Mose inquired about his brother. Some of them had heard of him, others shook their heads. "Allen Southwick? Don't rightly remember I ever hear o' him."

At one door, after he had pounded long and vigorously, a woman loosed the chain and put her head out. "What you want, man, beatin on a body's door like this? Ain't you see I was comin jest as fast as I could?"

"I was wantin to ask you is you know a colored man call hissef Allen Southwick."

"I never hear tell o' him." She slammed the door shut and rattled the chain into place. Mose turned and started down the steps. From the window the woman called after him. "Who is you?"

"I is his brother."

"An who was you wantin to see?"

"Allen—Allen Southwick."

"Well, now why didn't you say dat in the fust place? Jest you come back and set on the gallery. I'll be out terectly."

In a few moments the door reopened, this time with broad cordiality, and the woman stepped onto the porch, still patting her apron with regal regard for its neatness.

"So you is Mr. Southwick's brother. Well, I is glad to know you. I is Molly—Molly Anderson. I is Felix Anderson's wife. Felix, he ain't here."

"I is Mose Southwick. Dis the fust time I was ever in Lisbon. I is lookin for my brother. I was comin to think I wasn't goin to find nobody what knowed him."

"Yes, I knows him, Allen Southwick. Indeed I does. He out on Mr. Dancy's place. Out wid he wife an the chillen."

"Where Mr. Dancy's place at?"

"Well, now I show you." The woman stood at the edge of the porch and pointed off to the northwest. "You goes down dis here road to the church house, and you turns up there, and you goes on quite a way 'til you comes to a white house wid bee gums in the side yard. Dat's Mr. Dancy's house. Then you goes on down that very same road 'til where it goes through the new ground. You can tell the new ground. A little piece past there is Allen's very house where he live. It set under a big pecan tree. You can tell it cause it's de fust house you come to. You tell Mr. Allen I axed after him."

She stopped for a moment and then asked with open curiosity, "You jest visitin?"

"Well, no'm, not jest visitin. Course I does aim to visit a spell wid Allen." Then Mose explained to the woman his ultimate purpose in coming to Lisbon.

"Now shore nough that's nice. Allen, he'll shore be glad to see you."

Mose thanked her and continued on his way. He found the small weather-browned church with an old rusty plantation bell hung beside it. He would have liked to pull at the bell rope but refrained. But he did stop to peer in through the open door at the bare, rude benches and the rough, unpainted pulpit. Mose had not forgotten Brother Vincent's command that he carry the word with him.

Nearing his destination, he felt warmed at the thought of the coming reunion with his brother. The memory of his recent unhappy experience was almost completely gone. It had been many years since Mose and his brother had played together as boys, but Mose felt sure there was a bond of affection that had survived the separation. Clearly he recalled the day when they two had stood on the steps of the store house and the white man came out the door and cursed Allen. Allen resented it, and, being overconfident of his strength, had drawn his knife. Mose had pulled him off the white man before harm was done and got him home. Their mother had wisely bundled Allen to the edge of town and bade him depart before the white man's wrath descended on their house. News of his brother since that time had not come often, and Mose naturally wondered what changes time might have wrought.

Mr. Dancy's house with the bee gums came into view. It was a comfortable-looking place with a large rambling yard and extensive screened porches, carelessly kept but with a genial atmosphere.

The road continued further through the new ground where the burned stumps dotted the land. The partly decayed bark of trees was still mingled with the soil. The cotton plants were green and vigorous, nourished on the rot of centuries of fallen leaves and vines. Toil had at last broken the forest away, and the labor was being repaid by a luxuriant crop.

Just a short distance ahead was an unpainted shotgun cabin consisting of three rooms set one directly behind the other. The windows were shuttered. The roof was of curling hand-cut cypress shingles. A chimney on one side poured forth a thick gray smoke. In the back yard was a chopping block with the ax stuck blade-down into it. Pigs were grunting into the trough in the hog lot. In a shed a cow was nuzzling her food. The narrow front porch of the house was partly shaded by a gourd vine. Mose was not sure, but it seemed he noticed the smell of human habitation in addition to the pungent smell of the wood smoke. It was an inviting and substantial smell.

He opened the gate and went up to the steps. The door was closed, but he could hear people moving about inside and a subdued sound of soft voices. It was probably supper time. Mose stopped and listened with pleasure and contentment before he knocked.

A child opened the door and stood without speaking, looking at him.

"Where your papa?"

Without answering the child ran back into the house.

A chair scraped across the floor and a man came to the door, followed by a woman and children crowding out behind him trying to see who the visitor might be.

"You was wantin to see me?"

Mose hardly recognized his brother, and it was obvious he did not recognize Mose.

"Is dis where Allen Southwick live?"

"I is Allen."

"You ain't know who I is?"

"I don't think so."

"You shore you ain't never see me befo?"

"Well, maybe I is, but I don't remember." He turned to the woman. "You know dis man?"

"Ain't never see him in my life."

"You ain't remember a body name Mose?"

The man came out to the light of the porch. "Well, a body couldn't a told me I wouldn't remember my own brother. Charity, you jest step out here. Dis is my brother Mose. Mose, dis is my wife and these is our chillen." He seized Mose's arm and patted him, and the two examined each other carefully. The children, five in number, the oldest a boy of about twelve, old enough to be a hand in the fields, and the youngest a toddling baby girl, hung wide-eyed and silent about their parents, trying to establish the relationship of this man descended into their midst.

It took some time for the awkwardness to wear off. Putting two men together and calling them brothers is not enough to indicate just what the ultimate exchange of feelings may be. For Mose and Allen it was necessary to go back a long way to find any community of experience, but at least their last meeting had been of a tragic and dramatic nature, which proved a link of no mean value between them. Gradually the edge wore off and it became, "Well, now shore nough, Mose," and "Jest like old Allen."

Finally Charity interrupted them. "Maybe you all is goin to stand here makin talk like dis all night, but dese chillen is got to be fed. Allen, ain't you goin to axe your own brother in for some victuals? Where is your manners, man?"

By the time supper was eaten and the children gone to sleep on their pallets on the floor of the front room, darkness had come; and, sitting on the porch of the house, the two men, without either making any acknowledgment of the fact, were keenly aware of the presence of nature in the surrounding fields and woods. The earth seemed to be alive and close about the little cabin.

Allen had not remained the lean, awkward boy Mose had played with. He had never been tall and now, grown considerably heavier, he looked much older than his actual years. After eating he unbuttoned the top buttons of his trousers and opened his shirt both to relieve the pressure on his body and to be cooler in the oppressive heat. He had begun to gray, and flabby wrinkles gave his face a lazy kindliness.

His eyes were dull and sleepy as those of a dog before the hearth. He did not like labor overmuch, and weeds were not uncommon on his acres. Sitting now with his back against the wall of the house, he spoke without any noticeable movement of his lower jaw,—the words seemed to roll off his thick lips.

Mose had hoped to find a much more enterprising individual, but had no desire to criticize. Allen's family seemed well fed and cared for. Perhaps that was enough to ask of any man.

After all, Mose had notions in his head that did not bother most people; no use to judge all people by himself.

"What you think bout dis? Think Mr. Dancy could take on another hand?"

"Ain't do no harm to axe him. Mr. Dancy, he good to niggers, but I don't spect he goin to have nothin fer you to do, leastaways not befo next year. Crops is done all in the ground, and Mr. Dancy, he say ain't no use to have crops nohow cause you ain't goin to git nothin fer 'em. Last year they was many a bale what didn't git out of the fields. Waren't wuth pickin. Now what you think bout dat?"

"Hit don't seem right after a body's done worked the crop to lef it rot on the ground."

"No, course it don't, but white folks has to mess wid things like dat. Us niggers don't know nothin bout it. It like Mr. Dancy done say, jest do like a body is told to do an let de white folks do de runnin o' things. I looks to Mr. Dancy; all the hands on the place does. Mr. Dancy done look after his niggers. He a good man to work fer."

"You don't think maybe Mr. Dancy let me work fer him?"

"Ain't do no harm to axe him, jest like I say. If he don't want you, maybe he let you stay here wid me. You can help me long through the summer an wid the pickin in the fall. Course it wouldn't be nothin in it fer you cept a place to stay."

"Dat's obligin of you, but it ain't right to your chillen for me to be eatin of they victuals when my bein here ain't goin to make them victuals no more'n they is now."

"Don't you worry bout dat none. They'll be victuals nough for you, Mose. They'll always be a little extra pot likker an side meat. They'll be hogs to kill in the fall an corn comin on too; goin to be havin roasin ears fore long now. That cow done give a right smart o' milk. We goin to git by one way or another. But they was times last winter when they wasn't nough to eat. The chillen would roll an holler in they sleep thout wakin up; they stomachs was pinchin 'em fer victuals. That was jest what it was, an the Red Cross got plenty to do wid white folks down to Lisbon an Claksvul, let alone feedin niggers. But Mr. Dancy, he help the niggers some. He ain't goin to let us starve, not thout he have to to keep from starvin hissef."

It became very apparent to Mose that here was a fight for existence that would have to be won before there would be time for anything else.

"Well, ain't no use to bother no more bout that now; it can wait 'til mawnin, I guess."

"Ain't it de truf?" Allen replied. "Things generally does wait when you left 'em alone. But you can shore spile some things by pokin 'em too much. Now I got some melons over in that fur patch ain't goin to wait if dem chillen don't quit thumpin 'em to see is dey ripe. They goin to have my melons plumb wore out."

"Melons ain't ripe yit?"

"No, they was late dis year. Done plant 'em when the moon was wrong. Mr. Dancy, he say moon don't have nothin to do wid melons. Last year his melons done shrivel up an bust open an my melons was de best dis side o' Lisbon. Tell me moon don't have nothin to do wid melons."

Mose did not care to enter this controversy. When Allen had finished speaking, he remained silent for some minutes and then asked, "Allen, you ain't never axe me how come I done left Lousiana an come up here."

"Well, Mose, I figgers if you want to tell me, you goin to in yore own good time, an if you don't want to, you ain't, an either way what's all right wid you is all right wid me. But you can let that rest easy a while too. Charity, she goin to find out an when she do, she goin to tell me. Maybe I was jest waitin, knowin I was goin to find out after while anyway. Charity, she visits about wid the ladies in the church, an when somethin happen, it retches her all over 'til she find out all bout it an jest how it was, an don't nothin generally git past Charity."

"Well, den, I guess I jest wait an tell Charity."

"Save you tellin it twice."

For a long time the men sat talking. Mose was interested to hear Allen tell of the small happenings on the plantation that seemed to him the beginning and end of the world. "Is this man really my brother?" Mose asked himself. How strange that two men could walk the same road and each reach a different destination from the other. To Allen life was a series of days filled with tasks and pleasures and sorrows. Mose felt a desire to encompass these things somehow, to see beyond them. Even now, though he saw rather clearly the immediate problem before him, he had assumed a detached position. He wanted very much to be within life, but he was equally desirous to be without life.

"I thinks maybe I is goin to like it, bein here," he told Allen.

V

IF A man were seated before his breakfast table and saw two men approaching him with respectful manner, he might remark, "Two of my brothers in Christ's love are coming to seek me, and I shall inquire solicitously after them." But as Lucius Dancy sat before his table looking out the window down the road, he remarked to his wife, "That's a strange nigger coming down the road with Allen; wonder what the devil they're up to this early."

Mrs. Dancy finished pouring her cup of coffee and turned to look. "It's my guess they're headed this way and that if Allen has his way, you'll be a poorer man after they leave."

"Forewarned is forearmed," said Mr. Dancy. "With the present size of my pocketbook I'll be equal to them."

And Mr. Dancy smiled in pleasure at what he had said. He was a man whose wisdom consisted in repeating little phrases he heard here and there. He did not understand exactly what they meant, but accepted them if they had a good and orthodox sound.

To Mr. Dancy Memphis was a large and probably wicked city; he had been there. New York was mythological. The Sunday newspaper was his art, the hymn book his music. Between sleep and that amount of work necessary to produce a moderate degree of comfort it would be difficult to see which was vocation and which avocation. Yet Mr. Dancy was a progressive. He had a toothbrush which he used almost daily and a large tin tub which he used weekly. He had even written a communication to the Memphis *Daily Herald* on the necessity of malaria control. A copy of it was framed and hung in the parlor, but it was badly faded and would soon be beyond reading. It had represented a supreme mental effort and had lifted Mr. Dancy to a position of some importance in his own eyes. He exerted an influence and was a substantial citizen, he thought; not just a common down-at-the-heels farmer. This made life more vital to him. He served on the building committee of the church in Lisbon and had even sought to make himself known in Clarksville by means of his pretense of controlling the farm vote in his section of the county.

Mr. Dancy could not quite reconcile his position and his ability. He should have done so much better in other circumstances. He had informed his wife of this, and she did not disagree with him. True, it was her dowry that had paid for their land; yet he had wanted to go to Memphis to open some commercial enterprise. But his wife, being bred from the soil herself and having the authority of money, had voted for the farm, and he had been forced to submit. He had held it against her, not maliciously, for he was a just man, but rather as an academic question that could be discussed calmly. A man must make sacrifices for all things, he said. He had sacrificed much to the love of his wife. He would not complain. He and she had both been faithful and had lived righteously. That was no disgraceful fact.

That Mr. Dancy occupied a better position than most other men, for his land was free of debt and he was fairly well endowed with worldly goods, was surely no fault of his. He had in no way added to the sum of the gifts bestowed upon him. He took for himself the value which is placed by the world upon men in proportion to their wealth.

Mr. Dancy had that sleek appearance of worms on ripe peaches. He had not been observed in adversity. Stalwart and righteous man, blessed of God's ministers; for though he did not exactly tithe, he did support God's work sufficiently to be the subject of tribute from the pulpit, and to be called upon, not infrequently, to pray for sinners. All men were Mr. Dancy's brothers, except negroes and foreigners and certain other classes with which no white man could be expected to consort.

Mr. Dancy would not have lynched a negro; not under ordinary circumstances. But neither would he have tried to stop his neighbor from doing it. He was a prohibitionist and actually did no drinking himself. He did not permit his wife to employ brandies in her cooking, although he did indulge his appetite to the point of endangering his health.

They heard a scratching at the back screen door. Allen asked the cook if he could speak with Mr. Dancy. Mr. Dancy wiped his mouth and left the table.

"What can I do for you, Allen?"

"Jest wanted to have a word wid you, Mr. Dancy."

"Sure, Allen; why not? Like for the colored people to come to me with their troubles."

"Wonder if you would jest step out in the yard a minute." Allen had observed the cook was keeping an ear against the back door and he did not care to satisfy her curiosity just now. Mr. Dancy stepped out under the car shed.

"Well, Allen, what is it?"

"Mr. Dancy, dis here boy my brother, Mose. He done come up from Lousiana. He want to farm."

"What did you leave Louisiana for? It's a good state, ain't it? Didn't get into no trouble down there? We don't want no runaways around here."

"No sir," Mose replied. "Ain't been in no trouble never. Done live honest wid everybody. Done lost my job an couldn't git no nother one."

"So that's it. Well, a lot of people have lost their jobs nowadays; not to be held against them either. But I tell you, Mose, that's your name, ain't it, I don't see how I can take care of any more hands on my place now. Might use you in picking time, but wouldn't have no place for you right now. You look like a pretty good worker though, not lazy like Allen."

The negroes giggled at Mr. Dancy's joke.

"Mr. Dancy, you knows I ain't triflin. I done work good fer you."

"Oh, I'll admit you get by, Allen. Now tell you what I will do, Mose. I'll be going up into town today and I'll inquire around; I may run into somebody that could use you."

"I would shore be obliged to you, Mr. Dancy, if you would do jest that. I'd work hard, I shore would."

So Mr. Dancy dismissed them, and they returned to Allen's house. Mr. Dancy took out his pocket knife and cut a twig off the peach tree, which he chewed as he started his car.

Mrs. Dancy came out and handed him his dusty hat. "Going to Lisbon, Lucius?"

"Yes, thought I'd go in for the morning. Have several matters to attend to and wanted to see Colonel Stark about going to Marlin next week after those hogs."

"What did Allen want?"

"That other nigger with him was his brother. He sort of

turned up on Allen and is looking for a place. Lord, I can't put him up around here. We got more niggers than we can feed now. Guess I'll send him over to Rutherford's place. You can always find an empty shanty over there."

"Find little else," Mrs. Dancy said. "That's an awful place to send anybody, even a nigger."

"Well, what would you do? He'd starve to death in Lisbon. He can make some sort of a living over there the rest of this year, if he can stand it. Maybe I can move him over here in the spring."

"Lucius, I don't even like the idea of your going over to Rutherford's. They say awful things about Rutherford and those boys, and liquor isn't the worst of it."

"Now I wouldn't pay any attention to what you hear. Lon Rutherford was a fine man in his day. Guess he saw Pelham County when there wasn't an acre of cleared land in it. Sort of made this county and Lisbon too. Lot of fight left in him yet, I guess. Pity his boys didn't ever amount to anything."

"Sometimes, Lucius, I think this county would have been better off if they'd just let the woods keep it. A lot of thieving and murdering whites and a lot of mean niggers."

"All right, honey. Don't get yourself worked up. Pelham County's just growing up. Takes time. Everything takes time. I'll have a run by the Rutherford place after I get through in Lisbon; have a look around and talk it over with Old Lon; maybe it ain't so bad over there."

He motioned his wife back from the car and drove out of the yard into the dusty road where he turned toward the town, whose standpipe could be seen in the distance. Mrs.

Dancy watched him depart, shrugged her shoulders and entered the house.

Somewhere within Mrs. Dancy there was a quality that, had it been cultivated years ago, might have blossomed into nobility, but the numberless small assaults of the long years had so enclosed the seeds of that nobility in calluses that any hope of great activity motivated by the trait was gone.

Mrs. Dancy went back into her house, a woman of dead things. To do her chores. To throw out the refuse of yesterday and clean her hovel for another day. To be ground slowly but surely until her fiber could withstand the strain and tear no longer. Then to die and enter again into the ultimate stuff and source of all things.

VI

THE Rutherford place is back from the main road. The Minot branch of the Yazoo and Mississippi Valley Railroad runs on the north side of the plantation, as it comes west from Clarksville towards Lisbon. Coming from Clarksville, there are two trains a day now, one that leaves Clarksville about noon and another that leaves about seven-thirty, passing the Rutherford place a few minutes later. Once you could sit on Rutherford's front porch and see the train coming for several miles in the distance, but they have put in a drainage ditch that cuts obliquely across the road, and the high embankment covered with bushes blocks the view. Before the trains reach the ditch, they whistle for Lisbon, and it gives time to walk out on the porch to watch them, if one is interested. One usually is; there is little else to watch for.

In 1928 a young fellow who did not know the traditions of the country very well got the job of County Health Officer. He never came right into Rutherford's house, but he inspected all of the negro cabins on the place. He told Old Lon Rutherford they were not fit for human habitation, what with leaky roofs and contaminated wells often as not dug within a few feet of the backhouses. He stood in the yard; Rutherford did not invite him up on the porch, and he did not offer to come up, as he might have if he had wanted to. Rutherford would not have tried to stop him. He just sat there in the cane-bottom chair that Little Lonnie had brought him from the fair at Memphis. Occasionally he would make a brief comment,—"Well, confound it," or "I'll be dogged." He thanked the young fellow in a cold impersonal way and said he would look into the matter. The Health Officer got into his car and drove back to Clarksville and spent most of the rest of the day writing up a report on the L. R. Rutherford plantation, located in Pelham County, Mississippi, near the town of Lisbon.

That evening when Mr. Birney, the plantation manager, came over to see the old man, as he called him, Rutherford had left the porch and was sitting in the blue chair in his room before the fire in the open grate. His eyes were closed and he did not look up, just sat there with his hands clasped before him.

Mr. Birney did not speak first. He had not come about anything in particular. Finally Rutherford said, "I built every cabin on this place, had every shingle cut myself when there weren't a dozen more cabins in Pelham County. I don't feel like cutting new shingles this year. Fact is, don't believe I will. Be dogged if I will. The little whipper-snapper."

Of course, Mr. Birney did not know what Rutherford was talking about, but it was not the first time.

It was not until Little Lonnie came out from the store several days later that he found out all about it.

It was Wednesday when the Health Officer came out. On Friday Mr. Rutherford had Colin hitch up the buggy and drive him to Clarksville. Colin was a negro boy about the same age as Lonnie. Either one of his sons would have come from Lisbon to take him in the auto, but he preferred to go in the buggy. He went over to the courthouse, leaving

Colin to hold the horse, and stopped in at the Tax Assessor's office and made a public statement. Several men were in the room when he entered. He said "Good morning," and then went on speaking as though he were addressing a public gathering, without looking at any one person.

"The County Health Officer came and paid me a visit day before yesterday. Didn't let me know he was coming, or I'd have laid an extra plate for him. He was kind enough to go all over my place and check up on the roofs and back-houses just like a camp inspection. Told me they weren't fit to live in. Now you can just tell the County Health Officer that Lon Rutherford has been running his own business for about eighty years and he is still able to do it without any little damned wet-eared children to help him. General Lee didn't notice my horse was all saddle boils when I left the army. Good morning, gentlemen. You all come out and see me sometime."

And he turned and walked slowly out of the building. Colin helped him into the buggy and they drove from Clarksville, the old man holding his head up as if the place smelled bad.

Word of it got to the Health Officer and to everybody in Clarksville, for that matter, before the day was over. For some time after, people would ask one another how the shingling was getting on out at Rutherford's place. It taught the Health Officer that in Pelham County there were people you could deal with under the law and others you could not. Lon Rutherford was one you could not. You might as well try to get the courthouse painted green.

There were very few people in Clarksville who knew how long Rutherford had been in the county. As a matter of fact, he and Captain Winston had come down out of the hill country with their horses and a pet bear cub when most of that part of the Delta was a wilderness. They cut the limbs off a dead tree, made a clearing and camped. The dead tree was for the bear to play on. The bear amused them but he took to stealing the food. He would grab a piece of bacon and scuttle up into the top of the dead tree and sit there, and no amount of cursing would get him down. Finally one day Winston completely lost patience; the bear had gotten too big to handle anyway. He shot him off the tree, shot him just under the shoulder. The bear flattened out against the tree for a moment and then let go with all four legs at once, dropped to the ground, hit like a slab of dough.

Rutherford was gone at the time. He was a competent civil engineer and was running lines for the state. When he got back that evening and found the bear dead, he told Captain Winston it was a damned pity to have killed the bear without consulting him; the bear was half his; they had caught it together. Captain Winston told him he was just too hard to get along with, and they split up. As the years went by and other people moved into the county, there were many similar experiences. Rutherford had a great magnetism; he drew people to him through the force and command of his own personality, but usually when a person got in too close there was a quick rebuff.

He had been married twice and had outlived both wives. Orvil was his son by his first wife and Lonsford Robert Rutherford, Jr., whom they called Little Lonnie, his son by his second wife. Neither of the boys lived with him, though they both had a room at the house and often stayed there. They preferred to hang around the store in Lisbon, where they slept in the back room. No one had ever seen Old Lon in the store. He did his business in Clarksville and seldom went to Lisbon at all.

He kept a negro woman, Clara, at the house to cook and wash, and her boy Colin to wait on him. Colin served the table when the boys were there. When he was alone, Mr. Rutherford always ate in his room from a tray. Sometimes he would go off in the morning to shoot robins in the woods, taking Colin along to pick up the dead birds. Colin would dress them and cook them on a spit over the coal grate in Lon's room, with the old man sitting there in the blue chair watching him. He let Colin sit on the hearth at his feet and eat with him; he never permitted Colin to sit in a chair in his room.

Orvil and Little Lonnie both knew that Colin was their half brother. The resemblance between him and Little Lonnie was striking, only Lonnie was very blond and Colin was dark and kinky-haired.

It gave the ladies in Lisbon and Clarksville something to talk about. They said Lon had killed his first two wives, that only a nigger woman was a fit wife for such a man; yet for some reason the old man was looked up to and respected. Somehow the boys never seemed to resent Colin. He did as he was told, talked little and was faithful and devoted to their father. The state was full of mulatto children. If their father wanted to bring one into his house, that was his business as long as it did not interfere with anybody else's happiness.

But Colin being there, and Clara too, and nobody knowing but what she and the old man still had a more than master and servant relationship, even though Lon was past eighty, served to give the house isolation from the outside world. It was not the house a lady would visit. Most men did their talking from the yard. Mr. Dancy had done so when he came about Mose. Except Mr. Birney and the two boys, few ever entered the house.

After Martha, who was Mr. Rutherford's only daughter, died, when she was about twenty, her room had been made into a guest room, but the bed had never been slept in. There was an upright piano in the room; and Clara had made curtains for the windows and had cut some red wax cherries off an old hat of Martha's, hanging them on the wall, and had put a little bowl on a doily on top of the piano. But the rain blowing in the window cracks had stained and faded the curtains, and the wax cherries had become grimy with dust.

If Martha had lived, she would have been just a year or two older than Lonnie. She had been much like her father, headstrong and courageous, lovable and distant and alone. She had been the last bright interlude after which the old man had retired from the world, more eccentric and unapproachable than ever. Martha had lived her short life with a passionate energy that had burned out quickly. Pale and unsubstantial, hiding her inward bitterness, she glowed for only a short time. Her brothers had been unable to contaminate her; they endured her hatred and sighed with relief when she was gone. She had welcomed death and rushed forward to meet it. Her father knew that, knew also that he had no inducement to offer sufficient to make her want to remain. In his life he had not been able to make any resting place for beauty. All things about him decayed and fell to ruin, and he no longer had the strength or the desire to rebuild.

Nothing now to do but to sit there on the porch, looking out across the yellowed lawn, the dusty road, the fields with the negroes wearily plucking at the earth. It seemed that the earth was rising in waves about him, like an agitated and consuming primal substance. The cypresses, hoary, eternal, and the vine-clad oaks were growing feverish to extend their roots into his shroud to suck away the last bit of flesh from his bones. Walking down the cotton rows, slowly, holding himself quite erect in his last personal defiance, he would sometimes lean over and gather a bit of the earth into his hand and crush it between his fingers to feel its texture, and the black stain would darken his skin. If he loved anything, it was nature, but he knew there was no friendship for him there.

Or he would sit in the blue chair in his room before the coal grate, in which a fire burned even on summer evenings. The room was high, finished in long-leaf pine boards, stained brown, sweating out pungent resin. Above the mantel was a clock, advertising a jewelry store in Memphis, with a pendulum that clicked off the seconds in a monotonous, metallic beat. There were no pictures. His bed was in the corner with a washstand beside it. The carpet and the floor were dirty and bedaubed with his dried spittle.

This great, rambling house had been built many years before when he was a younger man and Martha and Lonnie were children, and he was having visions of gay house parties when the children would be older. But Lonnie had gone over to Orvil against his father; Martha's mother had died and Martha never had anyone at the house, and then she too had died. It was many years since he or anyone else had climbed the long, narrow staircase to the second floor, where there were spacious bedrooms with linen closets that might yet be filled with dainty linens and quilts unless the negroes had carried them off. He did not know, was not interested to look. Things would get on somehow a little longer, and he only needed that little longer to finish his allotted days.

He knew that Mr. Birney was a very poor manager and that it was Birney who had the negroes on the place making the whisky Orvil and Little Lonnie sold at the store, when they should have been tending the crops. But he did not have the energy to interfere. Not that he approved of it; he had never engaged in such business himself.

He could still take a rock from Colin's hand, throw it at a bird to make it rise, and lift his gun and kill the bird with one quick, carelessly aimed shot. He enjoyed these things he killed that Colin cooked over the grate. He liked the warm devotion of Colin, an image he had made from his basest self and yet more lovely to him than anything else that remained. But happiness had been laid to rest with Martha; and he remembered that Martha had loved him.

Orvil had been the first of his two sons to turn against him, and then Lonnie had followed in Orvil's footsteps. He did not quite blame himself for this, and yet he knew that he had never given himself to them as he had to Martha. Perhaps he had given so much of his love to Martha that none remained for the boys. And he was the only person who might have sustained their manhood. But that was all far in the past, and time had lessened his bitterness against them.

Evenings the negroes would pass the house in the soft darkness and would pause to listen, for frequently at such times they could hear the old man running his weary fingers over the keys of the piano and his dry voice wearily singing old church hymns.

VII

CERTAINLY, had he known, Mose would not readily have selected as his future guardians the Rutherford family with its boys, Orvil, a great black-headed, large-eared hulk of a fellow, and Little Lonnie, a blond thin lad who moved gracefully as in some mission of exquisite cruelty, these two running what pretended to be a store in Lisbon, peddling whisky and undertaking other undignified crime; and its aged patriarch, Old Lon, waiting with a desolate memory, for the end of time if need be;—and their plantation manager, Mr. Birney, who knew far more about a still than he did about a bale of cotton.

Yet when Mr. Dancy returned in the evening and called Mose and Allen up to his house, Mose was overjoyed that he could depart in the morning to go to work for Mr. Rutherford. It was not seemly for him to inquire of Mr. Dancy what manner of place he might be seeking, nor could Allen himself tell much except that it was close by and that it was known as a very dilapidated place where the hands changed almost every year. The negroes know that a house whose servants have been with it a long time is usually a good house.

When Mose came up the side road to the Rutherford house, Colin was in the yard making a desultory pretense of chopping weeds.

Mose approached him. "Mr. Dancy done sont me up here.

Say I is goin to work fer Mr. Rutherford. Wonder could I see him."

"He a settin in his room right this minute if you wants to go in, but I wouldn't do dat if I was you. The ole man, he don't low niggers come in the house, not ceptin me an mama. You better go see Mr. Birney. He run the place fer the ole man."

"Mr. Rutherford, he don't tend the place hisself?"

"Course not. Nothin but pore folks does that. He has Mr. Birney do it fer him."

"Where's I goin to find Mr. Birney?"

Colin indicated a little whitewashed cabin set in a clump of stunted trees further down the road. "You'll more'n likely find him down there, if he ain't out in the fields."

"I shore does thank you. I'll be seein you some more, I reckon. Likely I'll be here a right long time."

"Well, maybe so," Colin said. "I don't leave the old man much. I stays pretty close by the house."

Mose went down the road. Mr. Birney's house was little different from the other cabins. It had once been whitewashed, but the wash had mostly flaked off. There was a good roof and the windows had glass in them. There were no flowers, no garden; only a few stunted trees and bricks along the edge of the walk to the door.

Mr. Birney came to the door. His face had an expression of weary, stupid sensuality. His hands were short and fat, his neck flabby and red and the creases were lined with a leathery deposit of dirt. He wore a large Stetson hat, boots, corduroy riding breeches and a rotting silk shirt of uncertain color with an embroidered monogram on the pocket. A white handkerchief was tied about his neck. His dull eyes were round and reddish. He was as tall as Mose and much heavier. He spoke as though he were short of breath, fingering his face nervously all the while and pushing his hat from one side to the other uncovering his sweat-matted, soft, silken, black hair.

"So you're the nigger Mr. Dancy told us about. You think you can behave yourself and get along around here? Think you know how to work; think that, do you?"

"Yes sir, if you lets me. I can shore work."

"Got no family with you?"

"Ain't got no family no way. Jest me."

"Know anything about farming? Know cotton?"

"No sir, ain't never farmed. Done a little gardenin back in Lousiana."

"Well, I didn't figure you knew cotton from what Dancy said. I'm going to put you in with one of the other niggers this year. See how you get along. Put you on your own or make some other arrangement next year if you want to stay."

"That suit me fine."

"All right, we'll try it that way. You go on down to that house yonder by the drainage ditch and get that nigger Thurman and bring him up here with you."

Thurman Watson was an exception on the Rutherford place. He had lived in the same cabin since before they had dug the drainage ditch behind it. Thurman had his reasons for not moving.

He was what you would call a good nigger, always grinning out an abundant kindliness of character, a lazy but obedient servant. He lost no time in finding out who Mose was and what the white folks were up to. The idea of someone to help him with his crops seemed a great good fortune.

"Now that's what I calls right good. Ain't nough hands to work this place no how. Done told Mr. Birney that every year. Like he would pay tention to me anyhow."

He continued a steady flow of talk as they went up the road. "We better hustle ourselves on up to Mr. Birney's, cause he shore got a temper wid niggers. Ain't the kind that bile up. No sir, it's the kind that retches about inside him, and then it flash up a long time after, like a fire you done gone and left, thinkin it had quit burnin."

Soon they were standing together, hats in hands, at Mr. Birney's door, while he delivered their orders to them.

"Thurman, I'm going to put this nigger in with you for the balance of this year. He'll work with you on your land and along with the other hands in the general work on the place. You'll feed him, and when crops are in, he'll have to take his chances at getting a share. He won't get any at all if things are like they were last year. That suit you, Thurman?"

"Yes sir."

"Suit you, Mose?"

"Yes sir, seem liberal nough."

"One thing more, Mose. You're working for me. What I say goes on this place. You understand that?"

"Yes sir, I does."

"That'll be all. I'll come by to see how you get on. I don't want to have to tell Mr. Dancy he sent me a bad nigger."

Walking back, Mose told Thurman, "That man say nigger a funny way, like it was a hog or somethin like that.

Niggers calls each other niggers and it don't sound like that a tall."

"Guess you bout right on that. Mr. Birney, he think a heap more of hogs than he do niggers."

Thurman's household was long a matter for Mose to wonder about. His wife was a tiny negro girl, probably not over seventeen or eighteen years old, ignorant but industrious to the limited extent of her knowledge. She kept their small baby in a shallow box lined with quilts, where it slept fitfully. Many hours each day, it seemed to Mose, the child spent at its mother's breast, nuzzling animal-like for food that never seemed to satisfy it. The mother, Luella, was out of bed long before daylight, cooking over a little stove in the back shed room, and she was there after dark washing the pans. Hers was a slavery to which Thurman offered no relief. He came to her at night to eat at table with her and join her until she left him for the tasks of the ensuing day. He paid little attention to the child; only occasionally would he pause before it and thrust his thumb into its mouth to watch it sucking itself full of wind. Yet Thurman was not unkind. Mose never saw him strike Luella.

Beyond her cooking and tending the child, Luella's life was a boring, uninteresting effort to pass the time. Sometimes, at mid-morning or mid-afternoon, she would draw a bucket of cool water and walk out to the fields, carrying it to the men. Other days she would be asleep with her child lying beside her. She was not yet strong enough to work in the fields herself; she had had a painful delivery and dragged about the house in utter physical exhaustion.

Mose made a carefully calculated effort to do his part of the work and did not fail; for Thurman was all too eager to place the larger burden on Mose, whose superior physical strength and grace of movement enabled him to accomplish much more with less actual labor than the other negroes. He learned how to point and turn the plow through the newly cleared land that Mr. Birney was sowing in turnips. With his hoe in his long, powerful hands he never missed his mark. He enjoyed his command over his own body and was proud of his strength.

It was some time before he ever saw Mr. Rutherford close by, though frequently he saw him pass down the road with Colin beside him.

One morning when they were in the fields, Mr. Rutherford turned the horse up the path by the rows of cotton. He held the horse and reached in the bottom of the buggy for his long straight cane, which he pointed at Mose.

"Come up here, boy."

"Yes sir," Mose said, smiling, laying down his hoe.

"You must be the nigger Mose Mr. Dancy sent me."

"Yes sir. How come you know that? You ain't never set eyes on me before."

"Guess you're the only strange face on my place. Guess I didn't have to be so smart to figure that out."

"Shore nough," Mose said. "That's so."

"How do you like it up here farming, Mose?"

"Like it well nough, Mr. Rutherford. I shore does. Done git plenty victuals. Can't complain none."

"Come from Louisiana Mr. Dancy told me."

"Yes sir. Come from Biddyvul."

"Bideauxville? I've been there. Great state, Louisiana. Been many years since I was through there. Beautiful state, fine old homes, if they haven't all rotted and fallen down like the rest of this country has."

"Yes sir. Shore am a beautiful place. Done hate to leave there myself. Done seem more kindly down there."

"What do you mean by that?"

"Don't jest know, but it seem like down there things warmed to you and up here everybody done been watchin his own pot, and mostly glowerin at it too."

"Nigger, you think too much. You better tend your cotton. You'll be preaching, next thing you know." He clucked his horse and drove on.

Mose called after him. "I shore would like to. I shore would."

If Mr. Rutherford heard this, he did not answer.

Mose fitted easily into the life of the other negroes on the plantation. He rose at the first sign of day when the sun was beginning to cast a pale white shadow across the low wooded horizon in the east. The air was cool and perfumed with the smell of earth and growing things. After a hasty breakfast of corn pone and fried meat he and Thurman left for the fields. The hogs were still grunting into the trough and the cow swishing the hay as Luella milked her. Soon they were moving up and down the long rows, the sweat beginning to rise on their shiny bodies. The sun rose, red and livid, into the sky, and the soft twilight vanished as the day emerged with a pitiless heat of a texture one could almost feel. Sometimes the men dropped their hoes and bathed their faces and arms in the creek and then returned to their slow, rhythmical procedure. Someone would pass down the road and call a loud hello that would come to them like a sharp hollow sound that seemed apart from the person that called it, and the sound would sweep on to the woods that reëchoed it. Or the passer-by would stop by the field and exchange a more intimate greeting, and the workers would lean on their hoes and talk of the small things of their days and laugh into the hot noonday. When the sun was overhead, they went back to the cabin and ate and lay on the porch to sleep for half an hour. They returned to the fields, and the same working to and fro continued as the sun crossed over and began to descend. And they would begin to look back to where they had begun in the morning to see how far they had gone and they could hardly tell exactly which row they had started on, for the earth they had turned, soft and black in the morning, had been bleached and grayed by the sun. Fatigue passed into a state of half-suspended animation, in which it seemed one stepped out of his body and watched it, and it was still there, moving up and down the long distance from one end of the field to the other. When evening came and it was supper time, they turned weary steps homeward. In the long soft evenings the earth seemed to awaken again; the insects droned in a swelling rasp that rose and fell with a regularity that caused the listener to slow his breathing to keep time with the slow beat of this strange music. The negroes gathered, now at one cabin, now at another, to laugh and talk aimlessly in a complete surrender to the simple movement of life.

But the undertone of all this was sad and fate-loaded. The negroes are not a happy people, or rather they take much of their happiness in sadness; they have a ritual of sadness which transmutes the painful experiences of life into victory of a sort.

Because he is aware of his weakness, the negro for the

most part bears his burden with a cheer that is the honor of his race. He makes his mansion of the things others have cast off. To relieve his soul he is endlessly ritualistic.

Whether the wholeness in Mose was reasoned or instinctive is a matter beside the point. He felt within him the song of his people, that was forever pushing at his throat. He felt the necessity and finality of being as more important than becoming; he was in deep alliance with the universal movement which is life. He loved.

Such a man will express himself in the easiest means at hand. To Mose, preaching was not so much a matter of converting anyone to a given set of doctrines as it was bearing witness to the truth he desired to voice. He wanted to convey to others the feelings that came to him, for it seemed to him that these feelings would enrich and complete their lives. He was constantly aware of the many hindrances in life that irritate and make desolate. He wanted to relegate these to a minor position and sound out the more important, overlying movement.

It was inconceivable that Mose should in any way startle his world. His shabby attire, his half-barbaric language formed a barrier that tempted few to advance. Only the negroes, who did not notice these things, found his performance impressive.

And so, almost as though he were unaware of where he was going, Mose found himself frequenting the little meeting house at Lisbon. And soon he was in the pulpit teaching his people in his great love for them. With quiet force, tenderly, he poured forth the abundance of his own soul.

"The black chillen of the Lawd is born in toil, they lives in toil an they dies in toil. They shoulders is bent with burdens, they eyes is dim with weepin. They carries they new born close to they bodies, lest somebody strike it dead befo they eyes. They carries they dead in the dark o' the evenin to lay them in the groun in secret. They makes a sad song wid only the black trees an the Lawd to lissen.

"White folks done own the earth. Maybe the Lawd done give it to 'em. Maybe they stole hit. Don't make no difference which way it was. Cullud people can't take the earth for theirs. They must make them a spirit house, must worship the Lawd without no temple, without no gold banners. But the Lawd ain't care for temples an he ain't care for banners. He done turn he ear in the cool of the evenin to the forest an the fields, down to the cabin door an what he hear make a sweet music in he head. The Lawd done love the crippled bird an the animal with the stone bruise in he foot. All the things that must come a crawlin an a hobblin to the Lawd's altar to lay a piece of bread or a thread from the hem of they raiment for their gift, the Lawd he done love them an take them to he bosom.

"Let my people come down in the stormy night when the heavens done bust open an the rain fall an the lightnin strike an wound the biggest tree. Let them walk down the road through the soft mud what stick to they bare feet. Let them come without they hats so the rain wash clean they faces an anoint they bodies.

"Let them come across the fields through the woods, through the swamps up to the river's edge an lissen to the mournin of the water, strugglin against the land, fightin its way out to the great sea.

"My brethren, ain't you lost, standin there, watchin the great river rush by, cryin out the pain of the earth? Throw a stick in the river. Jest fer a minute you sees it an then it's lost an gone. Lift your head up; where is your troubles now; what do they mount to side the great pain an the cryin of the river?

"You is made whole again an strong. An little by little the rain an the thunder it die down 'til now you lissen hard to hear a rumble way off across the other shore. The river it done wore itself out an it quiet down an move more gentler. Now the light begin to come an the water it drip off the leaves an pitter-patter on the groun. The sun come up in glory that most blind the eyes. An my people go off across the fields an all day I can hear them a shoutin an a singin hallelujah an a makin a great noise fer the Lawd."

On another evening the negroes came in nervous silence to the church. During the preceding night a white fire had burned in the fields behind the town, and a man's body had been consumed for a crime that was less of him than of those that punished him. It had struck fear and dumb alarm into the cabins, for one never knew to just what lengths the white man's wrath might go when once aroused into this state of fury.

They sat there on the benches almost unseeing, swaying gently from side to side, moaning softly, "Oh Lawd Jesus, Oh Lawd Jesus." When Mose walked from his bench up before them, there were tears behind his eyes, and his heart was beating in pain within him. He longed to stretch his arms out over those people and ease their sorrows.

"Man's life am short an full of sorrow. Like the leaves befo the wind.

"But lissen, my brothers an my sisters. The Lawd have showed me a story so's I could tell it to you this night.

"I sees a great field with a tall forest on one side an rough land with gullies on the other side. An they is a great army movin back in the trees an they is another army in the rough land. The men is talkin low, a fixin theyselves for the fight, a crunchin on they biscuits. They can't be still; they has somethin a retchin about on the inside of them that won't be quiet 'til they has the battle.

"An after a little time the two armies begins to move slow like out onto the field an the fightin begin an it am most bloody. An soon the wails of the dyin an the moans of the wounded rise from the ground, an still the fightin go on. An then a man, a tall man with a long dark coat, he come out on the field an he walk bout mongst the fighters an they don't see him. Jest very slow that man walk round an about whilst the fightin am goin on, an nobody see him, an you can't see his face, cause he hold hisself all bent over with his face all covered in his great, windin coat. An he tremble like he was weepin.

"An then after the fightin been goin on all the day, the sun set, an most all the men on both sides been killed. An there in the first dark them that is left drag theyselves off the field, what's left o' one army goin back to the woods an what's left of the other back to the gully land. An there is no shoutin of victory an no song am sung. An then the man in the long, dark coat he lift hisself up an go walkin bout, layin he hands on the dead an the dyin an the wounded, an he bathe they wounds, an the faces of the dead they smile, an the faces of the livin they show radiant in the dark. An then the man he lay off his coat on the ground an it am the Lawd Jesus, all in shinin white, an they is a red place on his side an his hands am bleedin an he have the thorns on his head. They is a halo of light bout him. An slow he walk off the field an when he reach the edge of the field, a great blindin light come an take him away an leave only the wind sobbin in happiness across that place where he was at."

VIII

It was evening, and Mose and Thurman stood in front of the house. A gentle breeze coming off the river bore the sweet smell of the swamps, the heavy smell of luxuriant vegetation, rotting wood and stagnant pools. It was so quiet one would have expected the earth to cry out in sudden pain. The beautiful fields stretched away and merged with the forest, green leaves and black soil.

"Git along home wid you, been tellin this nigger for a long time now. But he can't git along. Been rooted too deep. Can cut him off but can't shoot the old stump out." Thurman spoke aloud his thoughts. "Been wantin to see my mammy down by the Yazoo. Done been wantin my mammy to lay my head on her bosom an I can't git away. Fore God, it ain't right. One of these nights I'se shore goin to do it, jest you wait. Old Birney, he goin to holler at Thurman's door, an ain't nothin goin to answer ceptin the hinge goin to creak in he face."

"How come you don't go if you wants to? Dere's the road; ain't nothin crost it to keep you from goin."

"Sometimes they's things crost a road you can't see." Thurman hesitated, half afraid to speak. "Mose, you is a good man. You talks wid the Lawd an walks in the Lawd's way. I ain't a bad nigger. I ain't never meant to do no harm. I wouldn't hurt nobody. You knows dat."

"What you tryin to tell me? What's eatin at you? You act

like they was a ghost in your house, like you was conjured."

"Wish it was jest conjured. You can git yourself unconjured. Ain't you ever notice the way Mr. Birney look at me?"

"No, I shore ain't."

"Well, next time you watch him an you notice. He done look at me like I was somethin dead an wouldn't lay straight in the coffin. Think sometimes he's goin to put me there hisself."

"How come all dis? What Mr. Birney got gainst you?"

"It's cause I done killed a man once fer him. Now I done told you an you can go tell it if you wants to. It was down in the field yonder." Thurman lifted his long arm, pointing off to the west. "Where the woods road come out. All evenin I laid there on the ground in the cotton patch, jest like Mr. Birney told me to, an when the man come by goin to the still, I give him both barrels in the back. He didn't holler or nothin, jest laid down dead; most cut him in two I was so close to him when I fired. That was the last time ary officer done come on this place. They was a terrible ruckus bout it fer a time, but it died down, an they didn't make no great try to find out who done it. An Mr. Birney he done told me if I stays here, he keer for me but if I tries to run off, he done turn me over to the sheriff an they hang me shore. Nigger's word don't mount to nothin when white folks talks, you knows dat."

"So dat's how it is. Done made a killer out of you." Mose felt sickened at this tale, weak and ineffective. "Pack of dirty hounds they is, rollin in they own vomit, cursin the land. Wonder the vines don't turn black an rot where they walks. Some day I is goin to blow up that levee an let the river clean this land what done been dirtied so long. No wonder the cotton don't grow big an tall like it did a long time ago. They done pizened the soil. But the little Jesus he done see us, an I feels his hand in the wind. Don't you, Thurman?"

"Sometimes, Mose, I thinks I does, an then I looks off to where the big house set yonder an it jest don't stand to reason the Lawd Jesus hang round a place like this."

"How long this sort of thing been goin on?"

"Long time, I guess. Since befo I come here. All de time done been the still down in the swamp through them woods yonder an the boys comin out from Lisbon to git the likker."

IX

IT WAS late afternoon when Mr. Birney entered the store. He let the screen door slam behind him.

"Hotter than a team load of hell." He slouched into a cane bottom chair and leaned back against the counter. He mopped his face on his sleeve and began moving his hat back and forth across his head.

At the back of the room Orvil was sitting on the counter, dangling his feet over the edge. He spit between his bear-like front teeth and did not reply.

Lonnie came out from the back room, walking slowly along behind the counter, his eyes bloodshot and heavy with sleep. "Meet the new deputy-sheriff."

Mr. Birney looked around the room. Lonnie laughed. Orvil reddened under his black stubble of beard.

"Deputy what?"

"Deputy-sheriff. Mr. Orvil Rutherford. Deputy-sheriff of Pelham County." Lonnie screamed with laughter.

Mr. Birney smiled sweetly. "Well, I'm damned."

"So you are," Lonnie said. "So are we all."

Orvil got up and thumbed his suspenders. He wore a large pearl-handled pistol in a leather holster.

"Guess that sets us up better than ever."

"Sure enough, I'll be damned," Mr. Birney said.

"Saves no end of trouble." Lonnie had reached in the glass counter for a sugar stick, at which he was biting. Finally he broke the stick in half, putting it all in his mouth, and his cheeks bulged around the ends of the broken pieces.

"How's everything at the place?" Orvil asked. "Anything to bring in? We need some bad. It's getting low."

"You all come out tonight," Mr. Birney replied. "Be enough to bring in, if you all think we can make it. Want you to talk to the old man too. He hasn't been doing well lately. You ought to send him off to the springs again."

"You don't seem to know papa even yet," Lonnie said. "I've tried to get him to go before now. But he won't do it any more. You couldn't budge him out of that house with a crowbar. He'll stay right there until he dies. That's papa all right. He'll sit right there in front of the fire and sweat to death one of these summers."

They locked up the store and got in Mr. Birney's car. Lonnie sat in the back seat and hung one leg out over the door.

The store was a dingy brick building with a gasoline pump in front of it. It was on the edge of town, like a wart on the weedy field, a dust-covered hovel.

They drove through the town past the one block of store buildings. Sallow-faced men were lounging on the sidewalk. The placards in the windows, advertising Coca-Cola, were dirty and ill-arranged. The graveled street was ribbed and rutted. Rotting vegetables had been thrown out of the stores into the street. Even the negroes refused to pick them up, and the curs drooled over them, ever keeping a wary eye heavenward. There were no buzzards in the street. Buzzards are not vegetarians, and meat is never thrown out in Lisbon. People knew the Rutherford boys and nodded to them as they drove past. Lonnie waved back. Orvil grunted.

"Guess what," said Mr. Birney.

"What?" said Orvil.

"We got a preacher out on the place. Your papa let Dancy send him over. And the dad-burndest nigger for work you ever saw. Working with Thurman. Has Thurman's tongue hanging out trying to keep up with him. They've got the cleanest piece of cotton you ever saw."

"That must be the new nigger preacher I hear them talking about in Lisbon. They say he knocks them down and drags them all over the meeting house."

"That's him all right. But I don't know as I like it a damn bit. He's not an insolent nigger. If he was, I'd knock him down and that would be the end of it, but when you talk to him, he just stands there and looks straight at you, not like any other nigger I ever saw. Won't say a damn word but 'yes, sir.' Never answers back. You don't guess he'd do any talking, do you?"

"Well, now I'm a deputy-sheriff, he can talk to me, if it's talking he wants. And I'll console him right enough; I'll console the hell out of him."

Lonnie's eyes seemed gleaming in the twilight and he laughed to himself, now softly.

They stopped at the house and went into Mr. Rutherford's room.

Orvil took his hat off. "How are you, papa?"

"Doing fine, Orvil. How are you?"

"Can't complain none. How's crops?"

"Ask Mr. Birney. He can tell you. I haven't noticed much. Do we have crops this year? That is, except the swamp crops?"

Lonnie said, "Oh, don't be a God-damned old woman, papa."

Mr. Rutherford never lifted his head. "I think somebody is calling you boys outside. You better go see."

They went out. Orvil stopped at the door. "You ought to stir about more, papa. Let us drive you up to Memphis some morning. Come over to Lisbon and we can arrange it."

"Yes, of course," Mr. Rutherford said. "I'll certainly do that. You boys come back soon; real soon. For Christ's sake, will you shut that door?"

They stood in the hall. They could hear the clock ticking in their father's room. They had never known the house without that slow beat, beat—beat, beat—without beginning, without end. It was like the endless catalogue of an army.

At the front steps Mr. Birney was rubbing out the glass of an oil lantern. He trimmed the wick with his pocket knife and shook the tank to see how much kerosene was in it. From the guest room Colin peered through the screen at them.

Lonnie said, "You better get the hell out of there or papa'll whale your hide." The face disappeared from the window.

They walked by Mr. Birney's house, and Orvil and Lonnie waited at the end of the brick-lined walk while Mr. Birney went in and got his gun. Then they marched off abreast, like three heroes, facing into the setting sun. That was coming up from behind them. In front you saw only legs thrusting out in front of one another and loose bellies; Orvil's hard, dark face; Mr. Birney's, heavy and foul; Lonnie's, thin, almost gentle, softly colored.

They cut across the fields about a half a mile until they came to a negro shanty on the edge of the woods. It was nearly dark. Orvil called out, "Binam." A voice replied, "Yes sir, Mr. Orvil, I is comin out. Wait 'til I gits my clothes on."

Lonnie said, "Don't be all night about it."

"Yes sir, Mr. Lonnie."

The door to the cabin was opened, and an old bow-legged negro ambled out, carrying a sputtering lantern. "It's awful dark to try to git down there this time of night. I'd a fotch it up if I'd a knowed you all was comin."

"You afraid to go?"

"No sir, Mr. Orvil; not wid you all here. Lawsy me, that shore am one gun you is totin."

"He's a deputy-sheriff, Binam," Lonnie said. "You're working for the state now."

"You ain't jokin, is you, Mr. Lonnie?"

They went off single file, Binam in front and Lonnie behind, trailing after them, scuffing the dirt. They passed the corn crib and cut across the sorghum patch, then on through a narrow strip of newly cleared land, covered with a thin stand of runty cotton. Then they found a path into the woods across dry ground. As they got deeper into the woods, the undergrowth grew more dense. Not a breath of air moved. The path was little traveled and the going was hard. The men breathed heavily and cursed in undertones, sweating freely. Some small animal, probably a rabbit, went running off to one side, and Binam started back into Orvil's face in fright at the noise.

"Ain't no kind a night to be goin through here. Copperheads in these woods thicker'n moccasins in the bayou."

"You go on," Orvil said. "You ain't as lame as you make out."

The land began to fall away to the creek, and the ground became soggy and soft. The men's shoes sucked at each step. Here and there on either side the glimmer of the two lanterns showed pools of black water and the bulging forms of cypress trees. Here the highest and the lowest orders of evolution met and seemed not at odds.

Binam stopped short. "Thar 'tis. You got to go careful now."

"What is it?" Orvil asked.

"Thar the bayou. It's slippery as a razor-back long here."

The path now followed a perilous course along the clay bank of the bayou. On one side it dropped off sharply to the water below. The lanterns drew swarms of mosquitoes into the men's faces, and they walked with arms uplifted before them, fanning the air. Mr. Birney stumbled and cried out as he fell. He swung the lantern up over his head and Lonnie bent to take it from his hands. The falling man clutched wildly at an overhanging bush and dug his feet into the soft bank. Orvil grabbed his arm and pulled him back into the path.

Binam said, "Done told you it ain't no kind a time to be comin down here. Lucky you didn't fall in the bayou. Moccasins would a done et you up befo now."

They resumed their march. In a few minutes Binam halted. "Dis here where we cross over. You got to go careful."

They held the lanterns high. The bayou divided, leaving a long island in the center. The channel was on the far side. The men waded through the shallow water, past the trunks of cypresses, to the shore of the island. It was black dark, corrupt and unspeakable night. The slime, broken apart by their feet, slipped noiselessly together behind them. A ripple showed something moving through the water. A rustling sound moved along under the vines on the shore. Nothing visible appeared. The men restrained their breathing, except Lonnie, who splashed along, making no effort to be quiet.

"God, what a stench. You can sure smell the mash," Lonnie said.

"Yes, it's bad all right," Mr. Birney said.

They came to the center of the island where there was a clearing in the trees. The dim light showed a gaping hole in the earth that contained a foul, rotting mess of wet grain. Near-by were a boiler and copper tubing. Stacked at one side of the clearing were glittering cans with screw tops.

"It's ready to take, if you all thinks you can carry it back thout falling in the water," Binam said.

"We'll take one apiece," Orvil said.

"Birney'll fall in sure as hell. We should have brought a gig along to fish him out with." Lonnie laughed.

Mr. Birney did not reply. They took up four full cans. They were heavy, and the men bent over them like gnomes bringing plunder from the bowels of the earth. Slowly they splashed and struggled through the water and along the bayou bank.

Once in the cotton patch, they stopped to rest.

"Lord Jesus God," Orvil said. "That's one hole, that is."

"Yeah. That place was your idea, Lonnie," Mr. Birney said.

"Well, what would you do? Cook the stuff up at the house? Papa'd raise hell sure enough. He'd come down and tear this up if it wasn't so damn hard to get to."

"Oh," Mr. Birney said. "I always thought it was the officers you was hiding it from."

They all laughed at this as they stood mopping necks and faces on soiled handkerchiefs.

X

THE high tide of summer came and spent itself. Fruits ripened and the boughs bent in full contentment, waiting to be relieved of their burdens. The long, feverish days of growing were past and there was an end to all this energy and a proper consummation. The red-yellow blossoms of the trumpet vines lay sleepy against the tree trunks they encircled. Already the leaves in the forest were beginning to be tinted and dry.

Soft and peaceful days of late August warmed the bolls of cotton, and here and there one burst in virgin whiteness.

Mose and Thurman watched the scene with peace and happiness at the fulfillment of their labors. Friendship and understanding had grown between them as they had toiled together. Not quite in vain had they joined themselves in their sincere efforts.

From the dusty cribs and outhouses appeared long sacks. A beam was hung up at the gin for weighing. High-sided wagons began to show on the roads laden with the white fruit. Low-bent singing figures were in the fields and hands deftly plucking away the lint and seeds. The South was kneeling once again in her annual reverence.

"Git a bale to the acre shore," Thurman said, and Mose did not dispute him.

Mr. Birney was at the gin, weighing. Even Mr. Rutherford came down with Colin and, standing always away from the traffic, watched the proceedings as if he wanted to be elsewhere and yet somehow could not keep his feet turned in any other direction. Too long he had done this himself. Cotton fibers were in his sinew, and even as he stood on the outer edge of life, his blood once more flowed warm at harvest time.

Thrusting his cane down hard before him, he came to Mose and Thurman, standing by the gin-shed. "Good crop you all had this year; best in the county, I hear." And the darkies grinned with sheep's faces and shuffled their feet.

"Shore done like to hear you say dat," Mose answered. "Done been glad you is pleased wid us."

Mr. Rutherford started to speak again but remained silent and turned away.

"Us done got a good crop," Mose said to Thurman. "But what he got? What sort of crop he done raised?"

During the long weeks until the crop was all baled and piled away in the great sheds at Lisbon, there was much talk about prices that the negroes did not understand. Only this much they knew,—that whether or not the white people prospered from the season's harvest, they would have lean days during the coming winter.

At the commissary Mr. Birney presented bewildering statements of advances for this and that item of food during the previous year, and explained volubly and with overwhelming rhetoric why the left-overs in cash were so appallingly small. The negroes scratched their heads and pocketing their small earnings, trudged off to rest for another year that would differ in no way from the one past.

Mose had been forewarned to expect little or nothing for his efforts and he received nothing except a five dollar bill and a promise from Mr. Birney that he could have an allotment of land to cultivate himself next year; and he was satisfied. Food and clothing in a minimum amount he most earnestly desired, but beyond that it never occurred to him to lay up a store of earthly riches.

XI

In the morning Mose walked down the road to Lisbon, singing to high heaven, the fingers of one hand thrust deep into his trousers pocket, caressing the greenback. Through all the stores he passed, lingering with fond glances before the brightly colored calicoes and knickknacks. Finally, his stomach bulging with chitterlings and strawberry soda pop and his pockets stored full of sugar sticks, he continued out past the meeting house to the Dancy place.

On Allen's porch he set himself down Silenus-like and bestowed candy on the shouting piccaninnies until at last their mother protested in the name of good health and moderation. All through the day he and Allen made small talk like boys let out of school for a long vacation.

In the evening, in company with the other negroes on Mr. Dancy's plantation, they walked down into the town to the meeting house, to sway and shout far into the night.

"What you say fer the Lord, Sister Whitley? What you say, Sister Lewis?"

"Say glory hallelujah fer the Lord," came the high wail in reply.

"Yas sir," Mose intoned. "Done been a great hallelujah fer the Lawd. He done riched the earth fer he people, an he people done come wid thanks to glorify the name o' the Lawd. The prophets done been a playin on they harps, an all the angels in hebbem am a singin an a stompin they feet on the floor."

An old woman in the rear rose and stood on her bench, and, raising her arms high above her head, "I done been a low-down sinner but I done see the light, an the Lawd Jesus am in my heart. I is been saved this night fer Jesus." And screeching in an unearthly harmony, she rushed down the aisle and flung herself on the mourners' bench. There she wept straight the ragged edges of her soul.

Tenderly and awkwardly Mose leaned over and placed his hand on her head. "Blessed am the one that comes back to the Lawd's fold. My people thanks the Lawd fer the good work done."

Soon others rose with similar shoutings, and the mourners' bench became full to overflowing.

Mose paused to observe in an undertone, "Done seem there been a power of sinnin goin on mongst my people," but his words were lost in the tumult.

From time to time as the fervor increased, couples left the room and disappeared in the grove behind the building, to return later quiet and solemn-faced and peaceful before their god.

Finally, as the most awful storm will eventually wear itself out, the ecstasy subsided and the congregation departed, leaving in the room a stillness filled with the memory of their voices. Blowing out the lanterns, Mose knelt long alone and in silence before the altar. His lips pronounced no words; there was no activity of any sort within him, only the joy at being there in solitude with the feeling that he was in harmonious accord with his Maker.

As he went out the door, he was startled by a figure of a woman sitting on the steps.

"I was jest waitin fer you, Brother Southwick," she said.

He peered carefully into the darkness at the woman, and then remembered who she was.

"Well, sholy if it ain't Sister Beatrice." He pronounced the word with a decided accent on the second syllable. "If I'd a knowed you was a waitin, I wouldn't a been so long comin out."

"I didn't have nobody to come wid me to the church from my house so I come long wid some other girls in the town. When the meetin broke up an we was standin bout talkin, like folks does, you know, first thing you know the girls I come wid had gone an left me. I didn't want to go home by myself, it bein so late an all, an I ricollict how you goes right past my house, so I says to mysef, I jest wait fer Brother Southwick an he go long wid me shore."

As she spoke, she cast calf-glances at Mose, which did not miss their mark.

"Well, now, that am so. You jest come right long wid me. Hadn't thought bout it but now I remembers I does walk right past your house."

Beatrice Curley was well known in Lisbon. The colored women called her a godless hussy. But she did not care. She was a graceful and well-proportioned negro woman of thirty. Her skin was almost white and her hair straight and black. When she spoke, she smiled and showed a double row of white, gleaming teeth. By Mose's standard she was pretty; sensual in her dark eyes that showed no depth. Her hands were soft and slender. She wore no hat. Her dress was green and her slippers scarlet.

For a long time she had been, in her way, and without knowing it, an outer rampart for the little decency that remained in Lisbon, and she had absorbed many a rude assault that might else have reached the inner circle; but like the seasoned veteran she did not see the business of the struggle.

Other women had cast soft glances at Mose, and he had smiled and passed on. But this was the first time that siege had been openly declared. If Mose had known Beatrice by reputation, it is doubtful if that would have mattered much to him. If he had really known her, then it might have been different.

Down the dusty street they walked and the perfume of the woman's body and the warm air of the evening performed their allotted task. They came to a small house in niggertown, Beatrice hanging on Mose's arm. At the door, she leaned over and removed her scarlet slippers and, leaving them on the door sill, entered into the house; and Mose entered with her.

When he left the house, as dawn was hardly breaking, Beatrice was still asleep. There was a child also, a young boy apparently, about three or four years old, sleeping on a pallet on the floor. And the scarlet slippers still rested, arrogant and precise, on the door sill. Mose long remembered the sight of them in the first light of day.

As Mose had feared, Thurman was stirring about when he reached home.

"Now jest whar is you been all night?"

"I done stayed the night in Lisbon."

"Whar you stay at?"

"Done stayed wid some folks there."

"Any folks I knows?"

"Don't know as dey is. Jest went long wid 'em after the meetin."

"Mose, why ain't you look at me? I can tell you ain't give me the truth. Ain't none of my business what place you stay at, only you been preachin a lot lately an I was jest wonderin."

"Thurman, I ain't did nothin I is shamed of. Only I didn't jest know what you'd say. I done stay wid Beatrice last night."

Thurman's eyes opened wide in astonishment. "Well, boy, you done picked the most slept-in bed in Lisbon. Wastin your money lak that! You is a fool in some ways an lak a chile too."

"They waren't no money to it; you understan that, Thurman. Maybe I is a fool; I don't deny that. I jest did it. That gal maybe done been misjedged. How you know?"

"Well, ain't matter how she been jedged. Folks in Lisbon done know fer a fact she got more mens than a woman her age got any business wid. An they ain't all cullud men neither. That cullud boy of hern; cullud nothin; he ain't had no cullud man fer a pappy. You know how long she been in Lisbon? Lessen three years. Whar she come from don't nobody know. But they's a heap of folks would be glad to see her leave. Mose, you done tore your pants fer shore."

"Maybe I is, maybe I is. But les us don't talk bout it no more."

Mose fled the house and kept out of Thurman's sight as much as possible that day, unable to ease the ache in his body and the confusion in his mind. He cleaned out the corn crib, raked the hog lot. He walked down into the woods with his ax and began cutting brush, but found no refuge and no forgetfulness. Some malevolent power, at least it seemed so to Mose, was conspiring against him. He resolved to conquer it and continue his life as before.

He went up to the big house, as he had never done since he had been on the place, and harangued Colin in the back yard until Clara came out and told him, "You git on off from here an left Colin do his work fore the old man done run you off hissef. You talk like somebody done lost his haid. Fore God, you do."

At dusk he went home and could not eat. The saliva refused to flow in his mouth and he could not swallow the dry bread. Thurman held a respectful silence, but he and Luella kept an eye of open curiosity on Mose. Finally he got up from the table, went into the kitchen shed, washed his face and hands and brushed his coat. Hatless he set out down the road to Lisbon without answering Thurman's, "Mose, why don't you bide it a day or two; it'll pass by like you say a man's troubles do if you gives 'em time."

Beatrice, sitting on her porch, appeared surprised to see Mose as he approached her. "Well, Mose, I hadn't figgered to see you so soon again. But I is right glad to see you. You come inside an set where people won't notice. People does talk, you know, an you has your preachin to think bout."

Mose felt the hurt of these words, but entered the house as she suggested.

"You acts, Beatrice, like it waren't right for me to be a comin back here. It don't seem no way wrong to me, leastaways it don't now. All of a sudden I done see some things like I never see 'em befo."

The boy whom Mose had seen that morning was standing

in the kitchen door. He was a large child, but still wore a dress that came just to his knees. Sucking his fingers, he looked at Mose without the timidity that might have been expected.

"Good evenin, jedge," he said.

Beatrice said, "Precious, that ain't no jedge. This here's Mose. Say good evenin to Mose."

The boy said, "Jedge."

Beatrice went to him and, picking him up in her arms, carried him to the back room. She returned for a quilt which she took to him.

"Precious, he ain't jest right. I don't let him go out none. But the other chillen they comes and pesters him through the door. They tells him his pappy was a jedge. That why, when a man come here, he call him jedge. He don't mean no harm. Doctor say he ain't never goin to have no mind at all."

Mose felt oppressed in the presence of this decay of mind and decay of body. He sat limp and unseeing in his chair, his mind confused. Now that he had been thrust, or rather had thrust himself, into this unnatural situation, he desired to find some means to clear the darkened environment of this house. But, being in the midst of these things, he was helpless, and his old fortitude and calm deserted him. He felt rising in him the lassitude of his people and the slow, rotting falling-away that seemed inevitably to overtake and overcome all men; as the parasitic, sensuous vines sweetly entwined the proud trees of the forest, by some enchantment, gradually but surely sapping first their vitality and then finally their very life until they stood gaunt and harsh and pitiful, their substance gone white and crumbling so that eventually they fell crashing to the damp earth; and vine and tree decayed together and mingled with the prime mud and the green slime. Was this then the predestined end?—that man should sink back to earth, having offered a denial to the last particle of nobility in him? Had he worshiped at some untrue altar, while all the day and night Colin moved about the white house that was a true shrine, harboring a wise devotee of the eternal truth?

But the woman came and sat beside him and took his hand in hers, and he buried all these thoughts in forgetfulness. The world and all its small symbols that had been clutching at him vanished. And sleep, soft and availing much, blotted out the last remnant of old associations.

But with the return of day the problem of the rightness of his conduct again dominated his mind and he found no solution. He only knew that he desired the woman near him. At times he seemed to see it all quite clearly, realizing that Beatrice was nothing more nor less than a parasite herself, growing in a society to which she contributed nothing and from which she took her life. But Mose had seen those things often enough before to realize that the question did not end there. Surely some connection existed between the phenomenon and the society in which it arose; there was a cause that did not lie in the woman.

And with weakness and a full knowledge of it he perceived, or rather felt, the devitalizing effect of the woman. Quiet, apparently without energy, she exerted to its full extent the female power, personifying perfectly the conjunction of creation and destruction, poisonous and inspiring, magnetic and forbidding.

It seemed he was standing at the rail of his dim vessel in

some mid-sea, feeling the desire to open wide his arms and plunge into that all-encompassing deep, to taste once the pleasure of a complete and heroic conflict and then be obliterated and commingled with the limitless, vital substance. He was approaching the mysterious source of life that seemed at once inviting and repelling, and its power resounded through his mind as the incessant roar of angry, rushing waters.

Mose had not forgotten the day when he had sat at the counter of the lunch room in Ventura. He had passed by that day. There had been other advances and withdrawals. But the why and wherefore of those other days was gone. Only the now seemed real. Mose was as the warrior who, tired from many struggles, at last gives up and rushes into the teeth of the unknown.

And Precious lay sleeping on his pallet in the back room that night, breathing a sputtering exhalation into the darkness. Lying there, he was no different from his fellow creatures. His skin felt the same to the touch; his body was composed of the same members; but Mose remembered him standing in the doorway in his dress, sucking his fingers: "Good evenin, jedge."

As the week grew older and the days passed, each like a month of the year, each with its separate significance, Mose became less tortured and resolved upon a plan of action which he refused to question and which at least gave life a course,—he would take Beatrice to the plantation.

The reason for Beatrice's consent to this plan is difficult to see. Perhaps she remembered too clearly the power that Mose had over his people when he was in the pulpit; she may have thought to find him elsewhere surrounded with the same pageantry and importance. She may have thought to find in him a stronger position in the world.

Allen heard of the strange goings-on and tried to dissuade his brother, expounding volumes of worldly advice, but Mose was adamant. On Sunday night he returned to the meeting house, looking a little worn, but outwardly at ease. Many of the negroes refused to attend. Others came and sat in hostile silence and watched Mose having his talk out. Then they bustled out shrugging their shoulders. Even this did not have any effect on the drunken man.

Beatrice did not come to the church. She waited at her house, commanding the situation without action, quite sure of herself. But she was not exultant. Probably she did not really care much either way. She had seen many men come and go. The world was full of men.

XII

ACROSS from Thurman's house a hundred yards away, a double shanty, for some years unoccupied, had been gradually falling to ruin. Decay had eaten into the walls, bricks lay about the bottoms of the chimneys on either end of the house, the porch sagged. The long, moss-greened cypress shingles parted here and there to show gaping holes.

To this house Mose turned his steps. He propped up the porch and nailed the walls together, chopped the weeds out of the yard. He begged a bed from one and an old stove from another. In the edge of the swamp he cut new shingles and closed the openings in the roof on one end of the house. Mr. Rutherford, passing by, thought of the Health Officer and whipped up his horse.

Allen came over one evening in a wagon and awkwardly made a gift of two of that year's hogs. There was no place to put them, so he and Mose by lantern light fashioned an enclosure in the back yard.

It was already too late in the season to think of a fall garden.

With all the bravado of a mariner, starting off on a long voyage, Mose drove Thurman's wagon into Lisbon; and, loading on Beatrice's possessions, handed her up to the seat, placing the child between them.

That night he stood on the porch, surveying his domain,

his house, a wife, her child, and, in the enclosure behind the house, two hogs.

On the following Sunday he did not go to the meeting house.

XIII

"I DON'T jest know how it happened," Mose told Thurman. "But thar it am an I'm bliged to bide what I done. I couldn't tell you how come I done it. I don't know mysef."

"Well, I can understan a man gittin hissef a wife. It's natural nough. But how come you to pick out Beatrice; that's what gits me. She ain't no farm nigger. You knows that. If you'd a got somebody could do choppin an pickin, it would a been all right, but how dat girl goin help you? Mose, you done laid up misery fer yoresef. Dat's what you done. Her settin on the gallery a watchin that boy o' hern an lookin off down the road. Mose, I done see trouble in that woman's eyes."

Mose nodded his head sadly. "Don't seem I never gits near to Beatrice. I tries to talk to her, an she gits up an goes off to Precious an jest sets dere, rockin the chile in her arms, singin to him, an he jest lay dere an don't say nothin.

"Can't git her to take no interest in nothin. She don't act like she want to be here an she don't never talk bout leavin none. She don't want to go back to Lisbon; I knows dat fer shore.

"She done been too high-toned. She done want things a nigger can't git. Her white hands, she wash an scrub 'em an won't hardly tetch a washboard, she so skeered she rough 'em up."

"Well, Mose, I hopes it work out fer you. Maybe after a time she git used to it an come to like it an make you a good wife. People maybe come to see different bout her. An then you can go back to the meetin house. I don't like to see you not goin, Mose." But behind Thurman's words there was a tone that showed clearly he did not believe in the hopes he expressed.

Like many another man Mose realized too late. He had always thought of himself as moving in his life alone and by his own strength. Now he had allowed himself to fall to dreary relaxation, to be overcome by an easy submission to the path of least resistance. It had been hard to fight his way alone, trying to keep his thoughts clear and his head high, but there had been a satisfaction that preserved his self-respect. Now he was given over to a petty life wherein he must be bound by all the common ties that destroyed his freedom. He had become as other men.

But, at least, Mose was not one to flee his obligation. There was no question about this. His duty he must do to the best of his ability. He took down all the outer trappings of his personal life and locked them deep within himself. His communions he continued to have, but in silence and in darkness.

Beatrice passed from resignation to sullenness and then became quarrelsome and finally openly defiant. The dreary monotony of life in the cabin, removed from social intercourse and the noise of the town, left her desolate and miserable. She came to hate Mose for his quiet way of going about his business. She longed for a flashing eye and a gaudy suit and the sound of heavy laughter. The humor that Mose made came seldom and was likely to be grim and double-edged.

Mose, in his desire to express some of the latent affection for the world that was part of him, turned to the child, Precious, who deeply reciprocated in action the feeling, but was unable to give it any coherent vocal expression. With his hand in Mose's he went about the place, staring before him with eyes that occasionally flashed as if in a sudden comprehension and then lapsed into long periods of blank dullness. Mose often talked to him, trying to stimulate some spark that might be in the locked brain, but Precious only looked at him stupidly.

"Ha, ha, ha; talk, talk, talk; why Precious talk? Why talk?"

"Precious, chile, don't go on so. You here and Mose here. Got a long time to be together. Just take it easy. Go slow. Listen to what Mose say to you. See, dere in the pen. Them is hogs. Now you say dat. 'Dere is de hogs.'"

"Precious can't say." And the child began crying with rage and rushed up to the pen, shook the gate and threw dirt at the hogs, but they paid no attention to him, rooting about over the litter on the ground. And Mose lifted the child and quieted him, saying softly:

"Don't you trouble yore head none, chile. Jest you rest here wid old Mose," and he sang to the child, making up the words as he went along,

> "The little Lord Jesus done come down the stairs,
> Done come down the stairs,
> Done come down the stairs,
> The little Lord Jesus done come down the stairs,
> Done laid his hand on me."

Beatrice came to the back door and watched them, then ran out to Mose and took the child from him.

"You done make fun of my chile. Don't pester him. Don't you try to hahm my chile. You leave him be. Don't you think I ain't watched you."

She continued, "The doctors in Lisbon done try to carry Precious off to the sylum an now you done try to take him away from me, but I ain't goin to let you."

She stood trembling, and the child writhed and screamed in her arms. Mose felt a deep pity for the woman and did not try to correct her.

"Honey, can't you an me do no better'n dis? I knows maybe I hadn't orter brung you out here where you is had jest one long misery, but we'd orter make better of it than we is. I tries hard an I knows I can't do much. Maybe if you'd tell me more bout how you feels inside, I could do better."

Beatrice paused for a moment; her eyes softened, but then the look of defiance returned to her face and she fled into the house.

Mose, looking about him, wondered at this situation he had created and saw nothing ahead except to be surrounded by an impassable barricade. He was suddenly impressed by the smallness of life and the pettiness of all of the things of life. They had never entered his mind before, because he had lived without and beyond them. But now it seemed he was drawn to their level and made a part of the dreary, rotting boards and the weedy yard where the hogs grunted into the filthy earth, and the stunted trees were uninspired and small; there in his castle a half-witted child and an abortion of civilization damned surely to be misfit and outcast.

Mose never came to lose his sympathy for Beatrice. Only

he knew that neither he nor anyone else could find a proper place for her.

Sentenced by his own judgment to be there the rest of his days until gradually he wore himself away against the rough surface of life. It was to live and perish with such insignificance. And he was now more intelligently aware of his people, for he had experienced their pain; and the black, heart-rending wail of his people rose in his throat. He lifted his arms high above his head, and the heavens did not open to him and the white graceful hand that he had known in former days remained withdrawn and the only sound that came to him was the snuffling breath of the indolent swine.

XIV

AND in the days that followed the only peace that Mose found was that of utter weariness. When he could return to his cabin at night so fatigued in body that his mind was benumbed, he found life in a measure bearable. He lived as a beast of burden, working and then sleeping to renew strength to work again. The words that Beatrice spoke resounded upon his ears as the sound of distant knockings on thin evasive walls. He hardly heard at all and seldom made answer. He longed with a definite urge to find eventually some way to appeal to Beatrice, but for the present he only waited to see what time might bring.

And in the rhythm of long toil he found there existed a consolation that was, though small, a certain reward. He came to realize a deeper communion with elemental life to which he was now quite close. For between him and his beasts, and the rocks and the earth they disturbed, there was a hard-fashioned link, a compact endlessly renewed by the sweat that dropped off to the ground.

"Done thought I seed it all so clear, Thurman; how what's a goin to be done lay down befo me like a long track. But it ain't never that-a-way. When you gits on down the road, it change. Don't nothin never rest long the same. What was a year ago don't seem the same now, and I knows fer shore that what am now goin seem different by the time muscadines done ripe again."

In countless centuries a man might sow the same field innumerable times and never twice would the earth crack in quite the same way to show the budding plant. Mose felt the deep mystery of this and held it in awe.

On returning to the cabin one evening in the late fall of that year, Mose found Mr. Birney standing in the yard, a little more flushed and explosive than usual.

"Well, Mose, well, now. A right smart darky, I'll say, making a house out of this place. Want you to know Mr. Rutherford spoke of it." And he fingered his hat from side to side on his head. "Just think, by golly, you're a sure-enough enterprising one, you are. Glad I got you on the place, I am. How are you getting on?"

Mose glanced up at the house. Beatrice was sitting on the steps, watching him closely.

"Oh, we done get on, thank you, Mr. Birney. Don't we, Beatrice?"

"Huh? What you say? Yes, we done get long right good."

Mr. Birney untied the reins from the gatepost and mounted his horse. "Want you to know I'm looking out for you, Mose. When you need anything, you come by the commissary. Guess you got a little credit." And to his horse, "Come up now," and he went off down to the road, his body rising and falling with the motion like a heavy, overripe melon.

"You done been makin talk wid Mr. Birney?"

"Yes, me an Mr. Birney done talk some. Oh, he done think a heap of you, Mose."

"Yes? He ain't never show it befo."

"Well, maybe you ain't never give him no chance. If you'd just play up to him now an then, maybe he'd help you to get on."

"Yes, maybe so." And Mose went into the house.

Beatrice came in behind him and busied herself about the large box that served them as a table. Her face was brighter and, though she spoke little, she was more cheerful.

When Precious had finished his food, she wiped the grease from his face and hands and went out on the porch, hugging him close to her, singing snatches of songs she half-remembered.

Mose puttered about the room, not wanting to question Beatrice further, and then lay down on the bed where they slept. It was perplexing, and he could not understand the change in Beatrice. But it was so much a relief from her usual mood that he sighed and was thankful.

A few days later Mr. Birney came to Mose where he was working and called him. Mose ambled up to him and stood in respectful silence.

"Mose, I've been down to Lisbon and had a talk with the boys, Mr. Rutherford's boys, I mean. I've lined up something for you. They say you can work in the store for them this winter. You can't do much good out here before spring now, and it'll give you a chance to get on your feet. Mind you now, they could find a hundred darkeys in Lisbon that would jump at the chance. How does it strike you?"

Mose's expression did not change. "I hadn't never thought bout it, Mr. Birney. I don't rightly know how it would be, leavin Beatrice out here by herself all day. The chile might tooken sick. You know how dat is."

"Just what are you driving at, Mose? You know there are plenty of people on the place all the time."

"Ain't drivin at nothin. Shore ain't. Only I hadn't thought nothin bout it. Dat's all."

"Well, if you got to think about it, as you say, you come by the house in the morning and let me know what you decide, because Mr. Orvil ain't goin to wait more than a week for you to make up your mind."

"I'll shore do dat, Mr. Birney, I shore will."

"Look here, Mose; can't you say thank you? Who the hell do you think you are anyway?"

"Oh, yes sir, Mr. Birney, I preciates what you does fer me; an fer Beatrice too. Thank you."

Mr. Birney muttered to himself, wheeled his horse around and rode off.

To whom might he turn for advice, Mose wondered. To the big white house perhaps. That was the proper place for wisdom's abode. But it was withered and stale. To Allen, then. As well to his mule that wagged with giddy laughter on one end and kicked with the other. At last he turned to his known refuge, to God, long and earnestly, with remarks respectfully addressed. But somehow in the long appeal there was a misstep, one number not quite achieved and the combination failed; the door remained closed.

So, heavy of heart, Mose sat at Thurman's door, hopeless of any counsel but rather seeking sympathy and the relief that comes from emptying when the bowl has long been overfilled and the bands are weary with strained tautness.

Thurman said, "They's some things in this world, seem a man need most, twell he gits 'em, an then they burdens him like a too tight collar done gripe a mule. But you can't fight back at white folks, Mose; ain't no need fer me to tell you that. You don't know nothin yet fer shore. Best think the best. You git long down to the store like he tole you to an think no more bout it."

It was a strange store, Mose thought. Hardly anyone ever came in; few people bought anything; mostly they sat about in the back room talking with Orvil and Lonnie. The shelves and counters were dusty and the concrete floor stained and tracked with mud.

At first they set him to cleaning the place, which he did faithfully, but after a time they forgot about it, and the dust and dirt seeped back to the accustomed depth.

On the cans of salmon, meats and vegetables, dampness loosed the labels and blurred the trademarks. The candy in the glass counter was wet and crumbly.

Mose waited on the few customers that entered, usually strangers who did not come again. He had only a vague idea of the prices of the goods, but as that did not seem to trouble the boys, he ceased worrying about it himself.

The real commerce took place in the back room where they kept the cans from which the jugs were filled. Sometimes they sent Mose to deliver in the town. He did not want to do it, but had reached the time when he did not care much one way or another. He had become resigned to the futility of his life. As he was bidden, he did.

But most of the time he sat in the store on the counter, leaning against a box, half asleep, unthinking, waiting for the day to pass. At noon he was permitted to eat his lunch from the shelves. It might be sardines, cheese or some canned meat, and always a box of crackers that were stale and full of weevils. Mose's lunches depleted the stock more than the customers' purchases.

There were never any inventories to be taken, never any bills to make out or orders to be placed. The accounting was all done at a drawer that slid under the counter. Whenever the sum got above a dollar, Lonnie or Orvil took out the surplus. They never questioned Mose about it and he never stole from them.

He came to work at six in the morning and left at six at night. The store was closed on Sunday. They paid him six dollars a week, a very generous wage in comparison to those paid by the other Lisbon merchants.

Not infrequently, leaving Precious at Thurman's house, Beatrice would come into Lisbon, stopping at the store to get a few nickels from Mose, which she spent on gaudy cloth at the other storekeepers'. Her hair now smelled strongly of scented oils; her lips and cheeks were over-rouged.

When Mose returned to the cabin in the evening, she avoided him as much as possible. Finally she moved a pallet for him to the back kitchen shed room where, she told him, he could sleep with Precious, as the front room was too crowded with both of them sleeping there. This, too, Mose endured.

He knew now without asking what was transpiring. He could read it in the other negroes' faces as they passed him on the plantation and spoke in halting embarrassment. He knew it most clearly from the way Thurman had difficulty now in finding anything to talk to him about when he went over after supper. All the talk was forced and spiritless.

But Mose dreaded to face the eventual issue. Anything to postpone action. To see with his own eyes he knew would provoke him to resistance. He hoped he would not see. He wanted to be let alone to go his way in a little semblance of peace.

One joy remained to him. It came in the early morning before and during sunrise and at evening after sunset.

As he opened his cabin door in the morning, the thick smoke from the chimney was hanging low and the now brown plants were cold and damp. There was a white spot in the east, cheerless and blanketed. He pulled his thin coat tighter about him and set out swiftly down the road, watching the patch in the east off across the quiet black forest growing brighter minute by minute. The cabins in the fields clung to the earth. Wagons and rusted plows were out on the ground where they had been the last day they were used, weeks before. The gravel in the road resisted his feet. A flock of brilliant black crows wheeled croaking off across the sky. In the ditch at the roadside the water lay still under a heavy green coat, and here and there showed cracked mud flats surrounded by withered, broken cat-o'-nine-tails. He walked as fast as he could and the blood coursed swift and hot through his body. And sometimes a surge of unaccountable joy swept over him and he pressed his arms across against his empty bosom and laughed in a high, ringing note of victory. Only when he reached the edge of the town where he could see dirty children sleepy-eyed at kitchen doors and the squat dingy brick buildings did he become oppressed and inwardly silent.

A strange figure he made,—tall, thin, graceful, walking hunched forward, drooping the high-foreheaded bony head out before him, swinging easily his long arms at his sides. A criminal he might have been, just escaped, headed off to timber country, or a lonely troubador. A lunatic perhaps.

And in the evening in the autumn early darkness he returned along the same road. The chill wind originating on the misty lakes hummed through the telegraph wires. Hawks sailed low. Like noises of some sad, distant, unreal land softly pulsed the voices of the negroes in their cabins, where blackened oil lanterns sulked and sputtered. And as the sound of the voices in the cabin he passed became faint and distant behind him, there arose the sounds from some other cabin before him, and as the one faded, the other increased, and it was as though someone were tinkling soft bells at him, now approaching, now withdrawing, as if to entice him from his path. He heard infrequently the sounds of singing and of feet beating on thin floors. A great limitless, strong-smelling earth, shadowy and harsh, and over all untold blackness and void.

He had then the joy of thinking how good it would be to run into one of these intimate cabins and sit down at table before a hot bowl of peppered broth and laugh heartily through one's teeth, to slap the fellow next down the table a great whack across his shoulders and jest with him,—and yet not to do it, to go on and on down the road as one was bidden, to thrust the tired foot out ahead into the crunching gravel,—crunch, crunch, crunch, until it became automatic and instinctive, not to waver or look back but go on into the throat of fate.

When it has been once aroused, there is no chaining the human mind. In most desolate circumstances it yet soars out and above all limitations, defying the bonds of the body. It is the one last solace of the lonely and defeated individual; it is a boon that can not be taken away by any usury or by the decree of any court. Witness the urchin seated on the sidewalk, his feet in the gutter, his hands rubbing a small coin and in his eyes a light that shows the mind has gone off a-visiting lords and ladies the like of whom no artist ever painted. So in most people of whom we say, he seems to get a bit of happiness out of life, we find some of that same sparkle that is in the eyes of children.

And going down that road, a criminal, a troubador, a lunatic? No, just a child, reaching out into thin air, building himself a momentary happiness.

There just ahead he sees a familiar light coming through the ill-hung shutter. The mind begins to slow its pace; he enters the house and, closing the door behind him, shuts out more of a world than is visible to the eye; but he has not destroyed it nor cut himself off from it; he is merely reserving it for a later appointment.

XV

It is late in the year, almost Christmas time. Women are going about the stores in Lisbon, making small purchases of toys and tinsels for a pathetic display about a candle-lighted tree.

The day has been cold and deadened. Only now and then the wind puffs feebly across the gray sky, disturbing loose papers that lie in the streets. Coat collars are turned up and shawls are drawn tightly over shoulders.

At the store the chill air comes in through the cracks at the door and the flames of the gas stove waver. The boys in the back room have been sullenly drinking. Death seems to have half a hold on everything.

In the afternoon large flakes of snow begin to fall. They melt in the dust, leaving the walks sticky and black. As it grows later, the temperature drops to freezing and the snow comes faster in a fine powder that begins to whiten the earth, making the buildings seem more squalid than ever by contrast.

Going home that evening Mose was sick with cold. His skin was dry about his body and his teeth chattered. With one hand he held his ragged jacket up around his throat; the other he kept in his pocket. He was unable to see anything through the blinding snow; only from having walked the road so many times could he tell approximately where he was.

Finally the embankment by the drainage ditch loomed ahead of him like a black shadow that the storm now concealed, now revealed through the wind-whipped snow.

The cabin was bitter cold. Beatrice had Precious wrapped in a quilt, sitting on the wood-box by the stove. Mose came and stood by the stove, holding out his long thin hands, working his fingers to stimulate the flow of blood.

"We goin freeze to death fer shore if this keep up much longer. Ain't never know such weather befo."

"Can't last long," Mose said. "Not more'n a day or two anyhow. Most likely it all melt off in the mawnin. Hope it stay cold 'til tomorrow evenin; then we can kill them hogs in the mawnin. Hog meat a heap better if you kills on a cold mawnin; meat don't spile fore you gits the salt on it, like in warm weather."

"How you gits off from the store to do hog killin?"

"I done axe Mr. Orvil fore I left this evenin. He say if it stay cold tomorrow, to go on an kill the hogs an don't come to Lisbon 'til after dinner, an if I can't git done by then, to left it go all day. Ain't no use me goin nohow. They ain't never nothin to do only set there an now an then go somewheres where they wants somethin took to."

They sat down on boxes about the stove, eating, Precious sucking the food into his mouth, drooling across the front of his sweater. The food was hot and the sweat stood on his forehead and his eyes glowed.

"You likes that, Precious, don't you, honey?"

The child whimpered.

Beatrice said, "How come you always tries to make him talk? You knows it jest riles him."

"How you goin help the chile, thout you done try to learn him to talk? You want him to stay a dummy?"

"He ain't no chile o' yourn. You left him be. I'll be bounden fer the raisin of him."

Precious paid no attention to them. Only that he moved and that his eyes showed life made him seem different from the inanimate objects in the shed room.

There was not wood enough to keep the stove fired all night. They lingered at their bowls, wiping up the gravy on pieces of bread, hating to face the cold sleep of the night.

They piled the dishes in a pan on the stove. Beatrice sloshed them in the water, and Mose wiped them on a torn meal sack.

Mose and Beatrice acted almost as if they were strangers. It would have been the natural thing for them to sit there while the stove was yet warm to stretch in animal comfort and make sleepy talk. But when they were finished, Beatrice went into the front room, turning at the door before she closed it behind her.

"You latch that back door. Precious likely to try to git out an it ain't no sort of night to be chasin after him."

Mose did not reply, remained seated by the stove, his forehead scorching and his shoulders aching with cold. Loose shingles flapped on the roof and the wind and snow groaned around the corners of the house. The lamp flickered, the bending flame blackening the chimney.

With dull unawareness he wrapped the child and laid him as close to the stove as he dared. He extinguished the lamp, and there was only the glimmer of the dying embers in the fire-box of the wood stove, showing through the crack in the draught door.

He lay down on the other side of the stove by the wall and drew over him the quilts, from which the cotton filler hung out through tears in the covering. He kept all his clothes on except his shoes, only loosening his trousers about his waist.

The wind abated some and softly hissed about the house, at times dying out altogether, leaving heavy silence. The stove creaked as, growing cold, it contracted. The glow from the fire-box died out.

Mose fell asleep.

He was unable to tell how long he had been sleeping when he was suddenly awakened. He was cramped with cold and thought at first this was the reason for his waking. It seemed that he could hear or had heard someone crying out; the sound of it was beating through his brain like a remembered dream. He sat up, trying to grasp his consciousness, trying to perceive some fact that seemed to be groping to imprint itself upon his mind.

The room glowed with a pale light. The outside door to the shed room was open. It had stopped snowing, the wind had ceased and there was brilliant moonlight flooding through the doorway.

He looked about the room. There was a knotted pile of quilts by the stove. Precious was gone.

Mose gained his feet and stood listening. He could hear nothing at first, then faintly from behind the house the sound of the hogs, grunting as they did for food.

He hurried out the door. The snow was soft under his stockinged feet. Whiteness was everywhere on the ground, and standing out from the ground black objects, the fences, stalks in the fields and the great trees in the distance; the silence of night reached out, encircling all, and beating back against it the throaty grunting of the hogs.

With impersonal aloofness, almost disdain, he stood looking at the form lying on the ground just by the hog lot beyond the reach of the snout that pushed out through the heavy mesh wire, slobbering to mouth the mound of flesh. There was no slow rising and falling under the dark sweater that breathing would have made. The knees were up against the chest, the head drawn to one side and the bare face staring with closed eyes up into the palely brilliant heavens. One arm lay on the ground, the other gracefully over the head, the fingers apart and extended, as if clutching feebly. The yellow-brown skin shone clearly along the top of the wide nose and on the cheek bones, giving way to the shadows of the eyes and the lines by the mouth and nose. The lips were full and dully colored.

An object not to be disturbed, to be studied and critically examined. But the hogs had no respect, butted against the wire and pawed at the earth, giving no thought to the morrow.

Mose remembered distinctly that he had latched the door. He remembered how the latch was rusty and had to be pushed down hard with the thumb—to keep the child from going out. He had tried the door to see if it were tightly latched. It did not give. He remembered it so clearly, just how he had done it—knowing well that he had never touched the door, had never thought of it after Beatrice spoke.

It was a dream. It could not be true. Like the boys at the store, like Mr. Birney coming to the house when he was gone, like the scent of perfume in his house. Untrue, false, a trick of his clouded mind.

He breathed heavily, agitated by ill-ordered passions. Then slowly, wearily, he walked to the body and felt it, dropped to his knees and placed his ear close by the nostrils. He thought himself smiling. What a show. Why not feel the pulse of the fencepost? He rubbed the cold wrists that were stiff in his hands, like the body of a bird killed by the hunters that the dogs overlooked picking up.

With difficulty he straightened the legs and forced the arms down beside the body. He lifted it and walked to the house, holding it out before him.

He was unable to feel any regret, any sorrow. He was only conscious of a fact. Not until he was standing before Beatrice, who sat cold-eyed with the dead child across her knees, did he feel, not his, but her pain.

He wanted her to ask him why he had failed to latch the door, to accuse him. It would have been a relief to confess his carelessness.

But she sat there chanting, her body moving slowly forward and backward, rocking on the box. Her face was colorless from grief and cold. He put a quilt about her shoulders. She acknowledged it by nodding her head.

"You better go lie down now. Best wait 'til mawnin." She rose and handed him the child's body and went back to the front room and lay down and he covered her.

He was afraid. Her failure to make any outcry was strange. He did not know what she might do. He sat through the night in the kitchen, watching for the child to begin breathing. He trembled with cold. Existence seemed an interminable extension.

As soon as the sky began to grow light, he looked at Beatrice. She was sleeping quietly. He crossed the intervening stretch of field, and calling Thurman from his bed, told him what had happened.

"I'm bliged to git back now. I dast not leave Beatrice by herself after she git up. You go by an see Mr. Birney. See what he say do."

Thurman obviously made more than one call on his way, for soon the negroes of the place began to edge up to the door with many awkward shufflings of feet. Such a mourning was not an event to be foregone.

They wrapped the dressed body in a sheet, and laid it on the floor in the middle of the room and mourned, audibly, beating their knees with the palms of their hands. Beatrice, apparently taking little notice of anyone, herself knelt and went through the procedure like an actress, capable in her part but lacking the power of reality.

Mose was embarrassed in the presence of what was to him a childlike demonstration and waited on the porch.

Presently Thurman returned. "Mr. Birney, he say, you got to bury him today. He say he ain't goin have the mournin go on tonight.

"You can use my wagon, an the others that wants to go long can git the other wagons on the place."

"Look, Thurman. There Mr. Rutherford, fer shore."

At the road Colin stood holding the horse, and Mr. Rutherford, bowed under his black hat, was stomping across the field to the house, his cane digging deep into the earth at every step.

As he neared the house, he removed his hat, showing his

fine head, resolute under its covering of dark hair heavily sprinkled with gray.

"Good morning, Mose."

"Good mawnin, Mr. Rutherford."

"Good morning, Thurman."

"Good mawnin, sir."

"Mr. Birney just came by the house and told me what happened. I was very sorry to hear of it. I understand the child hadn't been well."

"No sir, not that. Only he waren't right."

"Oh, I understand. I am told it was not your boy, Mose."

"No sir. Precious, he was Beatrice chile."

"Is she all right?"

"She seem to be bearin up."

"Well, I can hear the others in there. She will work it out of her system. Now I suppose you will bury the child today?"

"Mr. Birney, he say we have got to."

"It's not a question of got to, Mose. You do what you think best. But I think it would be better not to wait too long. Don't you think so?"

"I guess you is right. I guess so."

"Well, I'll just ride on in to Lisbon and see the sexton at the cemetery and have the grave dug and have the preacher arranged for. You all can come any time after dinner when you get ready to." He walked down from the porch. "I'll wait in Lisbon at the cemetery for you."

He turned and plowed his way back to the road and drove off as fast as the horse could go, Colin sitting beside him. A cloud of steam rose off the horse's flanks as they disappeared in the distance.

Graves in the negro cemetery are usually unmarked and if they are marked at all, it is with a wooden cross that soon falls and decays among the weeds. So there is a wide range of choice when the sexton digs. On that day he made two mistakes, and the mounds of earth remained to mock his forgetfulness.

They placed chairs in the wagons for the mourners to sit in, and it took some time for the procession to reach the graveside. Mr. Rutherford was there, waiting as he had said he would, and during the committal stood respectfully in the background.

When it was finished, Mose told him, "You hadn't orter come to stand so long in the cold. It make you sick fer shore."

He looked at Mose, smiled in astonishment, seeming to remember that no one had spoken so solicitously to him for a long time. "That's right thoughtful of you, Mose. But I'll be all right. I've seen a lot of rough weather off and on. This isn't so bad."

And then, as if ashamed of what he had said, he turned roughly away and clambered into his buggy.

The brief afternoon sun had melted the snow, making the earth soft. The wagons, entering and leaving the cemetery, rutted the ground, making black wounds.

Sitting in their uncertain places in the bumping wagons, returning that hushed evening back to the farm lands, the negroes were satiated and peaceful. Death is a powerful sedative. And that night in his cabin was more of desolation than Mose had ever known.

XVI

PERHAPS more than any other incident, the death of Precious served to crystallize in Mose's mind a feeling that had been growing in him since he had first become disillusioned about his relation with Beatrice; namely, that it was a futile enterprise, the sooner ended the better. But it seemed to him that quite possibly the fault might lie in the dreariness of their abode and the surroundings of their life. Perhaps if this sorrow could be in some measure alleviated, there might be constructed some basis upon which they could achieve a satisfactory relationship.

During the weeks he was at the store he had saved all he could, and when, with the return of spring, he left to go back to the field to make his own crop, he was able to improve their home considerably by a few small purchases of secondhand furniture and gaudy trappings in the Lisbon markets. Beatrice seemed not particularly impressed by this display, but Mose thought he saw some signs that he might take as encouraging. Beatrice questioned him with pronounced interest about his plans for the planting and how much profit he might hope to derive from the season. Mose did not have the vaguest idea about this latter question himself, but he endeavored to paint as pretty a picture as possible.

He was about the house most of the time at first. He never saw Mr. Birney except when he went to the commissary. Perhaps, he thought, that presence was gone from his house for good; he did not permit himself to think otherwise, so much did he desire to believe it.

Beatrice never spoke of Precious, and of course Mose did not. They never visited the grave, and when Thurman did on one occasion, he told Mose about it but not Beatrice. It seemed that every trace of the child had been buried with him, as a proper disposition for an unpleasant memory.

Mose resolved that the year would be one desperate effort to regain, not Beatrice, but, in gaining an adjustment of their relationship, himself. Surely the process of making the earth produce for their needs should have some by-product of spiritual value for them. At least he was not one to give way to resignation for long.

Mose had hoped he would be able to move to Mr. Dancy's place, where life would at least be more secure. He was disappointed in this, but Mr. Dancy assured him that quite possibly the next year some such arrangement might be effected. Mose did not know that Mr. Dancy would have been willing enough himself to have the removal take place at once. But Mr. Birney had had private conversations with Mr. Dancy on the subject, explaining how he had carried Mose through the fall and winter without any profit and indeed at considerable financial loss to himself personally, so now when Mose might be set at profitable enterprise, it was hardly an equitable act for Mr. Dancy to fetch him off to his plantation. There was further talk about the evil practice of stealing good niggers from one's neighbors, an evil which Mr. Dancy had himself condemned on numerous occasions; and so the matter was let rest.

But Mose was doubtless happier for his ignorance of this. There is a burden of pain that follows wisdom, increasing as wisdom increases. Pessimism is the price of wisdom.

XVII

THE return of spring on the Delta plain is no delicate phenomenon. It is the slow return of heat and movement in the body of a heavy, slumbering animal. And when the flanks begin to quiver and the nostrils to dilate, there is the acid smell of an awakened beast, and one feels the great, latent power that will soon realize itself.

It is a vast and fertile country, compelling and in many aspects terrifying. The blackness of the soil and the profuseness of the vegetation make a picture of a voluptuous luxury unequaled elsewhere. The man who dwells on the arid plateaus and the mountain dweller are unsympathetic and often repulsed. Only the valley people who like the taste of river water know that though they may not find peace dying with the heavy swamp mist in their lungs, they would assuredly be lost elsewhere.

The Delta rots a man's bones and eats out his fiber, but it also builds a hard cord about his heart, and he would rather lean against a cypress tree and fight mosquitoes than venture into any unknown land.

There was once beauty here. Its ruins can still be found. It might return.

And out from his house Mose turned his strength and his aspiration against the soil to see how they might avail much to the satisfaction of his own needs. Perhaps the life of man may be said to surge and then fall into a trough and then surge again. Mose was at the trough, floundering on a false scent. But the power for an onrush was building up in him.

All the energy he had held at quiet during the winter at the store now found an outlet. The dawn could not come too soon nor the darkness too late to suit him. He brought his fields to a state of cultivation that caused people traveling down the road to comment, "Clean as a hound's tooth, that field." But they were not led to emulate this display of energy, only interested in it as an unusual occurrence.

The green slime on the swamp pools awoke with vibrant life in countless forms. Water bugs churned across the surface, making little whirling wheels behind them. Moccasins slowly glided here and there; turtles basked in the sun. Willow saplings and vines hung out from the banks, holding the hot air suspended over the water. Even the cypress trees greened up a little at the top, as they pressed their gaunt roots into the cool deep mud. Could there ever have been any winter? It hardly seemed so.

Everywhere was life and growth displaying itself with such feverish insistence that it might have been the hour before doomsday when every natural accident was bent upon achieving its maturity before the end.

As Mose traversed the length of the field and the machinery of his body responded with competence, he found that many old aches and bruises fell from him and lost their power. But in spite of this he still held one eye fixed on the machinations of fate. He no longer believed that he was going to get any lasting reprieve. But he was not going to lie down and bawl and kick his feet against the ground. Let the future bring what it might. As for the now, there was a certain piece of ground that needed a little more breaking.

Perhaps he might not be there to see the end of his labors; that did not justify his forsaking the labor. The testimony of old frustrations was a distant wind that spent itself against some resisting hill before it found his face. Surely all this potent abundance about him was not so powerful but he could direct it down ways suited to his own needs.

Mose loved the earth as one must love all things that are known intimately. Knowing how it was not all good and how it could blast and curse, he also knew its strength and consoling tenderness. And when the earth filled his shoes, stained his body and mingled with his sweat to make a mud mask on his face, he loved the heavy scent of it in his nostrils. To drive the plow up against the hills and back down to where the ancient river rolls on is likely the most ennobling and fulfilling of all vocations.

If Mose had considered the possibility of the cloister at all, he had realized that it was not what he wanted. There were better and surer ways of fleeing life than that. He had not watched the river for nothing. But what he had realized was that in this world when one flees the first unpleasant situation, he usually finds himself thrust deep in the middle of another. No use then to go off hunting the utopia on earth. Best, as long as any hope remained, to do the business at hand.

Proud of self and eager in a justified self-respect, he stands at the end of the row, pulling the plow around behind the beast, pointing the curved steel just there at the precise spot where the row must begin. He halts the mule and as it stands with nostrils beating, showing red and wet within, he looks off across the field and the tree tops to where he knows the river of unity and dissolution is flowing, and his throat contracts and his breast rises. He throws his head back so that his bare forehead is thrust up, a black silhouette against the heavens.

"Great God Almighty," he cries, and, leaning forward, with his powerful shoulders gives the plow its first drive into the earth. He beats the lines, and man, beast and plow start across the field.

Strangely enough, Mose was not thinking of the pomp of kings nor the body heavings of dynasties. His world was small and yet important. A definite piece of land still unplowed. The sun so high above the horizon. Such and such a speed would be required in order to be finished by sundown.

But Mose was never able to arouse Beatrice's interest to the point where she was willing to share in his efforts as in a common enterprise. In the households of most of the negroes one found the women helping in the fields, and many of them could wield the hoe as well as their men and could deliver stroke for stroke with them during the long days when the crop was making. Beatrice never offered her help, and Mose had not the courage to ask it nor the desire to insist. He was reasonably sure that she had no strength for such work, and the thought of driving her, which was not an extraordinary practice, never occurred to him.

So during the hot days she remained at the house, only occasionally going off to Lisbon, bent on what business Mose did not know, as she never told him and he never asked.

He was so tired at night that quiet and sleep seemed enough. If Beatrice preferred to sit on the porch by herself, watching the gourd vine that grew up one end of the house, that was her business. Sometimes Mose went to visit with the other negroes in the evening. He invariably went alone. It was a relief and no one seemed to miss Beatrice, as she was always condescending to the other women. Her light skin and her dark eyes made her equally unwelcome in the home of the negro and the white man.

XVIII

It was on a Saturday afternoon early in June that Mose was sitting on his porch resting after his lunch before returning to work. Colin came across the field nearly to the house and called Mose.

"Mr. Birney, he say you come up to the commissary right now."

"What he want? He want me to leave the field?"

"He ain't say dat. He jest say you come on right now."

"You tell him I'm comin."

Beatrice came to the door. "Now what you reckon he want? You ain't in no trouble, is you, Mose?"

"No. How I know what he want?"

He got his hat and started across the field. He had not seen Mr. Birney for several days and he had a premonition that something might be wrong. Nothing he had done surely, for he knew he had worked his field as well or better than any other hand on the place.

Mr. Birney was sitting on a molasses barrel inside the commissary. His horse was tied to a post at the side of the building.

"You sont fer me?"

"Yes, Mose. Now I tell you what I want you to do. Want you to go down to Lisbon and get me a can of saddle soap. You can get it at the hardware store. Here's a dollar. Won't cost you more than half a dollar. You can keep a quarter for yourself."

"Yes sir, Mr. Birney, I can use a quarter. Only I is thinkin maybe I hadn't orter left the field whilst they is so much to be did."

"Well, guess your crops'll hold together until you get back. Now you go along like I told you."

Mose touched his hat and left.

As he turned into the road and started for Lisbon, his fears increased. There was no reason for Mr. Birney to be sending anybody to Lisbon for saddle soap. He could get it himself if he really needed it. He was usually in Lisbon once every Saturday anyway.

He turned and looked back at the commissary. Mr. Birney was apparently still inside; the horse was standing as before.

He continued down the road to where the bayou comes out from the woods. There he left the road, and entering the woods, made his way for about a quarter of a mile until he was beyond the path that crosses Binam's sorghum patch, leading to the still. He kept in far enough to be out of sight, but between breaks in the undergrowth he could see the commissary. He had reached a point where the semicircle of woods had curved back to within a few hundred yards of his house. There he decided to wait. The horse was still standing beside the commissary. Mr. Birney had not come out.

Probably he was wrong, he thought. He had better be getting back on the road to Lisbon, for if Mr. Birney's need for the soap were genuine, it behooved him to return with it in good time. He turned and started to retrace his steps.

At this moment Mr. Birney came out of the commissary

door. Mose halted, watching him. Mr. Birney untied his horse and mounted, then rode out to the road and paused, looking down in the direction of Lisbon. Then, seeming satisfied, he went the other way.

Mose was no longer in doubt. This was an affront too obvious for him to pass by. Keeping as low as possible, he began to make his way back to his house, approaching it from the side opposite to Mr. Birney.

He waited behind a small cotton shed close by. Mr. Birney dismounted at the door, tied his horse's reins, stood for a few moments scanning the fields about him, then went up on the porch. The door opened to him and he entered.

Mose came out from behind the shed and crept up to the house and on the porch. Faintly from within came the sound of their voices, Beatrice's slow and drawling, Mr. Birney's jerky and harsh, commanding.

Mose tried the door. It was bolted. He pounded on it.

There was complete silence.

"Beatrice, you come open that door. I done see him come in here. I ain't a goin to have it. Befo God, not in my own house."

He leaned against the door and broke it open with little effort. Then he stepped back. The sight that met his eyes was sickening, one that he would never be able to forget.

He did not enter the room, waited on the porch, his arms hanging at his sides.

Mr. Birney walked slowly out on to the porch, not speaking; then: "Mose, you're just a black son of a bitch and you don't know it. But I'll teach you, by God, I will. I never took talk from no nigger yet."

He went out into the yard and picked up a stick, and Mose followed him.

"I'm going to beat you within an inch of your life and if you don't like it, I'm going to kill you sure." He raised the stick.

Mose did not strike him, just caught his arms and held them so he could not move. It was not hard to do, not half so hard as holding a plow behind a fast-walking mule. Mr. Birney was a heavy-set man, but it was years since he had done any physical labor. His strength was no match for that of a good field negro.

His face became almost purple, the blood pounded so hard in his head. "You take your hands off me or I'll have you lynched, by God, I will."

"All right, Mr. Birney. I'm goin to let you go. But you ain't goin to beat me an you ain't never goin to come in my house no more. Iffn she want to go live wid you in yore house, dat's between she an you, but whilst she eat my vittles, ain't nobody else comin in there wid her. Now you go on away an don't you never come back cause if you do, I'm goin break your neck."

Mr. Birney clambered to his horse. "All right, Mose, you have it your own way. But just you wait. There's ways to handle niggers like you, and handle 'em plenty, what I mean."

Fingering at his hat, he rode away.

Mose did not go back into the house, but turned away and started across the field to the Rutherford house. Beatrice came to the door.

"Mose, you don't know what you're doin. You best leave

that man alone. He'll kill you shore. He's killed men befo."

Mose did not answer or look back.

"Well, don't say I didn't tell you. You goin put your head in where you can't get it out. Mose, leave that man be an come on back here."

If she spoke again, Mose did not hear her.

When he got to the back of the white house, Clara was at the kitchen window.

"Mose, now you listen to what I'm tellin you. Mr. Birney done been up here already an he done told Mr. Rutherford he goin to kill you sure. He ain't no man fer you to fool wid. You best clear out from here if you knows what's good fer you."

To the dark face pressed against the screen, Mose answered, "I wants to see Mr. Rutherford."

"All right now, you come on in. I'll see do he want to talk to you."

Presently she returned and told Mose to go to Mr. Rutherford's room. She showed him the way. As he came into the hall, he saw Mr. Birney standing at the front door watching him, smiling.

Mr. Rutherford was seated in his rocking chair, holding his hands clasped before him.

"Come in here, Mose."

Mose stood respectfully quiet, waiting for leave to speak.

"What's this I hear from Mr. Birney?"

"He say he goin kill me sure an I ain't did nothin to be killed fer. He was goin to beat me an I wouldn't left him cause they waren't no reason for him to beat me that-a-way. I done git my crop in the ground good an I don't want to run off. I jest wants to be left alone."

"Nobody's going to kill you, Mose. Nobody's going to beat you either, not without you need it, Mose, and not unless I say so. But don't you ever put your hands on a white man, not on my place as long as you want to stay here. You understand that?"

"But he had the stick to beat me."

"No matter. You can run, but don't you ever fight a white man. Nobody ought to have to tell you that. I'm telling you because you ain't a regular farm nigger and you need to be told for your own good."

Mose did not tell the real reason for his encounter with Mr. Birney. He did not think Mr. Rutherford would believe him.

"Now one thing more, Mose. If you're going to stay around here, you're going to have to get along with Mr. Birney. I won't have any fighting on my place. You ask Mr. Birney to come in here."

Mose went to the door and called him.

Mr. Birney walked in, appearing very affable and calm.

"Birney, I've had a talk with Mose. I think he'll behave himself now. I've given him to understand that you won't beat him and that you don't hold any hard feelings against him."

"Of course not, Mr. Rutherford. Mose and me'll get along just fine."

"All right now, Mose. You tell Mr. Birney you don't hold any hard feelings against him."

Mose felt a great desire to laugh but concealed his feelings.

"All right, sir, if he ain't goin to beat me, I'll jest be friends wid him."

As Mose passed through the kitchen, Clara said, "Well,

as old as I is, I ain't never yit see a nigger get off so easy as you is. But between you an me, I'd keep one ear open when I sleeps. If I knows Mr. Birney right, an I been seein him an them boys a long time now, you ain't heered the last of him. Mr. Rutherford, he ain't like dem, but he don't run this place no more an they don't pay him no mind never."

When Mose returned, Beatrice was waiting for him, trembling and afraid, whether of him or for him Mose did not know.

"Mose, you ain't understand; you ain't know how it is. A nigger woman ain't got no chanct wid white men. I done learnt dat when I waren't no more than a little girl. Mr. Birney, he'd a done whupped me, you know he would, Mose. I had to left him come here. He done give me money, Mose, an you an me done et what I bought wid it."

"He give you money?"

"Sometimes."

"Well, ain't no use you an me talkin bout it no more. If you wants to git out of here, you can git, an if you wants to stay, you can. Either way don't make no difference to me. Jest what's in your mind. But if you goin to live wid that man, or any other man, you goin git out fer good. I got my crop to tend an I ain't in no mind to be foolin round none."

"All right, Mose, be it like you says. Mr. Birney, he ain't did nothin to you?"

"No, it done been drapt. Mr. Rutherford, he say so, an Mr. Birney, he say so too."

"Mose, I wouldn't trust that man if I was you."

"How come he want to trouble me? I ain't did nothin to him. An I been a good nigger on the place, good as he got."

"I knows that, Mose. Trouble wid you is you jest don't know nothin bout folks like Mr. Birney. You better keep out of his way fer shore."

Mose could not believe it, even after they all told him. What under heaven could it profit Mr. Birney to go out of his way to hurt him? Was it not better by far to leave a good hand in the fields than to drive him off when he was needed most?

So he tried to forget it and went about his work as before. The next day he remembered he had not returned Mr. Birney's dollar to him. He did not go himself, but gave it to Clara with instructions to give it to Mr. Birney the next time she saw him.

Mose knew that Beatrice had lied to him about submitting to Mr. Birney because he had threatened her. It might well have been true with some, only with Beatrice it would not have been necessary. But why quarrel with her about it? Beating her would do no good. And for Mose she ceased to exist, was only someone that lived in his house, and he treated her with quiet kindness, never taunted her about her conduct or abused her.

He felt himself much to be blamed and was not sparing of self-condemnation as regarded Beatrice. He pitied her, living beyond the reach of God and man, in an exile she was perhaps born into. That she had waited on the church steps did not wholly free him from guilt.

XIX

On monday Mr. Birney had business in Lisbon which kept him in town all day. When he returned to the plantation that night, he had a look of deep satisfaction on his face. He went by and greeted Mr. Rutherford quite warmly.

"Yes, sir, going to have a right good crop this year."

"Expect we'll get anything for it?"

"No, sir, can't say as we will but we'll do as well as the next fellow."

"That's always a deep consolation," said Mr. Rutherford.

"Oh, it ain't so bad. Think we've run this place right well. Now don't you, Mr. Rutherford?"

"Yes, of course you have. Couldn't say I ever did better myself."

"Oh, I wasn't meaning that at all."

"What you got on your mind, Birney? You didn't just come over here to tell me how good crops were. I've got eyes myself, you know."

"Well, tell you what. Just tell you now. The boys got a darky in town been working for them off and on, for a year or two, I reckon. Long time anyway. Don't need him any more. Want to send him out here. You know. Hate to turn him off. Good nigger."

"Yes. But what do we need with him? We have hands enough, haven't we?"

"Well, the boys were out the other day, looking around and one thing and another, and Orvil was talking to me about how things looked a little run down and was sort of joking me and—you know how Orvil is."

"Yes, I know Orvil."

"So I says, 'What you think I can do about it?' And he says, 'I got a nigger in town that's a right good hand at carpentering; why not send him out here for a while and get some junk lumber and fix up these cabins?'

"Course I didn't think no more about it, and then today he had him up to the store. Right sharp-looking nigger. So I told him to send him out and we'd see how it would work out."

"What then?"

"Oh, I just wanted to know if it would be all right with you."

"That was right thoughtful of you. It sure was. Just what sort of a nigger is this; not another bootlegger, is he?"

"Oh, no sir, he's a carpenter; name's Willie Stubs; and a sort of handy man and one thing and another."

"Well, go ahead and try it. See how he works out."

"I knew you'd say so, Mr. Rutherford. I'll be getting on now. You doing well?"

"Yes, nicely thank you. Good-night."

Mr. Birney left him in the semi-darkness of his room. Mr. Birney knew that somehow he never came off in those conversations with Mr. Rutherford just as he would have liked to and it piqued him. He valued Mr. Rutherford's opinion more than anyone else's and would have enjoyed his approval, would have liked Mr. Rutherford to count him a powerful person. It never occurred to him why Mr. Rutherford always spoke to him with an ill-concealed contempt. He set it down that the old man was getting childish and grouchy and would likely be that way toward anyone the boys put on the place.

When Mr. Birney was gone, Mr. Rutherford called Clara to pour him a glass of whisky and water, and he sat there sipping it slowly, letting the warm liquid lie for a long time in his mouth before he swallowed it. Then he left the chair and lay across the bed, fully clothed, and fell asleep. His head was on its side across the pillow and from his open mouth the saliva flowing left a yellow stain on the pillow case, which would remain there until Clara changed the linen at the end of the customary two weeks.

Willie Stubs' wife, Lizzie, was a mature, heavy, lumbering negress with a slow drawling voice that was almost a whine. As she sat on the steps, Mose knew she was going to be a nuisance.

"Yeah, cose I is sure this is where we was comin. Mr. Birney, ain't he stand there an point straight here? But, Lawdy, dis am shore a ramshackle place. Hope it don't rain befo we gits a roof on it."

Mose had not bothered about the roof on the other side of the house. He never entered the rooms so what use to repair it?

"I guess it won't be so bad when you gits it fixed up. You all aimin to be here a long time?"

"Deed I don't know. You see, me an Willie ain't been married so long an I don't know what he aimin to do. He jest say this mawnin to git ready, an I did, an here we is, an dat's about all I knows cept I'd a heap ruther stayed in Lisbon."

"Willie, he a farm man?"

"I don't rightly know what he do. He come up here from Jackson bout a month ago an we been married since then but that was the first time I ever see him. Shore was. Lawdy, this goin to be a hell of a place to live in."

Beatrice said, "Oh, it ain't like the city but we'll be company. I'se glad to have somebody wid us."

Lizzie looked hard at Beatrice. "You was Beatrice Curley. Now I knows who you is. Shore nough I didn't spect to run into you out in no place like this."

Beatrice did not answer and Mose endeavored to rescue her from what might prove a very unpleasant turn in the conversation.

"Beatrice an me done like it fine out here. You goin to like it too when you gits fixed up a little. You say Mr. Birney done sont you up here?"

"Uh huh. Dat's what I said. Him an Mr. Orvil Rutherford. Willie done work fer Mr. Orvil befo."

"Oh, shore nough? Well, I tell you, maybe you all would like it better if you stayed up to Clara's. She work at Mr. Rutherford's. Her house heap better'n dis one."

"Maybe so, but I done hear Mr. Birney tell Willie that dis the very house we goin to stay at an no other one neither. He ain't no man to make no argument wid. I spect we goin stay right here."

Mose saw it was useless to discuss the matter further.

Presently Willie himself put in his appearance, seated on the top of a wagon load of household furniture.

"Dis the place, Lizzie?"

"Shore is. You jest drive up here by the side."

Mose offered to help unload the wagon.

"No," Willie said. "Guess me an Lizzie make out all right."

Willie climbed out of the wagon. He was a slender man with a huge bony head, high prominent cheek bones and a bulging lower jaw; unintelligent and belligerent. Mose remembered for a moment the same expression in Shorty's face the day of their meeting at Ventura.

Whatever business Mr. Birney had with Willie, it certainly was not going to be any sort of activity that Mose wanted to live beside.

He and Beatrice went back into their part of the house, listening to the knocking and banging that went on while their new neighbors got settled.

The partition that separated the two sections of the house was only a thin layer of sheeting that offered little resistance to sound.

Willie kept up a steady flow of talk about a deal between him and Mr. Birney, punctuating his harangue with profuse profanity.

"Yes sir, Mr. Birney done know a nigger what can git things done."

Lizzie said, "Well, it am shore a funny business, you comin out to a place like dis. You ain't got no more business on a farm than nothin. I'm tellin you I don't like it."

"Don't you worry none bout that an don't you give me no lip neither. It ain't none o' yourn to worry bout nohow. So you jest shut up bout it. Maybe we ain't goin to be so long out here as you thinks."

"You goin git yoursef in trouble. Them Rutherford boys

ain't done nobody in Lisbon no good I ever hear tell of."

Mose was unable to figure out anything definite from the conversation that ensued. Later in the evening the tumult beyond the partition increased, Lizzie protesting against something and Willie telling her to mind her own business.

Finally Mose ventured to the porch and called Willie out.

"Now what you want? I ain't like to be messed wid."

"I ain't tryin to mess wid you," Mose said. "I ain't keer much bout what you do. Only I lives here too an I got to sleep at night an I can't sleep wid all the argument goin on. I don't like all the cussin an raisin sand neither. You goin to have to cut dat out an be quiet."

"You a tough feller, ain't you?"

"No, I ain't tough. I don't want to bother you none an I don't want to be bothered none. Dat's all."

Willie took a good look at Mose and decided a physical encounter would hardly be wise.

Grumbling, he returned to his room and Mose heard no more out of him that night.

XX

THE next morning Luella knocked at the shed room door.

"Jest you step out here, Mose. Thurman done say you come by the house. He got somethin he want to tell you an he don't want to be heered by nobody. I'll go long now an you come on after a little."

Mose finished his breakfast and went out. Willie was on the porch.

"Hello, big boy."

"Good mawnin," Mose said.

"You sleep good?"

"Yes, I slept fine. I hopes you don't bear me no hard feelins bout what I said last night, only I jest wanted you to know how I felt."

"No, I thinks you is the best feller in the world. But don't git the idea you runnin this roost. Cause I ginly does what I wants to an I ain't nobody to mess wid."

Mose did not answer.

He found Thurman waiting for him.

"Mose, I done watch them movin that nigger in wid you yestiddy evenin. He's dat Stubs nigger been bootleggin in Lisbon. He am a low down, no count nigger an I jest wants you to keep your eyes open. He liable to figger dat bein one of the boys' niggers, he mount to somethin."

"I don't figger he want no good," Mose said, "the way he went on an cussed his wife an the way he talk an all. But

I quieted him some. I told him my mind. I could whup him if I had to."

"I don't think you goin git no chance to whup him. If you gits to fightin, they goin to be shootin done. Dat nigger ain't the kind what fight wid he hands. I know dat kind."

Thurman was insistent. "I still don't like it, Mose. I think Mr. Birney got a hand in this an he ain't meanin to do you no good. You do a heap better to git on way from here."

"No," Mose said. "I ain't goin to leave thout I is plumb run off. It would be plain stealin. I done most made the crop by now an by rights it's mine to git somethin fer it. I can handle that nigger. An I ain't fergit what Mr. Rutherford done say. I done pend on what he say. He ain't goin to let Mr. Birney do nothin like dat."

"Mose, he done been an old man an wore out. They steal from under his nose all the time an bootlegs an what he do bout dat? Then what you think he do fer you? Mose, you ain't reasonin right."

Mose was not being reasonable and he knew it. But he had been pushed, it seemed to him, to the far edge and there he determined to fight. There was such a principle as rightness of action. He was clear in his position. He felt that it would be weak and small to run away now, leaving the situation at loose ends.

Anyone with just a little more experience and detachment could have told him what he was facing and he might have believed it. But what the other negroes told him only made him the more determined to remain. The more the odds piled up against him, the more strength he poured into the breach in his own attack on life. Mose could no longer flee the dictation of his own self that told him to stay on and see the matter through.

XXI

ON FRIDAY of that same week Mr. Birney sent the teams to Lisbon to unload a car of feed and haul it to the commissary.

Thurman and Mose were on the same wagon and worked together.

But when they got to the commissary and were piling the sacks in the back room, it happened that Willie Stubs and Mose worked together. As Thurman told Mose later, "He jest hustled hissef up by you an I knowed he was lookin fer trouble an I left him go, not wantin to start nothin."

A sack between two men was no great weight to throw up on the pile. But Willie managed to let his side lag so that the greater burden fell to Mose. Mose said nothing.

Then Willie missed his hold, and Mose was unable to keep the sack from falling. He jumped aside and it rolled to Willie's feet.

Willie said, "You done try to drap dat sack on me. I see you do it. You been layin back on me all the time."

The other negroes in the room stopped their work and watched. They knew Willie was lying; they had seen him all along.

Mose said, "It ain't so an you knows it. You jest a trouble maker."

Willie reached in his pocket and flashed a knife. "I'm goin to teach you somethin, you low-down preachin devil."

With little effort, Mose knocked the knife from his hands

and sent him sprawling on the floor. He picked up the knife and, stepping to the door, threw it out into the field.

"Willie, I done told you to leave me lone. Next time you acts like this, I is liable to whup you good. Everybody done know how you act."

Willie kept silent and they finished the work.

When evening came, Mose went to Allen's house and borrowed Allen's pistol, telling him that thieves had been breaking in the houses in his neighborhood and he wanted it just in case anything happened.

XXII

THE week's work finished, Mose was lying down on his pallet in the back shed room. It was just growing dark and the lamp on the table was lighted. A gentle breeze coming off the river was beginning to give some relief from the heat of the day. The hot-bugs were at their rasping song and the bullfrogs in the creek were booming out their heavy notes. The odor of the evening meal was still about the house.

Peace was coming to weary bodies and Mose lay relaxed, thinking how good was rest after labor with the smell of the fields in the air, as the cool dampness of night came in the open window, making sleep desirable and soothing.

In the other side of the house there had been the sounds of Willie and Lizzie moving about at supper and then more shuffling about and then quiet.

Then Lizzie's voice. "You ain't goin to do yoursef no good, actin up this way out here mongst strangers. They ain't any nigger on this place likes you an you ain't been here a week."

Then Willie. "What you always mess wid me fer? Damn you anyhow. I take care of mysef. You old bitch, you keep your mouth shut."

Mose sat up listening to their angry voices.

"But suppose we tooken sick? Who'd nuss us an look after us? Way you acts, nobody wouldn't keer."

"Now you look a here. God damn what you say. I done

belong to the Lodge in Jackson. They look out fer me if I gits sick."

"Jackson done been a long way from here. You could die an be fergit about befo anybody git here from Jackson. An you hadn't orter talk the way you do. You don't hear Mose talk that-a-way to his wife. Don't hear him cussin an raisin sand."

"God damn Mose an his wife. They jest low-down niggers anyhow, sons of bitches."

Mose walked to the wall and pounded on it with his fist. "You quit all that goin on in there an you quit that cussin."

"God damn you an God damn your wife too. You keep out of my business."

Mose said, "You can't talk like that. If you ain't got no respect fer your own wife, you got to respect mine. I ain't goin to have you goin on like dis. I got a right to live quiet. I don't want to have to act wid you."

"I done say God damn you, Mose, an I'm a comin out an kill you."

Mose could hear him moving across the room to the front door. He ran back into the shed room and called Beatrice to him. "You stay back in here. They's goin to be trouble. That nigger's plumb crazy."

Beatrice said, "Fer Jesus' name don't go out there, Mose. You git killed shore. Is you blind?"

"Ain't goin do no good puttin off no longer. Left me lone. I knows what I'm doin." He got his pistol and went to the door, calling out to Willie, "Willie, you got to pologize fer talkin like that. I don't want to have no trouble wid you."

He pulled back the bolt from the door, opened it and stepped out on the porch.

It was by now what the negroes call first dark. Not far away he could see Thurman's house with lamplight at the window, and it seemed someone was sitting on the porch, probably Thurman himself, in the quiet and peace of the evening, taking rest.

But between him and the house was Willie, standing in the middle of the porch, near the steps. He held a shotgun in his hands.

Mose said, "You put that gun down." He held the pistol at his side, had not raised it.

Willie said, "God damn you, Mose," and, raising the gun quickly, he fired, and Mose felt the rush of the air as the charge passed by him. He was not touched.

Then he raised the pistol and fired, three times, without malice, calmly, acting from necessity. He saw Willie bend forward, holding his stomach, still clutching the shotgun close to his side.

Mose stepped off the end of the porch and around to the back window. He called softly to Beatrice.

"Is you hurt, Mose?" Her voice for once was tender and genuine.

"No. I can't understan how he missed me."

"Did you hit him?"

"Yes, once anyhow. I'm goin up to Mr. Birney's now an tell him what happened so's he can look out fer Willie an git him a doctor."

As he went across the field, Thurman called him and he turned aside toward Thurman's house and stopped by the gate. Thurman had come down from the porch.

"What's all dat shootin I hear, Mose?"

"It was Willie. He made a argument an come out to kill me. He made the fust shot at me wid the britch-loader."

"Did he hit you?"

"No. Didn't tetch me."

"You hit him?"

"Yes, I see him bend over. Guess I hit him somewhere in the middle. How many times I hit him I don't know. It was too dark to tell an I didn't go bout him."

"I hopes you didn't kill him, Mose. They would make it go hard wid you if you did."

"I'm goin by Mr. Birney's now to tell him. See what he say do."

He went up the road and when he reached the path that turned off toward Mr. Birney's, he saw Willie, preceding him, stumbling up to the house with the shotgun still under his arm.

He circled around the field and waited, lying in the cotton. He saw Mr. Birney come to the door.

"Good God, Willie. What the hell; you've been shot."

Willie dropped the gun on the porch. "I tried to get him but he got me fust."

"Didn't you shoot?"

"Yes sir, I made a shot all right but I missed him."

"You missed a man with a gun as big as that?"

"I guess I did. So I brung your gun back to you. Mr. Birney, I guess I'm did fer. My stomach pain me somethin awful and the misery am all over me." He fell sobbing to the porch.

Mose did not wait but returned to his house and again called Beatrice to the window.

"You done seen Mr. Birney?"

"No. Willie got there fust. He was doin it fer Mr. Birney. Mr. Birney done set him to kill me. It was Mr. Birney's doin. I see Willie give him the gun an say it was hisn.

"We got to leave here quick. Mr. Birney liable to come down an try to kill me hissef now. We better hurry."

Beatrice said, "I'se comin. Be right along."

When she came out, she had her hat on and was carrying a purse in her hand. She brought Mose his coat and hat, nothing else. "Where we goin, Mose?"

"I don't hardly know. I think we best make fer the ferry at Carter's Point an git on over into Arkansas. They ain't so likely to find us over there." As he spoke he hurried Beatrice along before him.

She stopped. "Mose, I can't go wid you. I'd jest hold you back. They ain't nothin no more between you an me nohow. I maybe better stay here. I won't go." She turned back.

Mose said, "All right, you do like you thinks. I'll be gone a long time. Don't spect I can never come back here. Don't you tell nobody which way I left. You tell 'em you see me set out fer Lisbon."

"Mose, I'll go on to Lisbon tonight an lay out. They can't catch me there 'til you has time to git crost the river. I got most five dollars; here, you take it."

"I'll take the half of it," Mose said. "I better git on now. You take keer yosef, Beatrice."

She stood there for some moments, watching the dark shadow of his form hurrying off into the darkness, noticing that he walked as he always did, stooped forward with his head drooping out before him and his arms dangling at his sides. Then he was gone, and as the breeze rustled across the fields through the green leaves of the plants, Beatrice cut across the back country toward Lisbon.

XXIII

Mr. Birney left Willie lying on the porch, and at the same time that Mose was fleeing across the fields, went up to Mr. Rutherford's house, the only place near-by where there was a phone.

He cranked the phone and asked for the store. In a minute or two he heard Orvil's voice, heavy and uncertain.

"Orvil, this is Birney. Been a shootin out here. Yes, Mose, Mose Southwick, that preacher nigger you had at the store, has shot Willie. Yes, of course it's funny. Tell you about it later. You drive out here in the car and we'll get him to a doctor and see just how bad he's hurt. Meantime you better have Lonnie call the sheriff's office in Clarksville and have them send someone out."

Then he went back to his house.

"I'm bleedin pretty bad, Mr. Birney, an I hurt awful." Willie's voice was deep and trembling.

It was nearly nine o'clock when Orvil got there. They threw an army blanket over the back seat of the car and helped Willie in. Orvil, when he had heard Mr. Birney's story, laughed and said to Willie, "What a hell of a shot you turned out to be, and you were set up to be a real tough nigger. Why, with that gun you couldn't miss a sparrow, let alone a man at ten feet."

Willie was moaning as the car bounced over the gravel and did not reply.

Lonnie was waiting for them at the store, with Dr. Shepard standing in the doorway holding a little satchel in one hand, the other hand clutching the lapel of his coat.

"Just you bring him in here and lay him on the counter and I'll have a look at him."

A large touring car pulled up at the door and two men got out, each armed with a pistol.

"Hello, Orvil," one of them said. "Had trouble?"

Orvil shook hands with them. "Yeah, a little. Mr. Birney, you know Mr. Holly, deputy-sheriff. And this is Mr. Morrison, nother deputy."

They all shook hands about and stood on the sidewalk talking. Dr. Shepard came to the door.

"How is he, doc?"

"Pretty bad. I can watch him here until five o'clock and put him on the morning train for Memphis. They might keep him in a hospital and pull him through."

Lonnie said, "That would cost like hell."

"He'll die here, Mr. Rutherford."

Orvil said, "All you docs alike. Don't never realize how tough niggers are. Give him something to quiet him and we'll take him back out to the place. He'll get well all right."

They went into the store and stood in a semicircle about the counter. Lonnie held the lantern high so the doctor could see.

Willie was barely conscious. The front of his body was dark with blood. The doctor wiped the needle of the hypodermic syringe on his handkerchief, filled it, bared the negro's arm and gave him the shot, then filled the needle again and gave him a second shot. "No use to let him suffer; that'll hold him a good while."

"Yes, of course, that's right, doc," Orvil said. "Now you all take a hold. Careful there, handle him easy, he's bad hurt."

They loaded Willie back into the car.

Lonnie said, "That back seat'll look like you've been sticking pigs in it."

"But you got to take care of the nigger," Mr. Morrison said.

They all laughed.

Orvil and Mr. Birney got in Orvil's car, and Lonnie rode with the deputies.

At the farm they put Willie in an outhouse behind Mr. Rutherford's. The cot they brought from Clara's was all the furniture in the room. They covered him with the same army blanket. Willie was unconscious from the drug and lay very quiet. He was obviously still bleeding.

They set Colin to stay and watch him and then they left the room.

"Now," said Mr. Holly, "we better spread out. Morrison and I'll work together and, Birney, you come with us; we'll go to Mose's house first. You all go to the other houses. You might find out where he is, but likely every nigger'll swear they never heard of Mose, much less know he shot Willie. If anybody gets anything hot, fire twice and we can get together. Everybody understand?"

They all nodded.

Orvil said, "Bout as much chance of gettin him now as flyin. Birney, if you'd a used your head, you'd a caught him when it first happened instead of waiting so damned long. He's miles away from here by now."

Lonnie said, "But, my God, he had to get Willie to the doc, didn't he? He might a died."

They went off, bristling, with chests out, talking loud. Lonnie said, "Don't you guys be shootin no birds around here; the season ain't open."

Mr. Morrison said to Mr. Holly in an undertone, "Little Lonnie, he's a sharp one for you, now ain't he?"

Colin waited in the room with Willie. After about an hour Willie began to rouse, moaning at first, then speaking inaudibly. Then Colin could hear the word, "Water."

He went to the house and called to Mr. Rutherford. "He say he want water an I don't know if I ought to give it to him."

"Sure," Mr. Rutherford said. "Give him all he wants. Is he hurt bad?"

"Pretty bad. He don't hardly move."

"The boys gone off?"

"Yes sir. They goed off wid the law to hunt Mose."

"I'll be out."

Presently Mr. Rutherford came out, carrying the lamp from his room in his hand. He spoke to Willie. "Willie, can you hear me?"

"Yes sir."

"You in pain, Willie?"

"Yes sir. Pretty bad. The shot am wearin out."

"How did the trouble start, Willie?"

"I wants to tell you. I'm dyin, I knows it. I wants to git right befo I dies. I wants to tell you. I made a argument wid Mose; I guess I started it. I done got what was comin to me shore. I made a shot and then he shot me."

"You don't blame Mose?"

"No sir, I don't."

Mr. Rutherford handed the lamp to Colin to hold. He raised the blanket and examined the wound. Then he went to the other side of the cot and looked at Willie's back. His hair fell across his eyes as he leaned over, and, as he brushed it back, the blood on his fingers left a dark stain on his forehead.

"Now don't you worry, Willie. Seen a lot of men shot worse than you that were walking around the next day. You're just hurt a little, that's all. You lay quiet. You'll be all right."

"Yes sir. Thank you, sir."

To Colin who followed him to the door, Mr. Rutherford said, "He'll be dead in an hour or two. There's a hole in his stomach I could put my fist in. If he seems to be suffering too much, you let me know and I'll have the doctor come out and give him another shot. He won't last long. You needn't tell the boys I even came out."

"No sir, I won't," Colin said.

Peering out of the door of the outhouse, Colin could see the flashlights of the searchers as they went from cabin to cabin on the place. After a time they all seemed to be gathered at Mose's house, and he could distinguish the shadowy forms going about the house and up and down the porch. The voices of the men were faint in the distance and he could not hear what they were saying. Then they separated and went on the rounds of the cabins again, pounding on doors and shouting to the frightened negroes within.

Willie lay on the cot, moaning monotonously with each outbreathing. Occasionally he opened his eyes, that showed glassy and dim. Then he grew very quiet and still. Colin walked up to him and touched the spittle that had run out of the half-opened mouth across the side of the face.

He went around just to Mr. Rutherford's room and tapped at the window.

There was no light in the room.

Mr. Rutherford said, "Who is it?"

"It's me, Colin. I think he's dead an I'm skeered to be out there by myself."

"Then you call the boys. Tell them to come up and get him."

Colin heard the bed creak as the man lay back on it. He returned to the shed and peered in. Willie had not moved and the lantern was still there on the floor by the bed.

He heard footsteps; then a flashlight turned on him, and Lonnie said, "How's he makin out?"

"I think he's dead, shore do. He don't move or nothin."

"That makes it murder," Mr. Morrison said.

"Yeah," Mr. Holly said. "We got to catch him now sure nough."

Lonnie said, "Oh, what the hell difference does it make anyhow? Staying up all night chasing a nigger ain't my idea of fun, not when he probably ain't within ten miles of here. He's a lot more likely to be in Lisbon.

"Colin, look here, did you tell papa?"

"No sir, sure didn't."

"You're lying."

"No sir, Mr. Lonnie. You know I ain't. You can axe him yosef."

"Lot of good that would do."

He turned to the others. "Oh, Christ, let's get on back to town. This place gives me the lousy creeps anyhow."

Mr. Birney said, "Well, if you all want to let that bastard get away with it, I guess I can't help myself, but how you expect me to run this place after this, I don't know. Why, every nigger'll be up at my house by daylight, thumbing his nose at me."

"By God, you're right," Orvil said. "Let a nigger get the upper hand on you and it's good-by. Niggers are all right in their place and all that but they got to be kept there. Only thing to do is to catch Mose and send him up."

Mr. Holly and Mr. Morrison stalked around with all the importance of the law. Mr. Holly said, "That's exactly right and the sheriff's office'll see to this thing, what, Orvil?"

"If my bein a deputy means anything," Orvil said.

Lonnie said, "All right; no use to stand around jawing all night." He walked into the outhouse, turned Willie's eyelids back with his thumb. "Dead; sure is. Funny how a dead man looks, ain't it? Christ, and didn't he bleed though!"

He pulled the blanket up over the face. "Colin, you might just as well leave him here until morning because there ain't a nigger this side of hell that would touch him in the dark. But you all get him out of here and buried in the morning. It's hot as hell. You get me?"

"Yes sir, Mr. Lonnie. He can jest lay there 'til mawnin. Won't nothin bother him."

"Not if you leave the door shut."

Mr. Holly said, "We might just speak to Mr. Rutherford for a minute before we go."

"No," Orvil said. "No use getting him out of bed at this time of night. He's a pretty old man, you know, and by rights oughtn't to be bothered with things like this."

"Just as you think best."

They got in the cars and drove away, leaving Mr. Birney standing by the road. Mr. Birney sighed heavily and started across the field to his house. Long before the noise of the cars died out in the distance Colin was safely in his house with the doors and shutters barred.

XXIV

WHEN Mose left Beatrice, he continued west and north to the levee, which he followed up to Carter's Point. He kept out of sight at the landing until the boat was nearly ready to leave, and then, seeing no one that he recognized and no one that seemed to be looking for him, he went on board and stood at the rail as they cast off.

The ferry landing was in the mouth of a large creek and on either side stretched the mud flats outside the levee. He could hear the water sloshing against the banks, could see the heavy growth of willows and beyond that the emptiness that was the valley of the river.

It was just about a year since Mose had crossed the river, that time at Ventura, and with what different feelings now. How the whole content of his mind had changed in that one rotation of the seasons, how his outlook on the future had been clutched away from hope and cheer.

Behind him, somewhere, across the levee, which lay like a long finger on the earth, was a man bleeding from a wound he had been forced to inflict, and how little he had ever wanted to cause anyone pain. And somewhere in that breathing obscurity was a woman who had profaned his house and whom he could not hate and for whose pitiful condition he held himself in a measure accountable.

The boat creaked in the sudden rush of water against its

sides, and looking up, Mose saw the limitless river flowing in the moonlight, like the unity and mystery of life, beautiful, silver ripples on the surface of a terrific, deeper force, rising out of countless springs on the bosom of a continent, moving on relentlessly to the sea, now calm and subdued, now thrashing over its shores like a wounded beast, dotted with islands without number, its shore line made irregular by inlets that lie leechlike against its sides, lovable and repelling, unknowable and tempting.

There in the distance a great log raft moved on to the south, its outline made hardly distinct by murky lanterns. Mose partook of the sacrament and his soul was refreshed and he lifted his head in dignity. Modestly he gazed at nature's great wonder and read its secret, feeling himself drawn to it by that community which is in all life.

Knowing the bitterness of life and how there is more blindness than sight, he retired there at the rail to renew his strength for a battle he now saw, not as peculiar to him, but as an endless life struggle in which he must make his way.

The boat butted her nose against the bank and Mose put his feet on the ground again.

A truck driver going north let Mose ride among his bales. They went through sleeping towns that rose like phantoms and fell away behind them until they were only tiny clusters of twinkling lights; through great forests they went, past long fields of corn and cotton, past the gloomy cypress swamps. At West Memphis Mose dropped off, hoping the driver would not notice, for he had no desire to leave any perceptible trail behind him. He turned toward the viaduct, and as the dawn rose behind the bluffs, he saw looming before him the great steel framework of the bridge that leads into Memphis, and beyond he saw the pile of the city, high above the river. A strange contrast, the sweep of fields and forest on either side as far as he could see, primitive, almost savage; and there, jutting against the sky, a steel skeleton, naked, massive, without imagination or beauty, only force, strength and utility.

Leaving the bridge, he found himself in sooty streets lined with blackened houses; then great railroad yards, warehouses, factories.

The air was foul and hot. He felt oppressed at the sight of mean people in the streets, people who were, even early in the morning, tired and pale, walking with wavering determination. It was the district of cheap stores, speaks, tenements and bawdy houses, the human dump of an aging, weary city.

Then on into Main Street and in to the business district, where traffic is regulated by blinking green and red lights. A large car stopped for a moment and a white-frocked, blond-haired girl took advantage of the pause to add a touch of color to her lips, and turning her head, she saw a negro standing on the sidewalk watching her with innocent curiosity, and she drove on, leaving Mose smiling at the thought of this pleasant apparition.

Mose stayed in Memphis a week, spending only a few pennies each day on food, for by careful analysis of the contents of garbage cans between darkness and dawn, he found that much is thrown away which the human stomach can yet assimilate. Probably he hardly noticed where he slept, but it was likely in alleyways and in the weeds along the tracks by the river. In the daytime he walked about the city looking for work, but he had had no experience in city ways and was often advised to go back to the farm. This amused him as much as it pained him. The farm hands wanted to get to the city and the city people ached for the farm. And Mose too, only he longed for the openness of the country and the absence of the dirt and smoke that hangs over the streets and buildings.

The first of July found him in St. Louis, whither he had journeyed by hopping freight trains. Here he found work for a few days on a river boat, but after the first trip they let him go, not because he was unsatisfactory but because the boat was lying idle. He went on into Illinois, now traveling by short stages, inquiring for work in each town. Only once was he set upon and robbed, but the thieves got only a small portion of his fortune, for he now kept his money divided, part in his pocket, the rest sewed in the leg of his trousers. The latter package escaped notice. Mose was learning. If he had had no scruples against petty thieving himself, he might have become an expert tramp.

But Mose disliked this swift movement of the life scenery. He wanted to take root somewhere and live with some semblance of order and security. And he began to think that eventually winter and bitter cold would be upon him and he turned his face south. Each day that took him further south found him happier. The few negroes he had encountered in Illinois scorned him and his drawling talk. He found it hard to be an outcast even among his own people.

He overshot his mark and got as far as New Orleans. Only then did he realize that this was not where he had meant to go. So he cut back over the river and began to move up into Mississippi. He avoided Ventura as though it were ridden by the plague. Finally he halted in the town of

Lebanon, which is not many miles below the Pelham County line. He was about forty miles south of Clarksville and Lisbon. He felt he would be safe here and yet close enough to establish contact with his brother.

Just why he wanted this contact he did not exactly know, for it could be of no financial good to him, nor spiritual good either, for there was no common outlook between the men. It was rather that he considered Allen as his one link in the social sphere. Not quite a stranger on the face of the earth. No indeed. "I has a brother what farms not so fer from Claksvul."

But this was only an inner comfort. He never mentioned his brother to anyone. He went under the name of Joe Haney. But the thought that his brother was not so very far away gave him for himself an identification; and he felt familiar responses in the scene that offered warm consolation.

By the first of August Mose had found work as a yard boy for a family of some means in the town. He began to think he might establish himself permanently in Lebanon.

One evening, as he was walking around the square, he found that someone was following him. He did not think he had seen the man before, so he stopped and faced him.

"You was followin me?"

"No. Why you think I was followin you? I was jest walkin long."

"Oh, I thought you was maybe tryin to ketch up wid me."

"No. But now I looks at you, your face do look like somebody I is seed at Lisbon."

"Ain't never been to Lisbon in my life."

"You look like a preacher name Southwick."

"No. My name is Haney, Joe Haney."

"Guess you ain't who I thought you was. Ain't dat funny now?"

And the man turned away and was lost from sight.

Mose hurried back to his room and gathered up his bundle. Then he stopped, defiant. He would not go. He was entitled to live as other men, unmolested.

On Saturday of the same week, about noon, Mose was sitting on the front steps waiting to be paid off. A white man turned in at the gate and spoke to him. "What's your name?"

"Joe Haney."

"Stand up. Take your hat off. I thought so. You're Mose Southwick."

Mose said, "Well, I guess you got me all right. I'm the very one."

"You come along with me. You're wanted in Clarksville for murder."

Mose walked beside the man. "The truf won't hurt nobody," he said.

PART III

I

When Allen had left Mary's office, after asking her to help him recover his stolen cow, it was her first thought to go directly to Mr. Caldwell. But she thought that possibly it would be wiser to approach him through Mr. Dancy. Probably she could prevail upon Mr. Dancy to recover the stolen cow for his tenant, which was no less than his duty. Undoubtedly, Mr. Dancy, finding that someone else was interested in the matter, would be shamed into action. And Mary also hoped that Mr. Dancy might be of some assistance in the real problem, which was the defense of Mose Southwick. At least she could sound him out.

When she went to Mr. Dancy's house, he was in the fields and Mrs. Dancy sent the cook to call him.

The two women sat in the parlor, waiting for Mr. Dancy, talking at first of the news of the town. They did not know each other very well but as they talked, the older woman responded eagerly to what Mary said; she seemed pleading for friendship and understanding, seeing perhaps in Mary what she might have desired to be. And Mary, sitting before her, was modest and yet direct, as if she felt quite sure of where she was going. Mrs. Dancy felt Mary's competence and the great contrast between Mary and her surroundings.

"Do you know, Mary," she said, "I've really been meaning for a long time to come by to see you. I admire your work a great deal. You wouldn't guess it, I know. It's the sort of thing I might have done. Maybe that's the way with all of us. It takes courage. I know it. You've done good in Clarksville.

"Of course Lucius is funny about things like that, a woman doing like a man, he says. But Lucius is a good man in his way. He's just old-fashioned. But I think it's splendid."

"It's kind of you to say that, Mrs. Dancy. I do appreciate it. I haven't gotten along as fast as I might have. But I haven't any complaint to make. Somebody has to make a beginning at everything."

Mr. Dancy came hurrying into the room.

"Well, Miss Winston, haven't got the law on us, have you? Can't tell about these lady lawyers." And he laughed heartily.

"No, not yet, Mr. Dancy." Mary's smile was disconcerting to Mr. Dancy. And the quiet, composed way she sat and looked at him was confusing.

"It's about one of your tenants, Allen Southwick, who has asked me to help him about a stolen cow. The thief in this case happens to be a lawyer in Clarksville, Mr. Caldwell. I think I am justified in calling him that. I've looked into the matter carefully."

"Now, now, Miss Winston, that's a pretty hard thing to say. Caldwell's maybe not the best man in town, but he wouldn't steal a cow from anybody, not even a nigger."

"You're quite sure of that?"

Mr. Dancy's face showed clearly he was not. "Quite sure," he said. "I guess Allen told you I went to see Caldwell myself. Drove right over to Clarksville first time I heard about it. And it's a thing I can't make heads or tails of. You know how niggers are. They'll lie to you and never are grateful for what you do for them."

"If you treat them right, they can be very grateful."

Mr. Dancy ignored this statement. "You couldn't expect Caldwell to defend a nigger for murder for nothing, could you? I expect Allen just tried to back out on his bargain. Allen's pretty shiftless and no count anyhow."

"Mr. Caldwell isn't going to defend Mose, if that's what you mean. I am."

Mrs. Dancy said, "I think it's wonderful of you to do it. Allen told me what happened. It was shameful."

Mr. Dancy turned to her. "Honey, you better not bother about this. You don't know none of the real facts in the case."

"I didn't mean to interrupt you, Lucius."

"Miss Winston," he said, "I don't see how you can lower yourself to a matter of this kind. Your father would turn over in his grave. Why, Mose is a nigger of desperate character. You don't know what you may be getting into. But it's your business; you'll have to decide it for yourself."

"I already have, Mr. Dancy. I couldn't go back on him now. I wouldn't if I could." Mary saw there was no use in expecting any help for Mose from this quarter.

"And as for the cow, Miss Winston, there's nothing at all I can do. I'm not one to go around making enemies and I wouldn't have a leg to stand on with Caldwell. He's not the easiest fellow to deal with. He'd think I was insulting him."

"I don't think it's a question of getting the cow now. It's probably been sold to the butcher. But I think Mr. Caldwell can be persuaded to pay the money over to Allen."

"You know, Miss Winston, I'd like to help you, but a man

can't go about stirring people up." For a moment it seemed there was a note of genuine sympathy in his voice. "I can't see what you are thinking about, really I can't. I look after my darkies real good, but there's limits to what a body is expected to do."

"I think I understand you, Mr. Dancy."

"I was sure you would. Tell me now, how's business? I hear you're getting on good."

"Couldn't ask any better in times like these."

And with smiling courtesies on both sides they parted. As Mary got into her car, Mrs. Dancy came around from the side door, carrying a bouquet of roses wrapped in wet newspaper.

"Oh, I was afraid you'd get off and I just hurried out with these. My roses were so pretty this year, and nobody out here enjoys them but me. I thought maybe they would look nice in your office."

"They are lovely and it was so thoughtful of you," Mary said. "I have a vase on my desk they'll just go in. I do like for people to give me flowers."

"But it's nothing. You can come out and have all you want any time. In the late fall I have fine chrysanthemums. Have for years.

"And don't feel badly about what Lucius said. He can't afford to do anything that might hurt him. You know how it is."

"Yes," Mary said, "I suppose so. I had hoped he might be able to help me with Mose's case. I will need all the help I can get."

"I could judge that from what Allen said. I told Lucius that Rutherford's was no fit place for anybody, not even a nigger. I wouldn't be surprised at anything those people would do. And a nigger hasn't got a chance. But to hang a man for a thing like that is terrible. You must stop them; I know you can. If there's anything I can do, you just let me know. But don't count on Lucius for anything."

Mrs. Dancy stood on the steps waving good-by. Then her hand brushed slowly across her already graying hair. She opened the screen door, and with shoulders drooping and the animation gone from her figure she entered the house.

II

When Mary had first opened her dingy office up over the bank, Clarksville was bewildered. No one knew quite what to make of it. It was contrary to all custom and tradition and therefore probably improper. The other lawyers were not particularly concerned. It never occurred to them that anyone would ever question the circular route of their little professional movements in which the client was usually an ignorant pawn for both sides to play.

People remembered Captain Winston, her father, and had liked him. They had seen Mary grow up like many other girls in the town, but somewhere in the process she had begun to get ideas of her own about life. She had tried school teaching for a time. She had been a worker in the local Red Cross. Then they learned she was studying law. It was too perplexing a phenomenon for Clarksville.

But there she was now with her shingle out, going quietly about her business, fiercely devoted to the interests of her clients. Although her appearances in the courtroom had not been numerous, she had shown ability as a strategist.

One of Mary's cases had brought considerable public attention. When old Mr. Christopher drifted from common senility to complete incompetence and his wife saw his money slipping through his unsteady hands, she talked to Mary about it, had Mr. Christopher declared an incompetent and Mary appointed his legal guardian. The bar association was genuinely alarmed. Estates not securely bound had been free fish for lawyers since the town began. But Mary not only kept the estate intact, she showed a profit on its operation. And Mrs. Christopher did not fail to give the town due notice of this strange legal performance.

It had been more of a struggle than Clarksville suspected. Clients without money had taken much of Mary's time. The already established lawyers kept a tight hold on most of the business that involved large fees. But Mary had come to the profession with more than one interest. She desired to penetrate and change the social order. So far a genuine opportunity had not come; there had never been a real issue with the ruling element; she had never aroused the dullness of local orthodoxy. And she had had no desire to force an issue; she was not a sensationalist.

Without ever having seen Mose, she knew that his was a case that would be an issue against the established order in which the particular problem might easily become lost in the interplay of attendant prejudices. Mose had already been indicted by the Grand Jury. It would be no delicate fight. The truth could never be told. His defense must be a half truth. To tell a jury that he had been defending his home from a white man, that he had killed an assassin sent by the white man and carrying the white man's gun, would be to end any chance for his freedom. No jury of white men could stomach such a tale. All the old racial hatred would flare up anew. Yet Mary felt sure that with all this left out, Mose could still be freed.

But it had never occurred to her just what sort of client she had undertaken to defend.

III

WHEN Mary went to the jail, they brought Mose into a small room adjoining the cell block. The jailer said, "It looks like a damn foolish thing to me, but you know your business, Miss Winston. You ain't goin to get nowhere mixin up with niggers. It'll ruin you."

Mary said, "You needn't worry about me. I can handle it."

Mose sat at one end of the little table and Mary at the other.

"You is de lady lawyer Allen done tole me bout?"

"Yes, I'm Miss Winston. I got the note you wrote me. I couldn't get down any sooner."

"Hit's all right. I don't mind waitin none."

As he talked, Mary watched his face. He sat quietly, his arms laid out on the table before him, his head bent slightly forward showing the high open forehead. He did not look aside but straight at her.

"Hit bothered me some when Allen done tole me bout you an all. Hit don't rightly seem a lady's business foolin wid me. Cause I done shore been in a heap o' trouble. An you maybe have to deal wid folks you ain't got no reason to be dealin wid."

"Mose, I'm glad you understand that. It makes it easier for me to help you. Now I'd like to get you out of here until the trial comes up, but I'm afraid that's impossible so it looks like you'll have to stay here until after the trial. It will be much better just to act very quietly about it all."

"I don't mind that none. I has lots to study bout, an hit ain't no worse'n when I was in Memphis. I'd ruther be here. Course hit would be better to be out workin, but hit don't seem no way to do that lest we gits dis here business fixed up."

"Mose, I want you to start in and tell me the whole story, just how it happened and all about it."

Mose told it easily, beginning with the first day he was at Mr. Rutherford's. He included much irrelevant material about himself and the church. But Mary let him tell it in his own way, only occasionally interrupting with a question on a point that was not clear.

There was no malice in the story. It was almost as if Mose were telling something about another person. And from time to time he smiled and then he would rub the back of his long thin hand across his chin. His deep voice was rich and compelling.

"Ain't it the most foolish thing you ever hear tell of? Hit ain't the sort of story a body would believe. I ain't never axed no more'n jest to be left alone. But Mr. Birney, he done sot his haid on doin way wid me.

"Tell me," he asked, "you think maybe dey kin hang me?"

"No, Mose, of course not. The trouble will be witnesses. Is there any white person who would testify for you?"

"No'm, I don't think so. I never bothered to make no frens wid white folks. You don't never think bout things lak dis fore dey happens."

"How about old Mr. Rutherford?"

"I couldn't tell bout him, fer shore I couldn't. He done

seem a man what think in he own haid. He don't deal wid Mr. Birney much. But he mout be skeered o' de boys; I is heered hit."

"I'll talk to him," Mary said. "He'd help the case wonderfully. Then I can get that darky who lived across from you. Thurman, was that his name?"

"Yes'm. But Thurman done been powerful boun to Mr. Birney."

"How's that?"

"I done promise I wouldn't never tell. Only Mr. Birney done know somethin to git Thurman in trouble maybe."

"Oh, I see."

"I wouldn't want them to hang me. Hit wouldn't be right Cause I done got a heap to live fer, done got a heap to do. You know I ain't never been ordained. I has things to study bout."

"Mose, if I could make an agreement with the State and have you serve a year or two, it might be a lot safer than going to court. Juries are mighty hard on darkies. You understand I'm not asking you to do this. I can only advise you. I'll do as you think best and you're entitled to be freed, but it might be better to serve a year or two than run the chance of getting a much longer sentence.

"You see, Mose, the story you have told me is not a story that can be told in a court room. You are a negro and Mr. Birney is a white man. A negro can't tell that a white man was living with his wife or that a white man sent a negro to kill him. No jury would free you if you made that your defense. All you could do in court is to plead self-defense. All you could say would be that Willie tried to kill you and you had to kill him. Do you understand what I'm saying?

That is why it might be better to keep out of a court trial if possible. It's hard to ask you to serve time for something you didn't do, but in court you might get a long sentence, possibly life."

"Yes'm, I'd do that. Two years ain't no time. I'd shore serve two years."

"But I won't do anything right away. I'll just investigate a little more and then I can tell better how things stand. I'll have to see how the District Attorney has his head set on this thing. He may be willing to talk reasonably about it. That depends on how much influence Mr. Birney has with him."

"Yes'm. You do jest what you feels am right to do. I been wantin to axe you bout Allen's cow. Hit done been a shore nough pity fer him to lose de cow over me. An he done need de cow too."

"I wouldn't worry about that. I'm going to see Mr. Caldwell." And she got up and knocked on the door for the jailer to let her out and to take Mose back to the cell.

Mose said, "Hit done been a heap o' trouble fer you."

Mary walked past the jailer, hardly seeing him. He said, "Anything wrong?"

She was not sure she had understood. "No," she replied.

It was not until she got back to her office and closed the door that she was able to think reasonably about it. She had the feeling that this experience did not tie up with anything she had ever known. The calm of this man, his nearly impersonal attitude, his solicitude toward others. And yet a negro, bound to all the associations that the word brings to mind. His inward contentment and order, his wealth in being satisfied with small things. The only time he had seemed concerned was when he spoke of Allen's cow. No, there was one other time. He did not want to be hanged. Only to be let live, to be left alone. Not any seeking for place or power, no public acclaim of his innocence, no indemnification for his loss, no desire for revenge. Only to be let go in peace. Things to study about, to be ordained.

How much she had wanted to question him about his attitude. But it was better to leave him alone to make only such statements as came to his mind. Better never to probe into any man's inner feelings.

And she knew how useless it was to go too far with a situation of this kind. To try to extend this man anything like his due might be to destroy him. Strange paradox and contradiction.

But they could not hang him. Surely some place could be found wherein this simplicity of life might continue unoppressed.

IV

"MR. CALDWELL, I have come to ask you to return Allen Southwick his cow."

The two men who were seated in the office with Mr. Caldwell looked up uneasily. They did not rise. Mr. Caldwell said, "You needn't go." He did not introduce them.

He said, "You can see I'm very busy, Miss Winston. We can talk that matter over some other time. I can explain the whole thing to you."

"I don't think I would be interested in any explanations until after you have returned the cow you took. I have a paper here which you represented as being signed by Allen. It is not his signature. You know whose it is."

"What kind of lies has that nigger been telling you?" He leaned across the table menacingly.

Mary did not retreat. Only her hands showed her nervousness.

"There's no need to talk like that, Mr. Caldwell. You and I both understand this matter well enough."

"I came by the cow legally in payment of a fee. By the way, how about your stealing my client? How about that?"

"I think it would be better not to go into that. I did not seek the case. You know that. They came to me because you had mistreated them."

"You may be getting into more than you bargain for, Miss Winston."

"That needn't worry you. Understand me, Mr. Caldwell, I shall have you prosecuted for this. And you are going to give that cow back to Allen. You ought to go to jail for what you did."

"I haven't got the cow. I sold it."

"I thought as much. What did you get for it?"

"Fifteen dollars."

"That's ridiculous. It would take thirty to replace it. Do you want to let me have the money now?"

"Don't be foolish. You know I'm not going to pay you a cent."

"I'll have you arrested. It won't do any good. I know that. They'd never convict you. But it would serve to warn people not to deal with you. That would be a service to the community."

"This is plain blackmail."

"No, I'm only representing my client in accordance with his rights. I'm not threatening you."

"You know well enough I'd pay for the cow rather than have a mess like this. I have a reputation."

"Yes, I know."

Mr. Caldwell sat down and wrote out a check. Red-faced and sullen, he turned and handed it to her. "I'm to hear no more about this?"

"I can't say anything about that. It's for Allen to say. But I'm sure he has no personal feeling against you. He just wanted to get his cow back."

The two men had quit chewing. It was a stupendous scene, unprecedented in their experience.

Mary turned and left the room. When she was in the hall, she heard the two strangers roaring with laughter and Mr. Caldwell cursing bitterly.

But it was a small victory. She could accomplish things like this. He would have fought a man. She could collect thirty dollars from a thief because it was the cheaper way out for him. But it was only a skirmish.

Mississippi *vs.* Mose Southwick for an offense against the dignity of the State. That was different. She walked swiftly down the hall.

She had not yet seen the District Attorney. Knowing how much might depend on this interview, she had postponed it until she knew exactly what she wanted to say to him.

V

The District Attorney was very affable. His short body and his small pointed face under his bulging forehead and heavy black hair gave him an unpleasant expression; and the constant sneering smile he had cultivated, until it had become a habit, made it hard for him to look genuinely friendly; but he obviously meant to be.

"I hear you and Caldwell had a little run-in and, though Caldwell don't just quite tell it that way, I expect you dealt him a short hand."

"No, really, I let Mr. Caldwell off pretty easy. He's not got what's coming to him at all."

"Oh, Caldwell's a fine fellow when you get to know him."

"Maybe so. Do you remember, Mr. Durden, when Mose Southwick was indicted?"

"No, ma'am, to tell the truth, I don't. I did look the indictment over and, as I recall, it was just one of those nigger shootings; happened out on old man Rutherford's plantation. The evidence showed he picked a quarrel with a nigger named Stubs, or something like that, and then shot him. The Grand Jury indicted him flat."

"Do you recall who testified?"

"As well as I remember, the plantation manager, Birney, and the deputies who investigated, including Orvil Rutherford."

"Mr. Durden, I have pretty clear evidence that the negro

Willie Stubs provoked the quarrel and fired the first shot. There is some ground to show that Mose was possibly a little hot-headed himself, but it was an obvious case of self-defense. I am wondering if we couldn't handle this a lot better to have an understanding about it. My client might be willing to plead guilty if the State would recommend the mercy of the court and have him serve a very short sentence of a year or two."

"Well, Miss Mary, if you have good evidence like what you say, I'm sure that can be arranged. I don't want to be bothered with the court work in a case like that. Every term is cluttered up with nigger cases anyhow. I never had given this case much thought. It isn't set soon, is it?"

"It's set now for early in October. That's only about a month off."

"I hadn't realized it came up so soon. I'll talk with the County Attorney and I'm sure this can be fixed up. I know you wouldn't misrepresent no facts to me."

"Thank you, Mr. Durden. Couldn't we arrange to bring it up before the judge at a special hearing? It shouldn't take long."

"I'll see what I can do." And he got up and, taking Mary's arm, walked through the outer office with her.

"You know, Miss Winston, I've tried mighty hard to do my duty as District Attorney. Anything you might have to say around among the ladies in town wouldn't hurt me none."

Mary laughed. "Mr. Durden, I'm not buying Mose off."

"Now don't misunderstand me, Miss Winston. I didn't mean that. Only you know a fellow has to toot his own horn a little in this town in politics."

"Yes, I know," Mary said. And she left the District Attorney standing at the door rubbing his hands, his dark face making a desperate effort to glow with friendly light.

Mary did not dare to believe what Durden had said. Yet perhaps what he said was true. Maybe it was just another nigger case, and if it could be finished, before it became generally known that she was working on it, she could gain her end. If it could only be done before Birney heard about it. He seemed the only one who had any personal grudge against Mose. Perhaps Durden did not know about that. If so, so much the better.

VI

THE jailer told one of the men from the sheriff's office, "Yes, sir, by all odds, the God damnedest nigger I ever saw in my life. Possessed or crazy, that's what I say. Gets under my skin. I've seen 'em all and all alike. But this one is different. Talk to him, and, by God, I'm not one to be taken in by no damn nigger preacher, and it makes me feel like I was an unwashed sinner. Don't hardly say nothing, he don't. Just stands there, so, with his hands in his pockets, looking at you, and for a measly plate of stinking beans says, 'Shore do thank you, boss,' and sets down slow like and eats 'em like they was king's victuals. It gives me the creeps. I'll be damn glad when they turn him loose or hang him, whichever they are going to do. This jail ain't been the same since he come here. He has every coon in here acting like a graveyard ghost caught naked robbing graves."

Mose's cell was on the north side of the building and so when he placed his stool by the window and, hanging his arm out through the bars, held his face pressed against the bars so that deep imprints were left on his cheek, he could barely see the sun rising in the morning and setting in the evening, because it was late enough in the year for the sun to have started south. But it was worth all the ache it gave him in holding that strained attitude to see the light coming out of and sinking into that black-tree horizon. For that was life there, extended and picturesque, primitive nature and, where hands had pushed it apart a little, the plots of field with cabins on them and people coming out, working and going in, and over it light waxing and waning and then darkness and a renewal of light. There was the great picture where you could see two children fighting over some object not quite distinguished, and you could narrow the focus until there was nothing but the hurt and excitement of that conflict, and then you could enlarge the focus and see the conflict in a proper perspective. Mose was not ungrateful for this leisure for contemplation and revery.

But Mose did not want to be hanged.

He felt a sense of having completed something, and death and the unknown after death meant uncertainty and a possible new conflict for which he did not feel ready. It was not that he feared death; only that it seemed out of place. He had envisioned a long approach to death that should be traversed slowly. It was not fitting to be snatched hurriedly face to face with the end. But if it was in and of life to die now, then let it be. Not—Thy will be done; but rather—Suffer what is to be.

And in this present completion there was an inward satisfaction and joy. He thought of himself as one who has been submerged in the great angry current where the present hindrances and annoyances are so potent that one is unable to see beyond them, and there is only the bewilderment that is associated with too much concern with small things. But now he was shouldering out of the torrent and looking about him, perceived that relatively the present hurts are insignificant, and it was this new and larger sight that blessed him with stability and balance.

Someone came to him and attacked him under cover of

a lie, and there was the personal burning resentment and the hatred that left him trembling and weak. But now a second self stood apart and saw the two real men standing there, all the resentment and hatred being left in the animate forms. And it became only a cold, impersonal fact, moving, to be sure, but not devastating. He was able to say, first, These things are, and then, These things are only parts and have their existence in relation to a greater movement.

There was no saying that these things are for the best, only that they are not of final importance. It was a more perfect understanding of the significance of being.

It was finally a merging of the two inner selves.

During the time that Mose was in prison they hanged a man in the jail yard. For two days workmen nailed the boards together until the scaffold took a form to which a rope could be attached. Mose did not go to the window during that time nor on the morning when the execution took place. But he could hear the men walking on the gravel in the yard and could hear their tense voices and the choking struggle of the man fighting to hold on to life, when the trap was sprung. This was the only real pain Mose felt while he was in the jail. He did not ask God to ease that man's suffering, for it did not seem a reasonable request. He knew it was a suffering of short duration. But it seemed such a denial, such an unmanly, cowardly act to take another's life in that way, when there was no possibility of ever knowing the truth about him or how he had come to his present difficulty, or through the unintelligent and misguided actions of how many other people.

During that time it never even occurred to Mose to wonder what had become of Beatrice. She seemed a stranger he had once in another life known in some intimate way, the exact nature of which he was unable to remember. And Allen and Thurman; they were strangers.

There was only himself now and his desire to lift his voice above the tumult, and to be heard. To set off down the highway with his head thrust out to the future and his throat echoing the harmony of his own soul, past the fields and their cabins, past towns and cities, across the true-flowing rivers, on to the very end where the sea surrounding all awaits to receive all things and reduce them to their elemental parts.

Mose had never before thought of himself except as a negro, yet he had always known that he was really only part negro. He did not find in himself the grossness and dullness of the negroes, nor did he find a complete resemblance to the white people.

There were in him the mystic singing and intuitiveness of the black race, and the intelligence of the white race, and yet he was not of either, a biological eccentricity of such form and dimensions that Nature, in one of her rare and infrequent outthrustings, found him prepared to shelter for a brief time a great soul.

And Mose was not unaware of the dignity of this choice and the obligation it imposed, though he never considered it in its precise terms.

VII

Mr. Caldwell was not a man to be trampled on without some show of fight. He made private inquiry in a quiet way and then called on Durden for confirmation of his facts. But he did not press the District Attorney; in fact, at that time, he made no statement of opinion one way or the other.

But he did call on Mr. Birney and found him sadly out of touch with matters in Clarksville. At first Mr. Birney was suspicious, for he had understood that Caldwell had been retained to defend Mose. But Caldwell explained how it really was, how he never believed in Mose's innocence himself, but how, a fee being a fee, he had let himself be led into the case. And now under his very nose a woman, an upstart lawyer, proposed to cheat him out of his fee by imposing on the negro's credulity and his gentlemanliness, and she had even gone so far as to try to railroad an arrogant miscarriage of justice right through the District Attorney's office and was even now well on her way to accomplishing this outrage against decent citizenry.

In apparent horror at this turn of affairs Mr. Birney lapsed into a profane babble. This was his only refuge. For Mr. Birney had not the intelligence to plan a counterattack himself. His blundering lordliness ended with the confines of the plantation, and, beyond, he was docile, even cringing.

But Caldwell was ready with suggestions. "It strikes me

Orvil wouldn't stand for a thing like this. Not if I know him. Not on his own place surely. Why, letting that nigger loose would be a damn crime."

"Yes, by God it would," Mr. Birney agreed. And he got in the car with Mr. Caldwell and they set out for Lisbon, boiling with wrath and self-righteous indignation in which they almost believed.

Even Lonnie, who was usually only half-hearted on such matters, became interested in Caldwell's story.

For Lonnie remembered that not many months before someone had taken a pot shot at a Federal Prohibition Agent right on the main street of Clarksville, but the shot failed to take effect and the Agent turned and drilled the man full of holes. It looked for a time as though there would be a case against the Agent, but this same Miss Winston had showed up with a list of bondsmen headed off by several prominent people with her own name included. The case against the Agent had vanished in the face of public opinion and he was not even indicted. And to Lonnie, who regarded federal agents as common prey, this Miss Winston became a very obnoxious presence in the community. And then, too, she was a woman, and Lonnie experienced somewhat the same feeling toward her that he had experienced as a boy when for diversion he had once tied up a negro child behind the barn and had beaten it with a surrey whip until it fainted.

But, as usual, it was Orvil who took matters in hand. As deputy-sheriff, and even before that, he had had dealings with Durden that gave him no small power. Durden was not a forward man himself; he was rather a pliable instrument, and he had not failed to benefit financially from his relationship with Orvil. The liquor business had been sufficiently remunerative to allow a good profit for more than one. Durden would not be one to crawl at a time like this; not that he would want to anyhow, once the facts were properly presented to him. And, as Lonnie pointed out, there was more than one thing to be considered here. Miss Winston might think she could snatch their fat out of the fire, but not while they could keep stirring the fire. And, most important, they knew they had public opinion behind them this time.

And Mr. Durden was astonished and ashamed of himself when they all crowded into his office; Caldwell sitting quietly in his neatly pressed dark suit there by the window; Orvil slouched on the table; Lonnie, bare-headed, walking up and down the room; and Mr. Birney standing timidly at the door hardly daring to take a good chew for fear someone would speak to him and he might swallow the whole quid in his nervousness. Mr. Birney had done that once and even his stomach rebelled. But Durden was glad to be able to announce that he had not really promised anything; he had actually said that it would depend on investigation, those very words. And now—why, he could even show Miss Winston how it was his duty to the State, except, he said, she was hot-headed to deal with, as Caldwell himself would have to admit. Caldwell did admit it reluctantly.

Lonnie said, "Why, what are you, a damn bunch of ninnies? That woman has got you so you all want to run for cover."

Orvil said, "All right about that. Only remember you can't go too far with a woman. There's people wouldn't stand for nothing high-handed. The way to handle this is soft like; be as sweet as pie about it. Work up your case good. She ain't got one damn witness, I don't suppose. Select the jury right. That won't be nothing to you, Durden. Sweeten 'em a little if necessary. Ain't no use to let anybody get on a high horse around here. She ain't no bigger than we are."

Mr. Birney ventured, "Imagine letting a nigger get away with a thing like that. Why, if I'd a ever got my hands on him—"

Lonnie interrupted him. "You had that chance once. And the night of the shooting I didn't notice you doing anything. You're a fine fellow, Birney, only light weight."

"Yeah," Orvil said. "You keep out of this, Birney. We'll holler for you when the time comes and we'll tell you what to say. No mistake about that. Durden, Birney'll be more trouble than the whole rest of the case, keeping him from making a jackass out of himself on the witness stand."

Mr. Birney hardly offered any show of disagreement.

And that same day Durden called at Mary's office. She asked him if he would not wait in the outer office just a minute and he sat down. For the first time, as he looked at this bare, dirty-walled office, Durden realized the position that Mary had made for herself in Clarksville. He would have liked being on her side in this case, but there was no way out now. He could hear her rustling papers on her desk, for the door was only half closed, and he wondered what she might be thinking about.

Mary sensed why Durden had come, and she was taking time to collect her thoughts. Apparently there was nothing she could say to him to change him. He was too deeply involved with the others. Durden made a true apology.

"You see, Miss Mary," he said, "I told you what I did that day because I was sure you had your facts straight.

And I'm not doubting you think they are. I give you that much, I sure do. But people have come to me and showed me how it was a plain premeditated murder, and I do represent the State and I couldn't lay back on the case."

"Orvil Rutherford and who else? Mr. Birney?"

"Well, yes, it was them. You see they was both there the night of the shooting and they both seen what happened and they have done some investigating since. They wouldn't stand for me letting down now when it all happened out on their place."

"I see how it is, Mr. Durden. But you understand I'm not going to let down either. I'm going to fight you to the finish and I'm going to beat you, too. I've got an ace that's going to wipe your whole case out."

"Don't count on it too much, Miss Mary. Really don't. Because the State's got trumps for that ace. I do wish to God there was somebody else defending that nigger, because I'm going to convict him sure."

Mary said, "I'm glad it is I, because you would convict him otherwise. But I'm glad you came and told me you have changed your mind about it."

"I'm awful sorry." Durden cringingly smiled out of the door.

Mary began to think of Mr. Rutherford. And she thought of her father, whom she remembered as an old feeble man who had told her about how he had shot the bear cub out of the dead tree. That had been a long time ago. She felt she almost knew Rutherford, remembering so many things she had heard about him. But she had only seen him a few times on the streets and had never spoken to him.

VIII

RUTHERFORD was sitting on the side porch that afternoon and he watched the car as it came down the highway, watched it turn and bump across the culvert into the road leading to the house. He did not know the car nor the woman in it. Then the car stopped and the woman got out.

"Well, God darn," he murmured to himself. He got up and sneaked back into the house, but not before Mary had seen him.

Clara came to the door, and Mary felt that the old man was back somewhere in the far darkness of that hallway, watching.

"Yes'm?"

"Is Mr. Rutherford in?"

"Yes'm. He shore am."

"Could I see him?"

"Yes'm. You jest set on the gallery an I'll call him."

Mary sat in the heavy wicker chair.

Presently the door opened and Mr. Rutherford stepped onto the porch. He had a collar on, but no tie. His hair had been brushed and it clung to his head like a dirty mat. He wore a gray, thin coat that had wrinkles under the collar made by the nail on which it hung in the closet. His trousers had once matched the coat, but now they were shapeless and faded. His shoes were high-top black buttonless slippers with tabs on the backs.

"Good afternoon, ma'am."

"Good afternoon, Mr. Rutherford." She extended her hand. "I'm Mary Winston." The name apparently made no impression on him. He took her hand slowly, he barely touched it, gracefully and with chivalrous dignity.

"Won't you set down? Better let me turn that chair where the sun won't get in your eyes. You know, funny thing, but the niggers on the place can tell time by where my chair is, and I wouldn't want to set in the wrong place; it might throw 'em off a whole hour or more."

She smiled at him, studying his face, wishing she had the power to read it all in one glance.

"You know, Mr. Rutherford, you and I should be good friends."

"You honor me, ma'am."

"And I reproach myself for waiting to call on you until I had to come to ask a favor."

He squirmed uneasily in his chair. Probably she wanted a contribution for a church building fund. No, not quite that. She was not that type.

"Anything in reason. I like to oblige the ladies."

"You are going to be surprised when you know who I am."

"By God," he said, and then, "I beg your pardon, ma'am, but you are like him as two peas. But you're too young to be his daughter."

"Oh, I'm not as young as you might think. Yes, Captain was my father."

"Confound it," he said. "After all these years. Did he ever tell you about the bear cub we had?"

"Yes, and how you quarreled over it."

"I always was a headstrong fool." It seemed he was reaching out for her friendship.

They sat for a moment or two without speaking.

Then she said, "I don't just know how to begin, but I think I'd best leave the preliminaries and we can get to them later. Mr. Rutherford, I'm a lawyer in Clarksville. I guess you know that. I've taken a case for a negro that was here on your place, Mose Southwick."

It seemed all the animation went out of his face. It frightened her. He was wearing a mask now, cold, lifeless, the mask of the other people she knew in the county. The defeated, withdrawing face of submission and superstitious cruelty, cowardice.

She became more direct, even pointed.

"They're going to try to hang Mose, not for shooting Willie Stubs, but because he refused to take a whipping from Mr. Birney and because he dared to resent the fact that Mr. Birney was living with his wife."

"You talk pretty straight about it."

She ignored this. "He was indicted by perjured testimony. I got into the case after that, only a short time ago in fact. They will bring that same testimony and other like witnesses into court against him. A negro is so helpless."

"Why do you come to me? What do you think I could do? I am an old man."

"Because you are Mose's guardian. Not legally, but morally you are. If they convict him, I think I would blame you more than anyone else. Not because you did anything against him but because you just did nothing at all."

She paused. He did not offer to speak. "Mr. Rutherford, it's not right to treat a human life that way. But forgetting that, leaving Mose out entirely, it's an issue involving justice, and it's time this country took justice out of the hands of mean people. The few that could do something, people like you, have carried their little bowls of water around under their arms, and every time something like this happens, they stop on the square and wash their hands. But that's not all there is to it. It degrades people to evade life that way. It's what's wrong with this community. Maybe one life out of the way isn't much, a little thing, but it weakens the whole people."

She was talking with passionate fervor, her hands holding white and hard on the arms of the chair. It seemed now Rutherford did not hear her; his eyes were staring, lost, across the fields.

"Your voice, ma'am, is like something I haven't heard for a long time. Like the dead crying at the head of an old man. Like the time before the end had got so little I could hear the noise on the other side.

"Only you're different, one that wouldn't die easy. You never knew her. Her memory will never die in me.

"You don't seem to understand. I couldn't get mixed up in a matter like this. I'm just trying to wait quiet. And you come trying to bring me back. I done with fighting a long time ago. I'm not a fighter now."

Mary said, "I don't know who she was. I didn't come to pry. Believe that. But if I could appeal to you in her name. To do it for her, for yourself. An old man rising still defiant. I'm a woman coming to the old strength of this country for help because I love what you were and what you and my father built and then neglected while it rotted away. It's that neglect I can't forgive. It's like God had gone back to the swamps to live with snakes."

"You tell me that. You think I have sat here these years

without knowing it. It's been creeping, crawling over the fields. No wonder the niggers chain the doors and shutters at night. Sometimes I feel like doing it myself. To look at my own monstrous children. What strange ends a man comes to."

She said, "Then you do love this country as I do, the greatness of it and how it holds you. The black sloping down to the walled river. And sometimes I hate it, too."

"I know," he said. "Only it's all nearly dead in me now. My body is yellowed paper like to be blown away or burnt up."

"But why not kindle the fire once more? Take the ax blade back against the forest and make a new clearing where our children can raise a new crop. That's what my life means to me. Fighting the onrush of human degradation to hold it back so life can go on and not fall before it."

He said, "I think I could do it if you would help me." He turned and looked about him, as if fearing something. Then he told her of the night Willie had been brought to the outhouse and how he had died.

"That would clear Mose before any court," she said. "Then we could send him away from here where they couldn't lay hands on him."

"Mose was a strange nigger," he said. "Must of been mostly white. A self-possessed one. I saw that, though I didn't see much of him."

"Not just self-possessed, God-possessed. Not like the church people, but truly humble, and proud too. He seems hardly interested in the case at all. He thinks about other things, his people, as he calls them. He was a preacher, you know. He wants to be ordained."

Rutherford said, "Maybe I'll go see him with you."

"It would be wonderful if you would. He'd appreciate it so much."

He got up and offered her his arm. They walked down through the fields, not speaking at first, she seeming to turn to his awakened strength.

Thurman laid down his hoe and gazed in wonder at the gray, hatless thin man and the woman beside him; and the other negroes peered from their cabins.

Once he stopped and lifted his arm in a broad sweep before him. "All this," he said.

"I know," she replied. "You and I together love it enough to make up for all it has been profaned. How glorious it could be. I don't see now how that will ever come. But it's worth all the serving it can get. It's worth fighting for."

He walked back to the car with her. "You live in Clarksville? Your mother still living?"

"Yes, mama and I live there together. Just where we always lived. When Captain died, I thought we ought to take a smaller place, but mama wouldn't have it. You must come to see us sometime soon. Mama would love to have you come."

When she had gone, Mr. Rutherford walked back and stood on the porch. Clara came and stood beside him.

"I done hear you tell her. Hit would be a blessed thing."

He turned on her. "You keep your damn mouth shut. You get back to the kitchen where you belong."

That night he did not eat in his room, but had Colin serve the table. And he kept up a steady flow of abusive profanity which did not make Colin any more at ease at this strange procedure.

IX

MR. RUTHERFORD was waiting on the porch, like an aged ruffled hen, when Mary went after him, proud of himself and somewhat amazed at himself too.

"I'll be cutting a new figure in Clarksville, going down to do business with a nigger in jail. I guess that'll give them something to talk over."

"Yes, I guess it will. They have so little. It may rouse a spark in them; at least it will be a novelty. It usually takes a lynching to really arouse Clarksville, that or an election where they can fight over the ballot boxes."

"I haven't voted for years. I'd have to vote in Lisbon. I don't like going there much. Not that I get to Clarksville often either. I used to know everybody in both towns and all their children by their first names; that was when Clarksville was just a little crossroads. Now I walk down the street and none of the children know who I am and they stare at me. It makes me feel uncomfortable."

He was balky like a shy horse at the jail, but Mary finally herded him in and kept him from telling the jailer too pointedly to mind his own damn business.

It would have been difficult to tell whether Mose or Mr. Rutherford was the more embarrassed.

"Boy, this lady here tells me I've got to get you out of jail. Just thought I would, by God."

"I done told her you thunk in yore own haid."

"She didn't believe it."

"She didn't say if she didn't."

"You know this means me fighting my own children, my own flesh and blood, to help you? I don't know why I do it. For a nigger. I don't know."

"It done been a hard thing fer a body to do. I knows dat. But hit ain't no more'n a body ought to. I ain't never hahmed nobody. Only bided and tried to keep out o' trubbul. You couldn't left them hang me, knowin as you do."

"It's not for you to tell me my duty."

"No sir, not urgin you none; jes speakin my mind. Maybe when I gits out, you help me wid my church, help me build a church on de place. It could do a heap fer de cullud people. I done have a heap o' power at persuadin my people."

Mr. Rutherford said, "I've built churches before. Here and in Lisbon. I wouldn't put foot in any of them. It would be funny now if I ended up by attending a nigger church."

"We'd done welcome you shore. We'd done come and fotch you. You'd give air to de church."

"You know if you get out of here, you'll have to leave this part of the country. That church was just talk. Somebody would kill you."

"Yes sir. I guess I knows it. I'd go off quiet. I wouldn't start nothin."

Mary said, "There won't be anything we can do today, Mose. I just wanted Mr. Rutherford to come to see you. I knew it would cheer you up."

"Oh, yes'm. Hit do indeed. Only I had done cheered a lot after you come de fust time. I knowed dey couldn't hang me.

"I would shore like to git back to de crops. I done started a clean fiel dis year. Hit done hurt me to run off."

Mr. Rutherford said, "It's still a good field. Thurman's looking after it. You better forget it. It won't do you no good." He stood there for a moment looking at Mose, and Mose returned the gaze steadily. He started to speak but turned away, and Mary followed him out of the jail.

"There was a lot I meant to say to that darky, but I felt like a setter the first time a quail rises under his nose, gun-shy and flustered."

"I know," she said. "He's not like anybody else. I felt that way, too. He has unusual qualities for a negro."

"Niggers have been the curse of this state, and of the South. It was too easy to live off them. But living off somebody else's strength makes you weak. That's what's the matter with my boys. They lived off me, and I guess it was pretty sour living, too. I don't blame them. I don't. Only now I just want them to keep out of my sight.

"They'll kick up a devil of a stir. I wouldn't put anything past Lonnie. He would burn his own mother and laugh."

X

DURDEN was almost glad it happened. There was no way around this, and it did not involve him in any way at all. They could not blame him for it.

"Orvil," he said, "he sat right there in my office with Miss Winston and told me."

Lonnie said, "I knew damn well Colin was lying that night when he said he hadn't told papa. Only I didn't guess papa had put his nose into it. God, that would sound lousy on a witness stand. They'd likely believe him, and you couldn't fix no jury on him."

"That's just it," Durden continued. "With him testifying for the nigger, we wouldn't have no case at all. I wouldn't be surprised if I got the Attorney General on my neck, and I don't hanker after that none, I can tell you.

"And there's more to it. There's a lot of people in Clarksville yet that would take his side. I don't guess there's ten people has had a talk with your papa in ten years, but he's better known in this county than Jesus Christ and looked up to more. It would raise a state-wide stink. I think we'd better drop the whole thing right now. It would look like hell in court. You all testifying to one thing and your own papa to another. And he had his mettle up. He gave me a good going over, and Miss Winston just sat there and smiled. I felt like Judas, I did.

"Yes, sir, this thing has gone far enough. He'd be the one

man I couldn't fix a jury on. Why, people around here think of old man Rutherford just like they do—well, like anybody that's been here a long time and was in the war."

Orvil said, "Aw, let it go. We can pick that nigger up later and handle him better than sending him to jail maybe."

Lonnie had been standing watching them. "You guys make me sick. You let her get away with this and she'll be running this county the first thing you know. The time to stop her is right now. You got to think about later on. There'll be other things coming up. It don't pay to sit back.

"You just lay quiet for a while, Durden. I'll think of something."

"All right, Lonnie, but you think fast. She's not going to wait around very long for us to make up our minds what to do. Pretty soon it'll be too late to do anything."

"I'll think of something all right."

XI

LONNIE telephoned to Clara. "You tell papa me and Orvil are coming out for supper."

"Yes sir, Mr. Lonnie, but he done been in a powerful tempah dese last few days. I don't know how you goin find him. He done been at Claksvul all day wid dat lady. He goin be wore out when he git back. He ain't took Colin wid him lak he ginally do. Colin kin look after him lak nobody else kin."

"You tell him we're coming out."

"Yes sir, I'll shore tell him."

Clara polished the chimney of the huge oil lantern that hung from the ceiling of the dining room and wiped the reflector. It lighted the room fairly well.

Mr. Rutherford was very tired. He helped himself and said, "Orvil, you take some and pass it on to Lonnie."

"Papa, I hear you have taken up with that lady lawyer, Miss Winston."

"I told her I'd testify for that nigger, Mose, if that's what you're driving at. This is one time you boys better lay off." He sat picking at his food. He would have preferred going to his room, but the laws of hospitality demanded that he remain at the table until they had eaten. He would not deny his children his table while he had food to put on it.

Orvil sucked heavily at his food. Watching Lonnie. Waiting for him.

"All right, papa. We don't see it your way, but if you want to get him off, it's all right with us. He's only a nigger. But I'd watch Birney. He might get other notions in his head."

"Birney wouldn't dare. By God, I'll run him off the place. I won't have him here any longer. And you boys can get that damn liquor off this place and keep it off."

Lonnie said, "That reminds me, papa. Me and Orvil brought you something. Only this is regular stuff. A feller from Memphis brought it down."

Lonnie got up and left the room. He told Clara, "You and Colin get the hell out of here and don't come back tonight."

"But we orter set the food in the pantry. The flies will git all over it and mess on it."

"I'll look after that. You get out. We got some business to look after and we don't want you all hanging around."

"All right, Mr. Lonnie."

He went back into the dining room and placed the bottle on the table beside his father.

Mr. Rutherford said, "This ain't any of that poison you make, fixed up fancy, is it?"

"Nope, it's the real stuff. Feller swore it come all the way from Canada. Christ, it cost me eight dollars. It's more than me and Orvil can afford to drink. Only we knew you couldn't get hold of anything like it."

"It was thoughtful of you."

His glass still had water in it, but he threw the water against the screen and poured some of the whisky. "You all have some."

"No, papa, we got plenty of the other stuff. You save it for yourself. You can't get it like that often."

Mr. Rutherford lifted the glass in his hand, sat looking at it with red, tired eyes. Then he turned the glass up slowly and drank.

"That's right good."

Orvil leaned over and poured him another drink. "That'll do you good," he said.

Mr. Rutherford looked at him curiously, wondering. "I don't think . . ." He did not finish the sentence but drank again. Then he leaned back in the chair, closing his eyes, rubbing his hands across his shirt front.

Lonnie got up and walked out on the porch, smoking a cigarette. It had become quite dark now. There was no light in the house save in the dining room. He could hear them talking. His father's voice was thick now, drowsy, querulous. He was saying something about Martha. Lonnie leaned across the porch rail and let the cigarette drop from his lips to the ground. It lay, a faint glow, on the thin grass.

He went back into the dining room. When he poured the whisky into the glass, his father took it in his tired hand and drank it without speaking. Orvil was hunched forward across the table, leaning on his cupped hands. A bottle fly hummed over the stewed chicken. The grease was beginning to congeal on the gravy.

Lonnie looked at his watch. "It's eight-thirty," he said.

Orvil got up from his chair. "Those niggers ain't around?"

"No," Lonnie replied. "Only you can't tell about Colin."

Orvil walked into the kitchen and returned. "They ain't here. Neither one of them." He looked at his father. "This place is ours by rights anyway."

XII

It is a building like many that stand in South Memphis, made of glaring red bricks that are dirty but still remain harsh in color. It has tin-roofed porches and jutting gables. The magnolia trees in the yard have black-green glassy leaves about black trunks. Concrete steps lead up from the street, where dinky trolley cars creak up the hill.

The heavy morning smoke of factories hangs over the streets and buildings; globules of soft soot fall gently earthward.

It is the only pretentious building in sight. The others are flat-roofed wholesale houses and stores and small manufacturing plants.

The reception room was probably once the library of the old home. There is still a great teakwood cabinet against the cherry-paneled wall. The other furniture is cheap by contrast, harsh sofas and brown varnished rockers. Long corridors lead off from the room, bringing to it a faint, unpleasant odor of acids and disinfectants.

The touring car stopped at the end of the walk. The side curtains were up except in front by the driver.

Lonnie was driving. He turned to the back seat. "I'll come around and help you get him out." They half carried their father out from the car and up the steps.

A man came and held the door open and showed them into the reception room. He was a short man with a heavy drooping face and waxy, bushy eyebrows over small, finely set eyes. He wore a narrow black tie and a black sack suit.

"I'm the house doctor. My name's Roberts. Which one of you is Rutherford?"

"We're both Rutherford," Lonnie said. "This is my brother."

"Well, gentlemen, could you just step into my private office where we can talk better? Will he sit quiet or had I better have a nurse sit with him?"

"He'll sit quiet, I think."

Dr. Roberts opened a door at the side of the room.

Orvil said, "I guess you can tell him. I'll wait here with papa."

"Yes," Lonnie said, "I guess that would be better."

The doctor took up a cigar stub from the edge of the desk and turned it cold between his yellow teeth. "You said over the phone he was your father."

"Yes."

"He have these spells often?"

"No, not often. He's getting pretty old. Eighty-four, I think. It's whisky, and maybe dope too. I don't know. The niggers say so. He don't know what he's doing. Ain't anybody to look after him at the place. Only niggers."

"We can get a doctor out from town, unless you just want me to look after him." His speech was noncommittal, impersonal.

"I don't want no other doctors. Just you keep him here, maybe permanently, if you understand. Don't let him see anybody or write to anybody either. You understand?"

"He got much property? Any other relatives?"

"A little property. No other relatives; only Orvil, that's my brother, out there, and me."

"Does he act up much?"

"He may act up a lot when he gets sobered up and wants to leave. Only if you let him know you ain't going to stand for any foolishness, he'll be no bother. He ain't as strong as a jay-bird."

"We can handle the case, Mr. Rutherford. You can pay in advance?"

"I can."

"You better let me know how I can get in touch with you if he should get sick or anything."

Lonnie took the piece of paper from the doctor, and as he wrote, he said, "He might. Might get real sick. Might even die. He's awful feeble. It's just old age with him."

"Yes, he looked like that. The natural decay of the body and the faculties."

"Is he likely to run into many people here? People that might know him?"

"We can attend to that. We got what we call isolation rooms. You like to see the rooms?"

"No, I'll leave that to you. I don't want you to muff anything."

"No, sir, this place is well managed, a good institution. I look after it all personally."

They went back into the reception room. Orvil had removed his father's hat. Mr. Rutherford was lying back heavily against the chair. It was stifling hot in the room. His eyes were closed; his forehead and eyelids were a yellow white, wet with perspiration.

Orvil sat meekly, nervous. He rose and waited with Lonnie.

Lonnie said to the doctor, "I guess you got me straight now. You know where you can reach me if he got real bad sick—or anything."

"I won't make any mistakes, gentlemen."

XIII

LYING there in the bed, he was unable to see objects. The dull blur indicated light. When he closed his eyes, there was darkness. That was the only difference.

He hardly remembered now. The faint struggle. The repulsion. Then lying quietly. Hardly thinking. Feeling the slight grasp on life weaken. He could feel the slow silent ebb. And no desire to hold on.

There were two concentric circles, revolving in opposite directions, slowly. There was a glowing spot on the inner circle. That was he. Now they began to revolve faster and the circles widened. The glowing spot dropped to the outer circle. That was the approach. The glowing spot would fall later from the outer circle too, off out into the great blackness. Then it would be lost from sight, lost utterly. That would be the end.

He was only faintly conscious for an intense moment of the gathering of phlegm in his throat, that choked him and made him want to vomit.

But it passed away, and he resumed watching the spot on the outer circle. It was beginning to fade now, to recede out into the blackness.

The nurse heard him cough. She went into the room. His hand was lifted slightly, as if pointing. He said, "You'll want to fill the lamps tonight."

There was no further sound.

She called the house doctor and waited in the hall.

When he came out of the room, he said, "You go to my office and look up that number. You put in a call for whatever that place was; you get his son on the line. Don't you say anything to him. I'll do the talking."

XIV

IT HAD been only a few days since Mary had seen Mr. Rutherford. She did not even know he had been gone. She saw the notice in the Memphis *Daily Herald* and read it, almost unbelieving. It was a very brief account of the man's life, giving the dates of birth and death and the names of his two sons who survived him. What impressed Mary most, beyond her personal grief, was that this would be nearly the last public notice of his life. He was gone now, obliterated, his effort and struggle ended. And all that he had accomplished he had lived to see perverted into avenues of decay, and that too was part of him and of his life and self-frustration. It was the pathetic tragedy of things that might have been, morbid sentimentality and melodrama.

For this man had chiefly sinned against his own self-respect, had denied the strength and intelligence that were his.

And the opportunity that might have been hers to call him back before the end, that too was gone now. Mary felt a sense of loneliness, realizing the futility of anyone's trying to find in others a bulwark for self-realization. For she saw that, paradoxical as it may be, the individual's proper pursuit of life lies in living externally without giving up the sanctity of self and without allowing self to be penetrated and disarmed.

For the moment she had forgotten the necessity for the

ancient gods and the reverence that must be shown them. It seemed to her that the unpardonable sin is not blasphemy against God but rather blasphemy against the integrity of man.

And when Mary went to the jail that day, she thought of herself as serving an exemplification of something that was to be esteemed in humanity.

It was Mose who said, "Hit do seem a downright pity to have a man tuk off that-a-way. Jest when he done heered right after livin so long heerin wrong. An I done like the man, done felt they was things I could a told him, only he done turned his haid so long he couldn't lissen. Hit ain't right fer a man to left he hands lay idle cause then he lay an rot like a plow lef out in de fiels in de rain.

"What a man do wid he hans ain't no more'n he insides comin out. What a man do am de spirrit in him a talkin. Cose hit ain't allus like dat, cause heap o' folks goes blusterin roun makin a show, but it ain't good fer de spirrit.

"A man can't lay hissef down an let de watahs roll by, cause effn he do, he drown. Maybe he keep on livin, but he done been drown jest de same. An hit am de same wid a man's spirrit. He got to keep a pokin it to make it do de fight, and when de spirrit lay quiet too long, it weaken. Misery am what all men done been bawn wid, ain't no gittin roun dat."

"You know, Mose, don't you, that this will make it mighty hard for you in court now. I have been trying to think how we could work this thing out. There will be so many of them to testify against you, and white people, some of them. I'm beginning to be worried and yet I don't see how they can possibly convict you; no jury will ever believe them. All the negroes know the story and they have promised to testify for you. Thurman has."

"Yes'm, Thurman will, ef Mr. Birney don't git to workin on him. I done tole you Thurman am afeared o' Mr. Birney.

"But don't you go lettin my troubles burden you none. I ain't doin so bad right now. I shore ain't. Long as dey lets me live, I goin git long well nough. I done got right wid mysef. Hit would take a heap to turn me over now."

"Well, Mose, we'll just do the very best we can. But don't expect too much."

"No ma'am. I don't do much spectin no more. I done cut all dat out."

That afternoon the gates at the cemetery were opened wider than usual, crushing the heavy growth of honeysuckle that lay banked on the fence. And Lon Rutherford came to lie at rest beside Martha on his left and three of the Sisters of Mercy on his right, three nurses who had died during the yellow fever and were lying now in a common grave marked with a Latin inscription on an iron slab that was half covered by vines.

In the slowly moving, heated air the preacher stood bareheaded beside the coffin, and as he addressed the multitude, the sweat gathered slowly on his worn gray chin. He was a preacher of the old order who had known Rutherford many years and he talked endlessly of the good works of this Christian man and he prayed with monotonous fervor as the people before him stood first on one foot and then on the other wishing he would have done. And yet they were drawn to come and linger in the satiation of their curiosity.

Before the coffin was lowered into the grave, it was opened, and the people pressed near to view the face of the dead man. Mary had no desire to see. And there was one other who did not approach, a man conspicuous for his being apart from the rest and for his dignified manner. During this episode this man found Mary looking at him, and he nodded respectfully and lifted his hand, extending one finger, as if to give emphasis to an unspoken question.

They closed the coffin and the men started to lift it away. Orvil stepped from where he had been standing, raised his hand to stay them and in a trembling voice asked them to reopen the gray-clothed box. He removed the white rose from his buttonhole and laid it on the glass cover.

The preacher was so touched by this impromptu demonstration that he delivered a blessing on Orvil, saying in conclusion, "That sacred flower will be there when the angels come to call forth our departed brother." And weeping that had hitherto been concealed now appeared in open demonstration. With difficulty Mary restrained the passionate cry that rose in her throat.

When the coffin had been lowered into the ground and the mortal earth committed to rest, the bystanders began to wander off to the waiting line of cars.

The man who had previously signed to Mary now approached. He was of austere manner and appearance, the color of his skin being rather more of bronze than of the yellowed white of the other men. His hair was well brushed and his pointed beard neatly trimmed. His suit was dark and well fitted. He showed no outward sign of grief, yet was respectful and courteous.

He said, "How do you do, Mary?"

"Very well, Mr. Higgins, thank you. I hope you're well. You're looking well. I had hardly expected you to come. It's such a long drive from Memphis."

"Yes, it is, but I felt I ought to. In a way it was a great shock to me, though I hadn't seen the old man for a long time. I was wondering if I couldn't see you for a few minutes before I go on back. There was something I wanted to ask you about."

Mary could see the people staring at them as the cars drove slowly out the gate. "You could come by my office in a few minutes. I'd like to see you."

"I didn't know if you'd be going back there today."

"It will be all right. You come over in a little while."

The man bowed slightly and turned away.

He did not let Mary precede him by many minutes. When he sat down in her office, he produced a small cigarette holder and placed his cigarette in it with fastidious touches. As he talked, he made small puffs of smoke, nervously but without any affectation or self-consciousness.

"It seems strange," he said, "that having grown up down here, I know so few of the people any more. I liked your father so much. But you drift away. Business keeps you occupied, enslaved.

"Tell me, did you know Rutherford well? He was a strange old bird."

"My father did, years ago. I never saw much of him until quite recently. It seems so strange." And she told him briefly of her reason for having sought Mr. Rutherford out.

"It's hardly possible," he said, apparently to himself.

"What do you mean?"

"His death seemed more than circumstantial. A nurse at

the sanitarium where he died phoned me, said he'd been asking for me to come to see him. He was dead when I got there. It seemed the nurse must have acted without telling anybody; I don't know. Apparently my visit wasn't in the schedule. The house doctor acted very strangely about it, I thought. It looked as though they resented outside interest. I guess it was my imagination. Maybe they killed him. You could never prove anything. He couldn't have lived much longer anyway. That's why I wanted to see you. I wondered if there had been any talk, anything to confirm my suspicions. Those boys of his are not quite human. They never were. You seem to have good opposition."

Mary was tense now, trying to follow the meaning of these staccato thrusts. "I've heard nothing," she said. "He seemed to be afraid of them. But I could hardly believe this."

"No, I suppose not. There's nothing you could do about it. It's useless to try to change things. But I half liked the old man. It looks as if you were dealing with people who would bear watching."

"It's such a cruel thing," she said. "They must be very determined. I don't see how it could mean so much to them. A negro's life, I mean."

"Oh, it's more than that. It's a sort of self-expression. It's the fault of the life here.

"But the negroes' position is so futile. They are so helpless and stupid. They can not cope with white people. It is utter folly to talk of equality.

"No, the problem is merely that the strong should not wear themselves out on the weak. Rutherford did that. Quite as sympathetic to the strong, that is, as humane to the weak. The negroes should be protected from gross injustices, and it will only be in accomplishing this that the white people can hope to progress socially. No society functioning as this one does could hope for anything but the savagery we find here."

He paused to expel the stub of his cigarette from the holder.

Mary said, "Yes, that is it exactly. Only I had never stated it so clearly. But why should Mose's case be so hopeless? Why should they be able to convict him?"

"A prominent white man could get him free. You were right. Rutherford could have done it. Maybe they figured that too. Maybe they had other reasons. I may be entirely wrong.

"But you will face a bribed or picked jury, or both, and witnesses that will be intimidated if necessary."

"Why do you say that? They wouldn't be able to do it."

"I'm only guessing, of course. I don't really know. But that's how things work out down here."

"It's not possible."

"Even not living here, I know this country better than you. I grew up in it. A man hears more about it. I understand these people.

"Did you ever see a man lynched?" He smiled urbanely.

"No. Thank Heaven."

"It is an enlightening spectacle. Your ribs like not to hold your insides in for a time. But you get over it. It matures you, acquaints you with your fellow men.

"Say, rather, it is interesting to realize the extent of man's nature. Far upward and far downward, even in the same man. God knows, Rutherford showed that. He was the one that got me out of here when I was a kid. But the two may not be coexistent. There's nothing tragic about that.

"But don't let a case like this worry you too much.

"What you are interested in finally—I guess I am too—is the social destiny of a people. You have to keep that in mind. My interest is not the kind that becomes action. Yours is. I want to talk about it. You want to do things.

"But I like this country with all its stinking old swamps and dirty yellow depots for the same reason, I suppose, that I like the odor of stale food. Of course there's more to it than just that. It's cruel, forbidding and challenging. It seems to be always slowly alive like heavy, smoky fogs.

"I think what holds us back as much as anything else is our own honest ignorance of the right way to proceed. I would part with much if I knew it would avail. But I could toss myself into the sea and be lost in an instant. I prefer to peck like a hen. I wait at my door scrawling on my slate."

He rose to go.

Mary said, "If this man had come to you, what would you have done?"

He looked at her closely. "That's a cruel question. A woman's question, if I may say so. Probably nothing. My business interests endangered for him? No, I would leave him for somebody else."

"Would you like to see him? Maybe you don't believe what I told you."

"Me? Good Lord, no. It would only be from curiosity. He may be a good darky. I'm sure he is. No, I wouldn't want to trouble you."

"You might think of something you could do to help him. He needs help desperately."

"I couldn't afford it. I'd do a favor for you, of course. But not this way. Say it's not in my line."

He added, hurriedly, "But I shall be interested to hear how it comes out. I wish you luck."

Courtesies were exchanged and he was gone, fleeing, it seemed.

Mary sat at the desk, letting the words he had spoken drift unguided through her mind. And she saw the picture of Mose sitting there in the heat of that small cell, at peace in the face of all that would have set other men to crying and cursing. Higgins was an intelligent man; she knew that; all brushed and polished, capable, perceiving but somehow beyond the reach of life.

She brushed her hand across the desk before her and noticed with calm interest the smears of coal soot on her fingers. For a moment it seemed as if her whole life were fatally enveloped in dirt and filth, surrounded by decaying evil walls and yellowed sickly plasters.

She rose and walked to the window. Across the flat-roofed buildings she could see the railroad embankment, with the train standing there by the station. Someone by the station restaurant was ringing a bell, calling the travelers from the coaches. The sound in the hush of twilight recalled the memory of twilights of earlier days with the sound of milk pails clanging in the milkhouse and the animals pawing at the stone floor. Now the train began to pull slowly away. And she could see on beyond into the west where the sun lay beyond the smoke, dimly red on the top edge of the forest blackness.

XV

Sometimes the most terrifying fact of life is its onward consuming movement, never any pause, never any alteration in speed. The principles deduced from today's experiences seem tomorrow to have lost their adequacy, for the new situations are not those of yesterday. Skillful is the man who can trace the thread through the weaving without losing it, for the very thread itself changes color and even texture as the cloth rolls past.

It seemed to Mary that she was being pushed slowly against a precipice where there would be no chance to stop and reorganize the fight. She was ambushed and in doubt.

With almost desperate energy she hurled herself back into the fight, determined that somehow this thing should be prevented.

Higgins had gone back to Memphis; back, as he had said, to write pertinent adages on his slate. But Mary remembered what he had said.

There was an old Frenchman in Clarksville who had had a shabby law practice for more years than most people could remember. An unkempt, hairy man who sucked continually at a short briar pipe. Explosive and good-natured, he was held an eccentric and not quite accountable to ordinary rules of good behavior.

His office was as disorderly as his clothes, dirty and littered with papers scattered on floor and tables. The windows were tightly closed and half covered with drooping velvet drapes. A faded flag lay on a match-marked mantel. Renard was the lawyer for fly-by-night merchants, foreigners and fruit-and-vegetable men. He was quick and shrewd in court, powerful in the community, and generally believed to be more honest than otherwise. But he had been known to wheedle a jury out of more than his client rightly deserved.

He uncovered a chair for Mary and put on his coat with a great, blustering show. He paced the floor, nervously, listening to her story.

"Ah, yes. You do honor me. But in my language I am the fox. I must remember that.

"It gives me great pain. I do not have a great business as you well know. But I cannot, as we lawyers say, place my life in—yes, it would be the triple jeopardy. I might curse your Mr. Wilson or Mr. Lee; they would endure it. But I cannot do this sort of thing. You ask for my life. I know it is nothing, but I save it all the same. Some day maybe I die a grander death, but not starve to death.

"I would like to help you. I would like to cry at these people and spit in their teeth. I tell you that, for I know you will not violate my confidence. I must endure these filthy animals that I may live. But sometime I am going to leave here so that at least I may die in peace.

"But for now I am not ready. No, Miss Mary, you must see, must know that. A fox may die stealing chickens but not die in a trap baited with chickens.

"Remember this. Do anything to people but offend their prejudices. They will endure anything else. But for that offense the sure penalty is death. I speak for myself. What you do is your business.

"I am sorry. I like you, Miss Mary. But you see. What can I do?" He lifted his arms in a sweeping gesture of resignation.

In spite of herself Mary was smiling at old Renard, but it was not ridicule, it was sympathy. Renard was no fool. How did he come here, she asked herself, this transplanted, lonely, nervous bit of life, pinching his livelihood off unwanted corners, living in the dreams of some other, distant world?

But she had hardly hoped he could or would help her. She thanked him for his time. He protested with vows of eternal friendship. And she left him standing in the doorway, still talking, gesticulating.

XVI

THURMAN said, "No indeed, ma'am, I shore don't want to see Mose hang. I done know how dat shootin was. An me an de other folks on de place done seed how Willie laid to make a fuss wid Mose. I done tole Mose he orter git on way from here cause Mr. Birney didn't mean him no good."

"But you must get this clear in your mind, Thurman. You can't bring Mr. Birney into this. That would turn the jury against Mose. All you can tell is just what you saw the night of the shooting and that you know Willie had tried to pick a fuss with Mose and that Willie had a mean disposition. Nothing about Mr. Birney and Mose's wife, nothing about Mr. Birney having sent Willie to kill Mose. Only just about Willie and Mose. Do you understand that?"

"Yes'm, I sees how it is."

"Now is there anything else that could help Mose that you haven't told? Is there anything else you can think of, any little thing?"

"Well, yes'm, they was one thing. De next day after de shootin when de people was all at de house mournin and at de cemetery when dey was buryin Willie, Lizzie she was dere, an she didn't hardly cry or nothin. She say to different people dat Willie didn't git no more'n what was comin to him cause he done made de argumint and done bused Mose, done cussed him, made de fust shot, she say. She done say Willie done got bought sense."

"Got what?"

"Got bought sense. Say hit was better'n no sense."

"What did she mean by that?"

"I don't know what she mean. But dat what she say. Say bought sense better'n no sense."

"Can we find the negroes who heard these things?"

"Yes'm, we can shore git de most of 'em."

Thurman accompanied Mary on her tour of the cabins, because alone she would have gotten no satisfaction from any of the negroes. She wrote down names, told them what she wanted them to do, and they promised with many a headshaking and giggle at their importance to the lady lawyer, who had come all the way from Clarksville. Colin and Clara had both left the plantation. Thurman said Mr. Birney had "done moved 'em off."

Then Mary secured the services of a Mr. Waldran, a planter from Lone River, who was a ballistic expert, an authority on the ways of moving bullets. He examined the house closely and found only two marks. They were on the floor of the porch on Willie's end of the house. Mr. Waldran showed Mary how the bullets had burrowed out a shallow mark in the boards before they glanced off. He said they showed clearly that the bullets had been fired from the direction of the other end of the porch, indicating that the line of fire was parallel to the front of the house, rather than toward it.

He went with Mary to Thurman's house, and Mary had Thurman repeat the story of the shooting as he knew it.

Mr. Waldran readily consented to come and testify. He

had no interests in Clarksville, no fear of anyone there. He understood the situation fully.

When Mary finally summarized her case, she had, as her strongest witness, Thurman; second, a dozen negroes on the plantation who could repeat Lizzie's statements, and finally, for technical information, Mr. Waldran. It seemed clear to her that this was sufficient to explode any case the State might build up. She did not fear that the State would introduce Mr. Birney's grief any more than she, for the State would know well enough that it might become embarrassing for Mr. Birney before he got through with it, regardless of what effect it might have on the jury.

The most pertinent facts of the case were not evidence that Mary dared to bring up in the trial. To build the defense around the actions of Mr. Birney would be to make the conflict one between a white man and a negro. To do this might be to get her client promptly murdered, and no one in the community would have any protest to offer.

No, if Mose were to be saved at all, it must be without offending race consciousness. Mary deeply longed for sufficient protection to be able to go into court and bare the whole story, but, lacking such power, she determined on the only expedient procedure, for she was primarily interested in Mose's freedom. It would be no part of justice to sacrifice him in an effort to expose other conditions, no matter what they might be.

As the time for the trial drew near, Mose was only slightly interested in the proceedings, as far as Mary could see. He seemed quite contented, sitting in his tiny cell, thinking his own thoughts. His complete and naïve confidence in Mary and his self-satisfaction frightened her. She did not feel sure that he would be able to hold together if the State gained a conviction and she wanted so much to have Mose prove out her high opinion of his character.

"Miss Winsun," he said, "I done been ready fer de trial. Done goin to tell hit jest lak hit was. Goin to tell de truf fer shore. Hit done been a body's bliged way to do dat. Hit don't hurt nobody to tell de truf. Hit done been more good to tell how it was, don't matter what de others says. Dey can't hurt Mose cause he done got de Lord on he side. De Lord goin be settin dere besides you an me. Now jest you don't fergit dat. De Lord done been trampled on befo. Fact is, Miss Winsun, de Lord done been de mos trampled on pusson I ever know. An hit ain't never ruffle de Lord none. Dey done nail de Lord up an poke a knife in he side an done laid de crown o' thawns on he haid, an hit didn't no more'n make him groan out wunst. You can't kill de truf; you kin mess on hit a heap, you shore kin, but when you lifts it up after it done been messed on an breshes it off, hit done shine out jest lak when hit fust wuz."

XVII

THE INDICTMENT
State of Mississippi
Pelham County
Circuit Court, —— Term, 193–.

The Grand Jurors of the State of Mississippi, taken from the body of the county aforesaid, duly elected, sworn and charged to inquire into and for the body of the county aforesaid, in the name and by the authority of the State of Mississippi, upon their oaths, present that Mose Southwick, on the — day of June, A.D., 193–, with force of arms in the state and county aforesaid, and within the jurisdiction of this court, did, then and there, willfully, unlawfully, feloniously and of his malice aforethought, kill and murder Willie Stubs, a human being, against the peace and dignity of the State of Mississippi.

(signed) JOSEPH DURDEN
District Attorney

XVIII

The large courtroom is on the second floor on the south side of the courthouse. The walls are painted a dark green but the paint has peeled off in places and is elsewhere stained and dirty. In the corners of the ceiling are wasps' nests to which the insects make regular trips through the open windows. The judge's rostrum is elevated and, as the judge faces the courtroom, the jury box is on his right and before him in the rail-enclosed rectangle is a V of long tables. On one side of this V are the District Attorney and the County Attorney and with them Orvil Rutherford. On the other side are Mary and Mose, facing the jury. The court stenographer has a small table under the rostrum and beside the witness chair. The room is filled with rude benches with failing backs from which the finish is cracked. The boards are marked with indecipherable carvings made over a period of many years by the pocket knives of nervous spectators. Cuspidors are placed at strategic intervals before the V of tables and in the jury box.

The first day of the trial was consumed in the examination and selection of the jury. Orvil was with Mr. Durden. They held whispered consultations over each name. Lonnie from time to time came from Mr. Durden's office and spoke to them. The questions of the lawyers and the replies of the jurors sounded metallic against the walls. Mose did not understand much of what was taking place. He sat very quietly, did not offer to speak unless Mary spoke to him.

Mary was suspicious of some of the jurors. But she could not be certain. It seemed as fair a selection as could be hoped for.

The judge said, "Gentlemen, this is a case of the State of Mississippi against Mose Southwick, charged with the murder of Willie Stubs; have you formed or expressed an opinion as to his guilt or innocence, any of you?"

"No, sir."

"Have you any biased feeling, prejudice or ill will against him?"

"No, sir."

"Or in the case?"

"No, sir."

"Have you any desire to reach any result in this case except that to which the evidence may conduct your mind, if taken on the jury?"

"No, sir."

"Have you any conscientious scruples against the infliction of capital punishment?"

"No, sir."

"Are you citizens of the State of Mississippi, over twenty-one years old, read and write, qualified electors?"

"Yes, sir."

"Have you ever been convicted of an infamous crime?"

"No, sir."

"Have you ever been convicted of the unlawful sale of liquor within the last five years, common gamblers or habitual drunkards?"

"No, sir."

The District Attorney said to the jury: "This defendant is charged with killing Willie Stubs in June of this year on the place of Mr. L. R. Rutherford. If the State proves to your satisfaction and beyond reasonable doubt that this defendant is guilty of murder as charged in the indictment, will you gentlemen, each of you, return a verdict of guilty as charged even though by your so doing the Court is required to sentence this defendant to be hanged?"

"Yes, sir."

Mary said to the jury: "Gentlemen of the jury, the Court will in all probability instruct you that the duty devolves upon the State of Mississippi to prove the defendant guilty of the crime of which he is charged, beyond all doubt and to a moral certainty, and that it is not encumbent upon the defendant nor is he required to produce testimony of his innocence until the State of Mississippi has met that burden to the entire satisfaction of each man on this jury. Will each of you jurors go into this jury box presuming this defendant innocent of this crime of which he is charged and require the State of Mississippi to meet this burden to the entire satisfaction of all of you; will you, each of you jurors, do that?"

"Yes, ma'am."

It was nearly six o'clock when the challenges of both sides were exhausted and the jury finally accepted. The Court called upon the jury to stand and be sworn. "Do you, and each of you, solemnly swear that you will well and truly try the issue binding between the State of Mississippi and Mose Southwick, charged with the murder of Willie Stubs, and truly verdict render, according to the law and evidence, so help you God?"

"Yes, sir."

XIX

The first witness introduced on behalf of the State of Mississippi was Lizzie Stubs:

"Did you know Willie Stubs in his lifetime?"

"No, I didn't really know him."

"You were living in the house with him, were you not?"

"Yes sir."

"How long had you known him when he was killed?"

"I had just got acquainted with him at Lisbon."

"How long had you and Willie Stubs lived in that house?"

"Hadn't been about. As near as I can get at it—I don't think it was. It hadn't been only a few weeks, a few days."

"Who was living in the other side of the house?"

"Beatrice."

"And who else?"

"That was all. Just Beatrice and Mose."

"State to the jury what happened on the night Willie Stubs was killed."

"Well, it was jest fust dark, an me an Willie was jest settin an we got to talkin an one thing an another, an he got to cussin. An when we was talkin, I says to him we had done moved out in the country with strange people an if—an we was liable to be tooken sick any time. He tole me he was a member of a lodge, an I says to him his lodge was mighty far for him to be out in the country that-a-way. Then he got to cussin an I called his hand. Don't be talkin so loud.

You ought to be more quieter. Then Mose he called him. Told him he jest dared him out here, 'You son of a bitch, jest come out here,' that is what Mose told him. Willie he say, 'Man, I waren't talkin to you, hadn't called your name.' Then Mose he say, 'Dare you out here.' An we hear him comin long to our door. Say, 'Dare you out here, you son of a bitch.' He had done made it along the gallery. Willie he walks to the door an Mose he jest commence shootin an say, 'You son of a bitch, I break you from suckin eggs.' Then Willie he come back by de bed an git he britch loader an go on out in de back yard an he make one shot out dere. I got skeered."

In the cross examination Mary was unable to swerve Lizzie from her story. The negress became defiant and grim in her answers. Then Mary began to name the other negroes on the plantation, asking Lizzie if, in the presence of any one of them, she had made the statements that Willie had fired the first shot and that he had got what was coming to him. Lizzie vigorously denied having made any such statements.

When court resumed in the afternoon, Durden was sitting talking to Orvil. As they talked, they were watching Mary and smiling to themselves. Then Durden rose. "Call Thurman Watson to the stand."

Mose leaned over and whispered to Mary. "Mr. Birney done got a holt o' Thurman. I done know how hit was."

"But, Mose, he talked so honestly. He said he would do anything in the world for you."

"Yes'm, he would. But you don't know how he skeered o' Mr. Birney. You can't blame Thurman. Dey'd kill him shore."

Thurman came and sat in the witness chair. He did not look up, just sat twisting his hat in his hands.

Durden did not rise from his chair. "Your name Thurman Watson?"

"Yes sir."

"Now, Thurman, you'll have to speak louder so these gentlemen can hear you. Do you know Mose Southwick here?"

"Yes sir, I does."

"How far is your house from Mose's?"

"Not so fur. Bout a hundred yards."

"Tell us what you remember of the night of the shooting of Willie Stubs."

"I hear them fellers git in a argumint down there. I hear Willie Stubs a cussin an a raisin sand. Den I hears Mose callin to him, Mose he say, 'Come out,' now it was some more words pass betwixt 'em of dat time, but I couldn't hear what it was. I had my little baby dere was a cryin an makin a fuss but I gits de baby quieted down. Den I hears Mose say, 'Come out, I dare you to come out,' an den de pistol went to firin an after dat hit quiet down a spell an den they was another shot, a hebby shot. Mose he run up into my yard an jest as he was comin up, I say, 'Dat you, Mose?' an he says, 'Yes.' I say, 'Did you tend to dat feller; what was you shootin down dere fer?' He says, 'I got dat feller.' I says, 'Shore nough?' I says, 'Did you kill dat feller?' 'Yes.' 'Where he at?' He says, 'Don't know.' He unloaded de gun right there in my yard by the gate. An I say, 'Go way from here. Don't want no shootin here.'"

"When did you see Mose again?"

"Not twell here in dis cotehouse."

Mr. Durden dropped his pencil on the table. "Your witness, Miss Winston."

Mose said in an undertone, "Hit ain't no use. Dey done got him."

Mary walked to where she could be between Thurman and the District Attorney's table.

"Thurman, do you remember when I came to your house and you and I stood there by your gate and talked about this case."

"Yes ma'am, I does."

"And do you remember what you told me then?"

"Yes ma'am. Told you de truf."

"You remember telling me how you heard the shot gun go off before you heard the pistol shots?"

"No ma'am."

"You didn't tell me that?"

"No ma'am. Heard de britch loader after."

"Do you remember telling me that you heard Willie make the fuss with Mose?"

"No ma'am. Didn't tell it."

"After you heard the shot gun shot, how long was it before the pistol fired."

"Heard de britch loader last. Yes ma'am."

"Thurman, I want to ask you if anyone has offered you any inducement to tell an untrue story or if anyone has threatened you."

"No ma'am. Jest tells de story like it was."

"Thurman, do you remember when a gentleman, a Mr. Waldran, came with me one day; and there in your yard I had you tell the story to him as you knew it, there in my presence?"

"Yes ma'am. I remembers."

"And you remember telling him how Mose had shot Willie in self-defense?"

"No ma'am. Didn't say nothin bout it."

"Do you remember telling Mr. Waldran how you heard the shot gun shot first and then later the pistol shots?"

"No ma'am. Didn't hear de britch loader twell after."

"Then if Mr. Waldran says you told him you heard the shot gun shot first, he is either mistaken or not telling the truth?"

"Wouldn't want to say. Don't know. Jest knows I tells de truf. Heard de pistol fust."

The State introduced as its next witness the sheriff of Pushmataha County, in which Mose was arrested.

Then Orvil was introduced and questioned as to his examination of the scene of the crime. With reference to Willie Stubs he said:

"After the doctor at the store got through with him, we carried him back to the farm and put him in an outhouse. My brother went off with the deputies and I stayed there with Willie in case he needed attending to. I asked him about where he had been shot and he pulled his shirt back; first he pulled the blanket back. He was covered up in an army blanket Mr. Birney give us. He showed me the bullet hole. He said, 'I am shot right through the stomach.' He says, 'I am going to die.' He says, 'I haven't got a chance in the world. My hands are getting cold.' I felt of his hands and they were cooling off a right smart, but it was so hot that night I couldn't tell for sure. He said he had heard the doctor tell Lonnie, that's my brother, that he couldn't get well. And I turned him over to see if the bullet came out. Looked like I could see a little lump right there on the skin of his back; didn't come plumb through. He was suffering a lot, said the shot the doctor give him was dying out. Said he was going to die and wanted to tell me how the shooting happened. I said, 'All right. Go ahead.' He says, 'Me an my wife was having a quarrel. I was cussing and Mose interfered with me and I told him, damn him, I was not bothering him, hadn't said his name.' He says, 'Then Mose come out by the front and called me, dared me out, you son of a bitch, dare you. Just dare you to come out.' And he says, 'Whenever I come to the door, he shot me.' I says, 'Willie, did you shoot him?' He says, 'No. I didn't have no gun. I reached behind the trunk by the bed and got my britch-loader and I went out of the back door and I was in such misery 'til I don't know, but I think I made a shot out there. Don't know, might not have.' While he was telling me this, he was kind of moaning, kind of groaning, shaking. Then he got quiet. About midnight I examined him and as far as I could see, he was dead. They buried him the next day so I guess he must of been dead by midnight."

Later Lonnie and the two deputies, Mr. Morrison and Mr. Holly, were put on the stand. The only additional evidence they offered was that they found bullet holes in the screen door leading to the front room of Willie Stubs' side of the house.

Mr. Birney was introduced and in cross examination told Mary that it would be impossible for the jury to go to the scene of the crime and see those bullet holes for, unfortunately, an old negro woman, the widow Black, who had come to live in the house recently and who was about half blind, had overturned an oil lamp and the house had burned to the ground.

This concluded the direct evidence for the State. Mr. Durden looked quite contented, and during Mary's presentation of evidence for Mose made only casual cross examination of her witnesses; some of them he passed by without any questions at all.

The State's case had been very brief. Durden, being thoroughly conversant with criminal law, had offered Mary little opportunity to oppose his method. His witnesses were carefully trained, and Mary was not successful in cross examination in materially breaking down the body of the story of the crime as Durden presented it to the jury.

Her hope lay in proving to the jury the lies told by Willie's wife and by Thurman. That at least would be sufficient to cast that "reasonable doubt" as to the guilt of the accused which was sufficient under the law to require an acquittal. She further sensed that the psychology of the situation was reacting in her favor. Durden had been overconfident, dominating. Some of the jurors had been irritated by it. Mary had been careful to proceed cautiously, with dignity. She felt sure of her ground.

The judge seemed to feel the tenseness of the situation and the determination of each side to win. He weighed carefully each point of law that was raised and Mary had no quarrel with the justice of his rulings.

In presenting the defense, she first used Mr. Waldran. He was an excellent witness. The State admitted his qualifications as a ballistic expert. He described the cabin in detail and the bullet marks on the floor of the porch. He repeated the story Thurman had told to him and Mary. The jury was sympathetic to him, even eager in following his testimony. It offered such flat contradiction to the State.

Mary knew that Mr. Waldran had delivered a telling blow and was amazed that Durden refused the offer of cross examination. But Durden knew well enough that any insinuation from him that Mr. Waldran might be lying would be a dangerous move. Mr. Waldran's reputation was too well known; he would have dealt summarily with anyone who cast aspersions on his character. Durden rather assumed the attitude that he regarded the testimony as too trivial to be worth answering. He acted as though he had private and good reasons for so believing.

Next Mary faced the genuine problem of getting testimony from a long list of negroes from the Rutherford plantation. For they hardly realized why they had been brought. They had a great fear of anything connected with a courthouse. They were suspicious and reluctant to make any direct commitment. Mary had to wheedle their stories out of them. But she knew that the jury understood farm negroes and could interpret what they said. The simplicity of their tales would strengthen the cast of truth.

The first of these was a large, raw-boned man with expressionless eyes and ridiculously small ears planted closely against his head. He shook his head slowly from side to side in keeping with the solemn dignity of his position on the witness stand, but he deceived no one.

"What is your name?" she asked.

"Name? Name Corlis."

"What's your last name?"

"Name Corlis."

"Yes. But tell me what your other name is."

"Knapp."

"Now, Corlis, tell me this. Do you remember when Willie Stubs was killed?"

"No ma'am."

"You don't remember?"

"No ma'am."

"But you knew Willie Stubs?"

"No ma'am."

"Did you ever see him?"

"Seed him in de coffin. Hoped bury him."

"When was this?"

"Not so long ago. Not so long. Dis summer maybe."

"Did you see Lizzie Stubs, Willie's wife, at the grave?"

"No ma'am. Didn't. Shore didn't."

"You didn't see her?"

"No ma'am."

"Did you talk to her?"

"No ma'am."

"Did you hear her talk about the shooting?"

"Yes ma'am."

"Who was she talking to?"

"To de other ladies dere. She didn't know me."

"What, if anything, did she say about the shooting?"

"She say if Willie done listened to her, he be a live man today."

"What else did she say?"

"Say he done brung it on hissef. Say he done tuk a shot at Mose yonder an he git what was a comin to him. Say he done bought he sense an he had it."

"She said Willie Stubs made the first shot?"

"Yes ma'am."

"You heard her say these things at the funeral?"

"No ma'am, I didn't."

"When did you hear them?"

"When Willie was in de coffin. I hope put him in de coffin."

Mr. Durden asked the witness, "Now, Corlis, who were some of the people Lizzie was talking to?"

"I don't know."

"Just name some of them. Tell me their names."

"I don't know who they was."

"Name one of them."

"Don't know. My wife was there."

"What's her name?"

"Mirna."

"How many people were there?"

"A right smart. How many I disremember."

"And you can't remember a single soul who was there but your wife?"

"I can't make no statement."

"What do you mean by that?"

"I don't know. I shore don't."

"You are a preacher, aren't you, Corlis?"

"No sir, only a Christian. Brother Southwick can tell you that. I goes to church."

There were six more of these witnesses who told substantially the same story that Corlis had told. Then Durden interrupted. He was jocular. "If it please the Court, I would like to object to this proceeding any further. There is nothing to prevent the defense from introducing a hundred similar witnesses, and this trial might go on into the winter.

There is nothing to be gained by spending further time on this sort of evidence."

Mary said, "Your Honor, I appreciate the District Attorney's desire to save our time. But here a man is on trial for his liberty. Surely the law does not deny him the right to present valid refutation of those who accuse him. Nor is it in the province of the District Attorney to say whether or not the evidence is worth the time of the Court."

The Court said, "The witnesses introduced have presented competent evidence. The District Attorney has not objected to testimony. He can not object to witnesses not yet heard. If their testimony is incompetent, let him make his objection when it is offered, not before it is offered. Please proceed." He spoke with stinging emphasis. Durden glared at him, then smiled and slowly sat down.

Mary went on to the end of her list of witnesses. There were five more of the negroes who repeated Lizzie's conversation at the grave and elsewhere.

It is not customary in the conduct of criminal trials for the defendant to testify. The risk is too great that he may make some slip that will leave the impression that he is either crudely lying or has been taught to recite parrot-like a story his attorney has prepared. It is not detrimental to the defendant's case if he declines to testify; on the other hand, it is decidedly in his favor if he can testify coherently without allowing the State to confuse his story in any way.

Mary had discussed Mose's testimony with him. She had listened to his story as he related it, but there had been no need or desire to alter it in any way. She only cautioned him to answer slowly, to be truthful in every detail as he remembered it and to avoid any reference to Mr. Birney. She was not afraid of Mose's losing his self-control and had no reason to suspect that he would be awed by Durden.

"I wish to introduce the defendant, Mose Southwick."

He sat quietly in the witness chair with his hands clasped in his lap in schoolboy fashion. He held himself hunched forward, his head to one side and, as he spoke, he turned his face first to Mary and then to the jury. Once during his testimony he turned slightly in the chair and crossed his long legs. This was the only time he moved his body.

By now the courtroom was packed. People entered quietly and others left. Children stood in the doorway. From the corridors without came a steady hum of voices. It was an unusual drama. Tense whispers sounded in the room. Eyes long dull half glowed. Heads covered with tawny hair leaned forward and ears were cupped by rough-skinned hands. Mouths drooped, showing yellowed broken teeth within. The hot room was permeated by the smell of dirty bodies.

They studied the jurymen, who shifted nervously, trying to look dignified, realizing they were being watched. Mostly it was Mary who was watched.

The lady lawyer against Durden. What were the odds? Could anybody beat Durden? What was it? A nigger shooting? Really over a nigger girl? The nigger's wife? Was that it? Or something like that? Rutherford's boys trying to hang the nigger? And old man Rutherford not dead very long. What would he have done? Probably left town. He hated all of them. Why didn't anybody tell about the nigger girl? A damn fool question. That couldn't be done. Anybody knew that much. And Waldran from Lone River. Durden laid off him like poison. He gave them hell. He could talk wonderful, Waldran could, could shoot straight as an arrow too. No man to fool with. Durden used his head. Durden was keen, smart as a whip. That man on the end seat in the jurybox. Didn't he used to sell whisky for the boys? Sure he did. And, good Lord, there was Warren in the jurybox too. He'd run with the boys. Durden had outsmarted her. But how could she know? She couldn't know everybody in the county. Who is that now? The nigger they're trying to hang? That's a bad move. Durden'll tie him in knots. But he don't look scared. She must be mighty sure of him. It's a long shot. It'll be good if it works, but if he lets Durden break him, it'll be like roping a sick hog.

"Your name is Mose Southwick?"

"Yes ma'am."

"Mose, did you know Willie Stubs in his lifetime?"

"Yes ma'am. I did."

"I believe you and Willie Stubs lived in the same house on the Rutherford plantation."

"Yes ma'am."

"Was this a single or double tenement house?"

"Hit was a double house."

"Tell who lived in one side of the house."

"Me an my wife an Precious, her boy. But he died. He got out one night an frize to death. But that was befo Willie come. Willie an he wife they come an live in de other side o' de house."

"Do you remember distinctly the night of the killing, Mose?"

"Yes. Yes ma'am, I does. It was in de fust part of June dis year."

"What year?"

"Nineteen thuty—"

"Were you in your side of the house that night?"

"Yes ma'am. When de night started, I was."

"What noises did you hear at that time from the other side of the house?"

"Well, Willie he commence cussin, raisin sand, cussin he wife."

"Willie Stubs?"

"Yes ma'am."

"Making trouble with his wife?"

"Cussin, makin a fuss, raisin sand wid he wife."

"What did he say?"

"He told her, 'God damn it,' cussin her, fussin at her, as usual, you know. She told him he mout git sick an no people to help him out. He say if he git sick, all right, he blong to a lodge in Jackson an he won't be out nothin. She say, 'Well, you got to die sometimes,' an he say, 'If I dies, send to Jackson fer de lodge.' An she say, 'They is a preacher in de other side an I don't never hear him cuss none.' "

"Was he cursing at that time?"

"Yes ma'am, he was cussin right along."

"Yes. Go on."

"She say, 'I never hear preacher cuss at he family.' "

"Yes."

"She say, 'You ought to respect dem.' He say, 'God damn them sons of bitches.' "

"Who said that?"

"Willie Stubs say dat. And that time I spoke to him. Told him to recognize me."

"How did you speak to him?"

"I hollered. Said, 'Willie Stubs.' "

"Did you curse him?"

"No ma'am."

"Did he curse you?"

"Yes ma'am. I said, 'You got to respect me an my wife. If you don't respect yourn, you respect me.' "

"What did he say then?"

"Say, 'God damn son of a bitch, I am comin round here an kill you.' He made a big rumple in dere like he was comin. I'd been in de kitchen, lyin down in de kitchen."

"You were in bed then?"

"Well, not on de bed, no. They waren't no bed in dere. I was lyin on a pallet."

"What happened then?"

"So I goes to where my pistol was an gits hit an walks out to de gallery. He had come cross his'n, opposite like, standin by de steps, you know, had he britch-loader down side o' him. Well, when I walks out, I was tryin to talk to him, tryin to git him to pologize. An when I gits out dere, gits to talkin, he says, 'You son of a bitch, youse bad anyhow, I'se goin to kill you.' Throwed up an shot, an de meantime he shoots, I jest reached in my pocket . . ."

"Where were you then?"

"I was standin by the far end of my gallery. So I jest pulled up my pistol. I shot three times. How many times I hits him, I don't know."

"Mose, at the time you shot Willie Stubs, did you believe your life was in danger?"

"Yes ma'am. He'd done made one shot at me. I knowed it."

"Did you know at that time whether or not you had hit him?"

"Not fer shore, but he kind o' bent over like he was hit."

"Where did you go from there?"

"I went on— I started over to Mr. Birney's, an Thurman he hollered at me."

Durden interrupted. "I object on the ground that only the State can prove flight."

The judge said, "Yes, you can't prove anything after the shooting. It's not part of the res gestae."

Mary continued. "All right then, Mose, did you hear any shots after those three you fired?"

"Didn't, no ma'am."

"That is all."

The witness chair was raised somewhat from the general level of the floor, being on the same rostrum on which the judge's bench rested; so Mose's head was higher than Durden's by two feet. Durden asked his questions rapidly, pecking. Mose answered slowly, deliberately. It was with the same expression he might have had if brushing gnats from before his face as he followed the plow. But it was in no way disrespectful.

"Mose, how long had you lived in this house?"

"Some time. Since befo de last winter set in. Since right after crops was in las fall."

"Now, as I understand it, when you first came to live in this house with Willie Stubs, you all had an agreement that if at any time he cursed in his side of the house, or you cursed in your side of the house, you were to call each other down?"

"No sir."

"No such agreement?"

"No sir."

"So everything was peaceful all those months, everything was harmonious?"

"He hadn't been dere dat long."

"But there wasn't any trouble after he moved in?"

"Yes sir."

"Then you overlooked telling about that just now?"

"No sir."

"You didn't overlook it?"

"No sir. I waren't axed."

"Well then, it comes up to the night of the killing. You were in the kitchen, you say?"

"Lyin down, yes sir."

"And they were in their side of the house and he was cursing his wife?"

"Yes sir."

"He didn't say anything to you?"

"Called me a son of a bitch."

"That was after you interfered with him?"

"It was she spoke to him of me. He say, 'God damn them sons of bitches.' That was when I called his hand."

"What was that; you said you heard a rumpling sound?"

"Yes sir. I was scared he was comin to kill me."

"And you dared him out?"

"No sir."

"That didn't happen?"

"No sir."

"So he took the shot gun and shot at you."

"Yes sir. He did."

"You believed you were in danger?"

"Both of us was in danger."

"How far was he from you?"

"No piece a tall. Jest a few feet."

"And he didn't hit you at all?"

"No sir."

"Did he hit the house?"

"I don't know. It was dark. I didn't hear it if it hit."

"And then you went up to Thurman's house?"

"Yes sir."

"And you talked to Thurman Watson there in his yard?"

"Yes sir."

"And you emptied your pistol, didn't you?"

"No sir. I didn't."

"You didn't empty your pistol?"

"No sir."

"You didn't have five empty cartridges in your pistol?"

"No sir. I didn't only have but four cartridges in all."

"And you didn't leave any empty shells lying there in the yard?"

"No sir."

"When you shot Willie Stubs, you were standing then sort of up toward his door?"

"No sir. I was on the back end of my end of the gallery."

"But his door was in the general line?"

"No sir. He was out some by the steps."

"After you reloaded your gun there at Thurman Watson's, what did you do?"

"I didn't reload. I didn't have no cartridges."

"Where did you go from there?"

"I went by Mr. Birney's."

"You never got there, did you?"

"I got nearly dere. I seen him give Mr. Birney de gun."

"All right, then where did you go?"

"Back home. Knocks at de window an calls my wife out."

"Then what did you do?"

"Went to Carter's Point."

"You went to Carter's Point?"

"Den I cotched a truck, went to Memphis."

"How long did you stay in Memphis?"

"Jest a few days. I didn't have but a little money. I couldn't find no work."

"Then where?"

"Went to St. Louis."

"Stay there long?"

"Not long. I wuked a steamboat but hit laid up."

"After you got through visiting in St. Louis, where did you go?"

"Up to Illinoy."

"Didn't go to Chicago?"

"Got pretty close. Got to Peory."

"Got up that far before you used the telephone?"

"What's that?"

"Didn't you phone back to let people know where you were?"

"No sir. I never even written a letter."

"Then where did you go?"

"New Orlins."

"Didn't get to California this trip?"

"No sir. I didn't."

"Utah?"

"Never been dere in my life."

"When you were in New Orleans, what name were you going under?"

"Goin Mose Southwick. Went Mose Southwick twell I gits to Lebanon."

"That Lebanon, in the adjoining County of Pushmataha?"

"Don't know what county. Hit was Lebanon all right."

"What name did you go under there?"

"Joe Haney."

"Joe Haney?"

"Yes sir."

"You also called yourself the Reverend Haney, didn't you?"

"No sir. I won't be Reverend twell I gits ordained."

"You haven't been ordained?"

"No sir."

"Why did you change to Joe Haney?"

"I was afeared I'd be cotched."

"Scared they would catch you? You said you hadn't done anything. You acted in self-defense?"

"It was self-defense. I believes in God."

"And so, because you thought this man was coming to kill you, you shot him?"

"No sir. I didn't fire on him. He fired on me but he miss me."

"Then you shot him?"

"Yes sir."

"Then you decided to travel."

"Yes sir."

"When the sheriff came up to arrest you, where were you standing?"

"I waren't standin. I was a settin."

"Where were you?"

"I was workin fer Mrs. Wilks. Had wuked all week, wuked twell Saddidy dinner, waitin to go to my dinner, waitin fer her to pay me off an I was settin on de steps dere."

"What did the sheriff say to you?"

"Says, 'What is my name?' I says, 'Joe Haney.' He says, 'Come up dere an pull my hat off.' He says, 'You is Mose Southwick, you come long.' I says, 'You got me. I is de very one.' "

"You said, 'The truth ain't going to hurt nobody?' "

"Truf ain't goin to hurt nobody."

"And then you told him all about your travels?"

"He axed me."

In redirect examination, Mary asked, "Had you known Willie Stubs a long time? Did you have a long-standing quarrel with him?"

"No ma'am. Never see him befo he come to de place."

Mose had been sitting so long with his legs crossed that one leg had gone to sleep. When he rose, he stumbled. He caught at the table and steadied himself. Mary said, "Is there anything wrong, Mose?"

He laughed. "No ma'am. My foot's done went to sleep. Hit like to have throwed me." He reached his chair and sat down.

It was all over, Mary thought. No, there was something else, one more thing. She could see him coming down the aisle now, old Lon Rutherford, dignified, arrogant in his worn suit, holding his hat at his side, not deigning to look at the people who stared at him. He was on the stand. Durden was afraid. Orvil and Lonnie had gone from the room. He was telling them what happened. The judge was leaning forward, amazed. He was rushing on, talking rapidly about things that did not concern the trial. The judge was banging his gavel, trying to stop him. She must quiet him somehow.

She brushed her hand across her face. No. He was dead

now, beyond the reach of anyone. Even Truth could not penetrate the inaccessibility of the grave.

The Court was waiting on her. She turned to Mose. "Is there anything you can think of to tell the jury that we haven't told them?"

"Well, no ma'am. Done seem like you tole 'em a right smart already. Only I'd like to tell 'em how I feels bout hit an all. Jest like to talk wid 'em a little bout hit."

"You can't do that, Mose, of course."

"Den I don't guess dey is nothin more."

Mary rested the case for the defendant.

It was early afternoon. The judge said, "It seems that the issues in this case are pretty clear. I don't want to deny anybody's rights and if you don't agree with me, you can say so. But I would like to wind this thing up. I wonder if we couldn't adjourn for an hour and then have the arguments of counsel and get this case to the jury maybe by supper time. I don't want to hold this over until tomorrow."

The lawyers agreed. Mary did not leave the room, but sat with Mose.

He said, "What you think? They hang me maybe?"

"You can't ever tell what a jury will do with a negro, Mose. It's not like it is with white people. But if I know anything at all, those men haven't got any notion you are guilty."

"Yes'm, dat's jest what I figgered mysef. I been settin here studyin dey faces. Don't look to me like dey thinks much o' Mr. Durden. An dey's some o' dem what didn't look kindly at him. He ain't de mos pleasin man. But hit done been Mr. Orvil an Mr. Lonnie what's runnin dis place."

Mary said, "Yes, that's the trouble. That's what I'm afraid of more than I am of Mr. Durden."

Mary knew about what Durden would say to the jury. She had heard it all before, a hundred times, couched in different language, perhaps, and adjusted to other circumstances, but in essence the same. She was wondering how sometime it might be different.

But it seemed useless to hope. The practice of criminal trial by jury is so ancient and venerable that few dare to question its fundamental strength and rightness. For so many centuries it has functioned largely in the distribution of essential justice that like many other institutions it has withstood changes that would have made it parallel to the changing social order instead of anachronistic. Trial by jury is undoubtedly a praiseworthy attribute of society, but it is no longer needed to protect a weak people from a monarch. The power now lies in the people themselves. They need to be protected from themselves. That, she remembered, was what Higgins had said. That the strong should not wear themselves out on the weak.

She thought of the bitter clamor of hatred that would meet the suggestion that negroes be tried before negro juries. That was what trial by jury meant, to be tried by one's peers. It was not a desirable change. Yet the difficulty remained.

The everlasting fallacy of judging the present solely by the past.

Awaiting Durden's words and listening to them, Mary knew that these reactions had no practical value. Not in a short hour could those men sitting there, mouthing their tobacco, be changed. There was no hole in their armor where the shaft of a new idea could break through. No, they must be appealed to in the manner of their fathers and grandfathers.

Durden was talking to the jury, and they were sitting as onlookers will at a spectacle where life is in danger.

"I appeal to you as good, true gentlemen, substantial citizens, guardians of this community. I call upon you to do your duty in preserving this community from the menace of a murderer. You have listened to the testimony of men who have been for many years prominent and respected in this county. Against their evidence you are offered, for the most part, the word of a handful of farm negroes come to try to keep a friend of theirs, their preacher, from paying the just penalty for his crime. Gentlemen, I ask you, in all fairness, if you can properly consider the testimony of those negroes as important beside the testimony of the witnesses of the State? You know negroes, gentlemen. Can you turn this murderer aloose because they say they heard somebody else say that somebody who is now dead did something that only two people can actually testify about, and those two are Lizzie Stubs and Thurman Watson, and you heard what they said? The evidence of the murderer himself you do not need to consider. What else could he have said? What would you have said if you had been in his place? Exactly what he did, of course.

"Now, let's go back and take up that testimony just as each witness gave it. . . .

"In conclusion, gentlemen, let me remind you what you swore to when you went on this jury, that if you thought this man guilty beyond a reasonable doubt, you would return a verdict of guilty even if by so doing, His Honor were forced to sentence him to be hanged. Gentlemen, there is only one law in a murder case. Counsel for the defense will have a whole book of instructions read to you. And why? Just to befuddle your minds. Mose Southwick thought maybe he could kill that man and be justified because he hadn't been ordained. I asked him that. He said he hadn't. I'm wondering, gentlemen, if he ever will be ordained."

When she spoke to the jury, Mary tried, as far as she was able, to address them quietly, as she would have done if they had been sitting in her office, asking her thoughts on an important question.

". . . The thing to consider is that we, you and I, as members of this social group here, owe it to ourselves, to our own self-respect, to act justly in the problems of our lives. It is up to us to meet each situation as it arises by calling upon the best that is in us. It is this which makes for the progress of our community. That man sitting there is innocent. If you convict him, you will be wronging this state as much as him. Believe that, gentlemen, and weigh your decision carefully.

"You have considered with me the testimony of each witness.

"The law says that you have no right to convict that man as long as any reasonable doubt remains in your minds as to his guilt. Can you believe that the evidence offered in his behalf does not create even a doubt about his guilt? That law reads that way to protect innocent men. Some day you and I may have need of the protection of that legal principle. It behooves us to strengthen and not weaken it.

"Objection has been made to the character of the defendant's witnesses. Remember this, gentlemen: he is a farm negro, living isolated in his cabin, and his closest associate outside that cabin is his mule. The negroes that came to testify for their friend, for he was their friend, he was a friend to all men, did not have the gift of learned speech; they could not be expected to, but what they said is as highly valued under the law and in the sight of God as the speech of men who have had better advantages.

"I feel very deeply, gentlemen, that you and I are not so much trying this defendant as we are trying the State of Mississippi; we may all have different reasons for loving this our home but I am sure you feel with me that it should not emerge from this trial with a name less fair than before."

Murmurs of approval rustled about the courtroom as Mary sat down. The judge blew his nose and rapped for order.

When the bailiff came to conduct the jurymen from the room, one of them gathered up the written instructions of the Court and carried them with him to the jury room. Before the sheets were divided up among the several jurors, who used the backs of the pages to make notes, one of the men read them aloud. It was on these sheets that were written what might be termed the rules by which the game should be decided. Some of these rules echo those high moments when legal phraseology has come close indeed to poetry:

> "The jury cannot find the defendant guilty merely because they may believe that it is more probable that the defendant is guilty than that he is not, and if the jury believe that there is only a probability of his guilt, it is the duty of the jury to return a verdict of not guilty.
>
> "The presumption of innocence in behalf of the defendant is not a mere idle fiction of the law but is a

substantial muniment of his defense, following him from the inception to the conclusion of his trial and as the voice of a living witness of unimpeachable character testifying in his behalf.

"It is the policy of the law to require that the life or liberty of a human being shall not be taken as punishment for a crime charged against him unless and until his guilt is so clearly established that there remains no reasonable doubt of it.

"Before they can convict the defendant, the jury must believe from the evidence beyond a reasonable doubt, both that the defendant intended to kill the deceased, and also that he did not believe, and had no reason to believe, that he was in danger of death or great bodily harm at the hands of the deceased; for, if he did so believe, and had good grounds so to believe, he had the right to take the life of the deceased intentionally."

Mose was taken back to his cell to wait until the jury had agreed on a verdict. The spectators filed slowly from the room to return to their homes or to near-by lunch stands for supper. The air was hot and close and the sounds of the moving and talking people in the somber corridors were as the insistent beat of self-animated wooden drums. Mary felt the pressure of her wet hair about her head under her tight hat.

She wanted to stand forth from the crowd and call upon them to stop and realize the importance of the outcome of this present deliberation. But the people shuffled slowly about the dirty floors, talking among themselves. This decision meant nothing to them one way or another. It was a fight on which they had no wagers, nothing at stake.

Mary went back to her office and sat at her desk writing at a paper that was to be filed on the following day at the County Clerk's office, trying to get her mind off the case at hand. A servant girl came to the door.

"Yore mama done sont me down wid some supper." She laid a sack of sandwiches and a bottle of milk on the table. "She done know you'd likely be goin thout yore victuals."

Mary thanked her, and when the girl had gone, she placed the sack and the bottle on the window sill. The cream was thick and yellow in the top of the bottle. It should be put on ice, she thought. Otherwise it would be sour in a few hours.

It was after eleven o'clock when the phone rang.

The voice said, "The jury says they have come to an understanding. The judge says he'd like for you to come right over. The District Attorney's already here."

They came and sat at the tables again. The jury filed in slowly and took their places in the jurybox. The door to the judge's office was opened and everyone stood as he entered the room. Above them the insects were a black whirl about the electric light globes.

"Gentlemen of the jury, have you agreed on a verdict?"

The foreman stood up. "We have, Your Honor." He took a piece of paper from his pocket and handed it to the clerk.

The clerk unfolded the paper and read it. "We, the jury, find the defendant guilty as charged and fix his punishment at life imprisonment in the penitentiary."

The judge said, "Let the defendant stand up."

Mose got up, leaning against the table.

"Mose Southwick, the jury has found you guilty. Have you anything to say before this Court passes sentence on you?"

"No, jedge, only begs fer mercy."

"Under the law of the State of Mississippi, I have no alternatives in this sentence. Wherefore, Mose Southwick, for the murder of Willie Stubs, this Court hereby sentences you to be confined in the state penitentiary for the period of your natural life for such offense of murder. It is further ordered by this Court that you, Mose Southwick, shall stand committed until all of said sentence shall have been served."

The judge paused only for a moment. "Court is now adjourned."

Mose turned and steadied himself on the table. "Miss Winsun, he didn't say nothin bout hangin, did he?"

"No, Mose, nothing at all about hanging."

"Will dey take me straight off to de pen?"

"No, Mose, I'll try to get you a new trial, and if I can't do that, I'll take it to the Supreme Court. That will mean a delay of several months. They'll have to keep you here until then. Keep your courage up, Mose."

"Yes'm, hit ain't botherin me none. We done did our level best. I was jest flustrated a minute, you know; he mout a said somethin bout hangin. I didn't know."

The noise of voices in the courtroom rose to a hostile clamor, harsh, clashing. Many stood staring at Mose as they took him from the room. The people began to depart in small groups. The sounds of voices became less frequent, echoing between the dark walls. Mary finally rose, took her brief case under her arm. The janitor was coming in to turn out the lights. He said, "Good evenin, ma'am," and touched his hat. When Mary reached the street, the courtroom above was a dark recess behind the high narrow windows.

The cell block was very hot. Mose could hear the breathing of the other prisoners. A drunk in the far cell was crying. Mose listened to the persistent sobbing. The man was hardly conscious of what he was doing, it seemed. Mose knelt and lifted his face toward the window and the stars without, his lips unmoving, his eyes almost unseeing. Then for a long time he walked barefoot up and down the cell waiting for the torment within him to cease. He lay down on the bunk, his hands under his head, his eyes open wide. After some time he could tell that dawn was about to break. He could make out the bars of the cell now. He rose and placed the stool by the window and leaned his head heavily against the bars. Out there it was quiet; a gray behind the black was coming to life, bringing with it the trees and cabins, restoring the world that had been taken away. He got down and washed his face, lay on the bunk again and slept.

XX

DURING the week that followed the trial Mary found that the town had been far more interested in Mose's trial than she had suspected. Groups of men discussing it on the street corners and in the lobby of the Alhambra Hotel would suddenly become silent when she passed. But now and then some individual who was sure he could not be overheard would come by her office or stop her on the street.

"It was a great fight, Miss Winston. It plumb done this town good. Ain't nobody in years throwed such a scare in the District Attorney's office. They ain't likely to pull off no such stunt as this again soon. I don't think this town would stand for it. By golly, Miss Winston, you just ought to have gone in there and told off on old Birney for sure."

But to her question as to what could be done now for Mose there was no ready answer. No one was willing to help or to do anything where his name might be known.

Then one afternoon a member of the jury called her on the phone. "I'd like to talk to you, Miss Winston," he said. "That is, if you wouldn't mind running by my house. I'd rather not come to your office because everybody knows I was on the jury and I don't want nothing said about this."

Behind the closed doors of the man's home Mary began to get a definite confirmation of rumors she had heard. "They's several of us was on that jury that's downright sorry what happened. I just wanted to tell you I was sorry. Don't want you to think it was nothing you did. You put up a good show and you got the jury with you. Only they was picked men on that jury and they was things come out in that jury room on that nigger that like to have got him hanged. Sure did, Miss Winston."

"Could you tell me what was said?"

"Well, no, I can't. You see here is how it was. One of the men on the jury said he had some information of a very private character about that nigger that we ought to have the benefit of, but he'd be letting himself in for it if anybody found out he had told us since he had swore he didn't know nothing about the case and all. So we all made an agreement that we wouldn't never tell what it was. But it was pretty bad, what he said about the nigger. We couldn't turn him loose after that. I just wanted you to know how some of us that was in on it felt about it when we come to see how we had been put on."

"Would you give me an affidavit about this?"

"Well, no, I couldn't do that."

"Would you be willing to go before the judge and testify to this, if the Court would permit it?"

"I might do that. I'll see about it. I'll let you know."

XXI

RENARD was more explicit. "Oh, I heard it all," he said. "Haven't hardly been in my office for days. You gave them a good run. It was well handled. But the game was all decided before you started. Don't you see that?"

"You know that?"

"Durden had his picked men on that jury. That fellow with the gold-rimmed glasses. They tell me he's been running with those Rutherford boys for years. Seems like everybody knows it now. Only nobody would do anything about it when they could have. It's bad luck."

Mary said, "I know pretty well what happened. But nothing very definite. Nobody will talk. I don't see why they are all so afraid of Durden, but they are. I guess it's because Durden's crowd has been running the county so long, doing whatever they wanted to. But I think I can get one of the jurors to go before the judge; maybe I can get a new trial. I'm sure Durden wouldn't have the nerve to try the case again."

"Don't you see you can't do it? Durden knows his game. He has the law now to protect him. No juror can impeach his own verdict. That's a good law. It works hardship sometimes but it's a good law all the same. Like all things, some good, some bad. I just thank the Good Lady when there's more good than bad."

"You mean that if these facts were presented to the judge he would still let the verdict stand?"

"Oh, he probably knows all about it by now without you to tell him. But he is powerless. He can't hear such evidence. It's strictly forbidden by the law. He might have thrown the jury out when they returned the verdict on the ground that they had not acted as reasonable men would; he has that power if he wants to take it; he might have instructed them to acquit the defendant. Nobody would have disagreed with him. But he has elections and one thing and another to think about himself. It takes a strong man to be a fine judge. He can't take any chances with his political future over a nigger. I refused to, didn't I? You're trying to fight too much all at once."

"Then we can't get a new trial?"

"No, there is no way. It is all over; forget it. But think this: you have got people interested in what's been going on. Durden is scared himself. He didn't think it would amount to as much as it has. He wishes to God he'd never seen that nigger. You have done Clarksville a service."

"And Mose goes to the penitentiary just the same?"

"Don't take it so hard. There is the governor. That is the way. We could get him a pardon maybe. Wait a year or two until it all blows over. Then get your client free in a quiet way. No one knows then. It's all forgotten. Get some good, representative people to petition the governor. The governor's no fool. He can see through what happened just as well as you and I. He knows how these little towns work. He'd likely be willing to help you."

"I'll take it to the Supreme Court first."

"Yes, you might. But I think it's useless. The judge was

very fair to you in the conduct of the trial. There is no reason for the Supreme Court to reverse him. The jury is everything in the criminal case. The Supreme Court is very careful about reversing such decisions. They are so far from the scene of the trial. They can not act except on points of law. None were violated."

"Mr. Renard, would you argue it for me before the Supreme Court if I prepare the briefs? I couldn't do it myself. You could. It wouldn't take much time."

"Yes, Miss Winston, if you ask me, I just will."

"Thank you. I'm going to count on you."

"I'll do my best. I don't promise it will help any. But you have thrown a scare into Durden. It did my heart good."

XXII

IN SPITE of what Renard had said, Mary entered a motion for a new trial. Perhaps by some chance she could gain the judge's approval of her motion, and if not, she might be able now to get some evidence into the record which would give the Supreme Court an idea of what had happened in the lower court.

She persuaded the juror to come and testify. She placed him on the stand and began to question him, but to every question Durden made the same objection, that a juror could not impeach his verdict. For a long time Mary tried framing her questions in different ways, hoping that the judge might allow one of them. But the judge was firm in his adherence to the letter of the law. Finally he said, "It seems that counsel for the defendant has only one purpose in this action. The Court has now ruled on that point several times. Do you have any other point to raise?"

"I believe not, Your Honor. But I think these questions should be entered into the record."

"Under the law," he replied, "they must be stricken from the record and the Court so rules.

"The motion of the defendant is overruled."

Durden gathered his papers into his brief case and hurried from the room.

Mary stopped and spoke to the judge. "Judge Rutledge, could I talk with you a moment?"

He appeared anxious to hear what she might have to say. "You certainly could."

"It is irregular, I know, for me to ask you about this case. But it is out of the jurisdiction of this court now. It was in your power, arbitrarily, to grant a new trial. Why didn't you do that?"

"Well, I tell you, Miss Winston, I could have done it. But it's a dangerous thing to do. Your client was well defended. I'm not trying to flatter you. He had every benefit of the law. Maybe he is innocent. That is not a matter on which I can ethically express an opinion. But the point is this. When I grant a new trial, I am establishing precedent. Precedent is a mighty important thing in court practice, as you know. The body of the law is a sacred thing and not to be dealt with lightly. I do not feel that I have the right to exert the power of my court too far. There is no telling what evil effects it might have if precedent permitted this power to be used freely. It might be a source of endless corruption, thwarting the only protection of society against criminals. Once in a while an innocent man suffers. It is the price we pay for protection; it is the cost of human imperfection."

"Frankly, what do you think the Supreme Court will do on an appeal?"

"Although no one would believe it, I hope they will reverse this case. Of course, that's my personal feeling, Miss Winston, and I know you would not repeat what I have said. But what I think they will do is another matter. There is only one place where you have a chance."

"You mean the governor?"

"Well, yes, you can try to get a pardon. But what I really meant was the Supreme Court of the United States. I have great faith in them. If they wanted to turn our court procedure topsy-turvy, I would feel confidence in their ability to foresee what it might lead to. Perhaps I am only admitting my own weakness. I am a smaller man who must lean where there is greater strength than I have."

"It is out of the question. It would cost a great deal of money, which we do not have. But I wish it could be done. That's thinking of Mose, of course. What I really want is to see this situation remedied right here. If the Federal Courts interfered in a case of this kind, it would do more harm than good. It would stir up everybody in the State of Mississippi to bitter resentment. And we have no right to expect that every time something like this happens, we can make somebody else bear the burden of setting things right. These courts belong to the people of this state, and no lasting good will come until the people themselves take action. This is not the business of the United States; it is Mississippi's business."

"I hadn't thought of it that way. I guess you're right. I was only thinking of it from the point of view of the law. I love the law, Miss Winston. It's a noble institution."

"That has suffered a sad profanation," she added.

"Remember this too. Perhaps it's not to my credit. I'm not a young man any more. It would be difficult for me to re-enter the active practice of law. I have served on the bench many years. I have tried to be a fair judge. I depend on this job now for the support of my family, my children. There are limits beyond which I can not go. The people elect the officers who prosecute for them. I have nothing to do with that. The people get what they want."

"Thank you, Judge Rutledge."

XXIII

THE year was drying up. The cold smoke of winter was beginning to drift across the town and fields in the early mornings, carrying the dampness and chill of the river.

They said that, Mr. Rutherford being dead, Mr. Birney was drunk most of the time now and seldom at the plantation at all. What had become of the crops was a subject for speculation and doubt.

It was a source of sadness to Mose when he heard about it. He had somehow identified the making of that cotton with the fullness and competence of himself. He wondered if there might be anything symbolical in this general waste and neglect.

"Me an Thurman would a shore made fur fly if I'd a been out dere dis fall. Hit was a sweet field, Miss Winsun. Jest you go out some time an take a look at hit. I'd a made a fust class farmer."

"I've been out, you know, Mose. I've seen it. It was fine."

"Miss Winsun, you ought to git yosef a farm. An when we gits dis here bizness fixed up, I kin wuk hit fer you. I kin handle niggers good. I'd wuk like de mischief, I shore wud. Hit would be de beatenest farm on de whole Delta. Wouldn't be a weed nowhere."

"Don't you forget that, Mose. I'm going to hold you to it."

"Yes'm, I don't fergit nothin. Once sumpin git inside

me, I holt on hard. I shore does. I'd like bein on a good farm where wouldn't be nobody to bother me, where a body'ud jest left me do my wuk. I'd like to take Thurman wid me. Me an him could wuk fine togedder.

"When you goin hear word from Jackson?"

"Not much before spring, Mose. And we must be prepared for anything that comes."

"So dat's how it stand? Well, jest like I tole you, we done did our level best. Can't nobody blame us."

Mary could not be sure if Mose meant to be joking her or not. He was not looking at her, but rather toward the open window and the shadows the bars made across the floor. He was leaning across the table, so she could not see his face except from the side. But he spoke very seriously, with an abstract sadness it seemed, distant.

"I don't want to be no bother. If you didn't have nairn you could jest say so an hit would be all right."

"What do you mean, Mose? Is there something you want?"

"Yes'm. It's gittin long where it cool off a heap toward mawnin an I can't sleep sometimes I git so chilly. I shore could use a little kivver. I couldn't never stand much cold. I axed de man here fer some but he ain't give me any. But don't bother none."

XXIV

In the spring Renard went down to Jackson to argue the case before the Supreme Court. When Mary received his wire stating that the Court had refused to reverse the original decision, she was not particularly surprised. She had hardly believed the outcome would be different.

Later she read over the decision feeling that somewhere here existed a fault in the technique of legal procedure for which some day she would find the practical solution.

The Court said:

"The appellant, Southwick, was tried and convicted of the murder of Willie Stubs, and was sentenced to the penitentiary for life.

"A statement of the facts of this case would not be profitable. Suffice it to say that the evidence offered on behalf of the State, if believed, made out a case of murder. The evidence offered for the defendant, if believed, established self-defense. The defense offered a dozen witnesses who contradicted Lizzie Stubs, a witness for the State, in that she had made frequent statements that Willie Stubs, the dead man, was to blame and had fired the first shot at the appellant, Southwick. There were other contradictions of witnesses in the record, all of which made it a case of conflict on the facts and a question properly and only for the jury. So, there is no merit in the contention that this Court should reverse the case, because the evidence overwhelmingly preponderates in favor of the appellant.

"It is insisted that this case should be reversed because of the argument of the District Attorney, reading as follows: 'Gentlemen, there is only one law in a murder case. Counsel for the defense will have a whole book of instructions read to you. And why? Just to befuddle your minds.' Objection was made to this argument. The Court did not, in words, rule on the objection, but said, 'It is argument; you can reply to it,' to which exceptions were made. This was equivalent to an overruling of the appellant's objection.

"We are not of the opinion that the argument in this case permitted by the Court constitutes reversible error; but it is our opinion, from an ethical standpoint, that such argument should not be permitted. Counsel ought never to suggest to the jury that the instructions given by the Court should be disregarded.

"We have quoted the language in the case at bar in order to disapprove it, and to warn those officers of the law, whose duty it is to present cases to the jury on behalf of the State, that it is far better to stay within the beaten paths of legitimate argument; and courts which grant instructions ought not to be inferentially changed with befuddling the jury in granting instructions.

"We find no reversible error herein."

Cold, impersonal, those words. The law become articulate; mutterings from a distant impenetrable shrine; oracles not to be questioned. This decision had as much relation to the truth about Mose Southwick as if it had been a page from a story book. And yet there it was, dogmatic and final, like the seals placed on a tomb, as binding as a potent and awful curse.

And how seldom, Mary thought, men are judged on the facts of their lives. If you would attack a man most forcefully, there is no need to study the weaknesses of his character, for that is too arduous a process. Rather seek out that day in his career when he has offended against the common level of society. Perhaps you will call him Tory, Hessian, Red, atheist, communist, socialist, nigger or Christian. It only depends on the date and the geographical location as to what label will be most effective in rousing men against him.

XXV

DURING the following week, there being no further legal means to prevent such a move, the sentence of the original court was carried out and Mose was taken from the jail to the penitentiary or prison farm situated some few miles out from the town of Collinsville, which is south from Clarksville.

Mary had previously told him of the decision of the court, but on the morning of the day when he was to be taken away she went to the jail and asked permission of the jailer to speak for a few minutes with Mose. The jailer said there was no reason why she might not do so as the officer who was to take Mose had not yet arrived nor was he likely to come much before time for the noon train.

Mose was seated on the bunk which was attached to the cell wall. Mary stood by the door to the cell and talked to him. He had prepared himself for departure. A small bundle of possessions, the nature of which Mary did not know, was tied in a blue rag ready to be carried with him. His face was washed and shiny and he sat in an attitude of quiet expectancy.

"Good morning, Mose. The jailer said I might have a little talk with you before the officer came to take you away."

"I preciates you comin. I shore does. But effn you hadn't come, I would a knowed you had good reason. I did sort a want you to come an say good-by like. Maybe I don't git to see you no more."

"Oh, yes, you will, Mose. Now I want to tell you a little about the life on the farm. The work will not be unlike the work you knew at the plantation. Only of course you will be in a prison. They will guard you in the fields. You will have to work hard. If you should be disobedient, they would whip you; if you tried to run away, they would shoot you. I want you to be good, Mose. Then after a time they will make you a trusty, and it won't be so hard on you."

"You needn't worry none bout me not bein good. I don't mind workin. I never did. Body ain't got no right not workin. He mus earn he keep."

"And I don't want you to get down-hearted, Mose, and get to feeling sorry for yourself. Don't do anything desperate. They would be sure to catch up with you. I'm still trying to help you and I won't be able to unless you make a good prisoner."

"Miss Winsun, you knows I wouldn't do nothin to dispoint you. I'm goin to do my level best. Ah'll git trusted. Folks dat knows me always trustes me. Always has. I don't know why hit is, but people turns to me. I done been boun to hold up."

"I am going to the governor for you, Mose, to try to get you a pardon. But we can't do that yet. We must wait, maybe a year or two, until the people who have been against you have forgotten about you."

"Yes'm."

"I did the best I could for you, Mose, and I'm sorry I couldn't do any better than this. But it was no use. They had it all fixed beforehand."

"Yes'm, hit was use. I don't see why you says hit waren't."

"I'm glad you feel that way."

"You know, Miss Winsun, dat man can't git here too soon to git me way from here; I done want to git my feet on de groun again. Hit's been powerful cramped here. Hit ain't de sort a place a body gits tatched to. No'm, hit ain't. No chance to do nothin. Only set an study. I has been here mos goin on a year. Dat's a long time to study. A body git hissef mos studied out. Hit won't be so bad at de farm. I'll have somethin to do, more folks to talk to.

"Tell me, did you ever git ary word from Beatrice? You know Beatrice was my wife."

"I know who you mean. No, Mose, I never did. No one seemed to have seen her or to have heard where she was."

"Well, de night I left she was standin dere in de fiel. I didn't see which way she tuk out. She said she was goin to Lisbon. I guess she changed her mind. Beatrice was good to me dat night. She want to give me her money. I tuk de half of it. It ain't dat I keers bout seein her but I worries sometimes. Beatrice waren't nobody to look after hersef. I spec she done got hersef in trubbel. When you has lived wid a body, you don't never fergit 'em."

Then Mose began to laugh, quietly, to himself. It was a deep, booming note, rising resonant in the small cell.

"Hit jest struck me funny. Hit done make me recollict, you an me here wid long-drawed-out faces like somebody was goin to die.

"Dey was a old cullud woman live down crost de bayou frum de plantation. Didn't nobody know how old she was or nothin bout her. Dey said she could cunjur. De cullud people was skeered o' her. I don't take no stock in cunjurin mysef. But she was a hand to lay misery on people. Said we was all a bunch o' sinners an she was goin to call de wrath down on us.

"Say she done sont a dollar to Memphis an got hersef a member o' some lodge. She say de man at de head o' de lodge had a third eye an he talked wid de Lawd an could see what was goin come to pass. Every once in a while she git a letter frum Memphis what would lay out to her what was goin to happen.

"Den she git one what say dat on count o' her sayin how we'd done been such sinners, de Lawd done decide to swallow us up. She say dat come midnight on a Friday bout two weeks off dey would be a stawm an de river would retch out an swallow up dat whole section down roun de bayou. Wid dat she go off to Lisbon an tole evybody else to repent an git out too. Well, didn't nobody else git out, but hit was talked roun a heap. Dey all say she didn't know what she talkin bout an dat de man at de lodge didn't have no third eye anyhow.

"But, Lawd, Miss Winsun, late dat Friday afternoon de clouds laid down all roun black as tar an de lightnin commence to poppin an evy once in a white hit would split a limb offn a tree. Den hit git dark an commence to rain. An hit roared an hit thunder like de end was comin shore nuff. By evenin evybody on de plantation had done tuk to de road fer Lisbon. I was settin on de gallery watchin 'em an dey waren't losin no time neither. Looked like a bunch o' drowned rats carryin lanterns. Some of 'em was in wagons an some of 'em was on de groun. Dey'd holler at me, 'You better come on, Mose. Dat river's shore goin retch out an swallow you up.' But I know hit was jest a stawm."

"Weren't you even frightened, Mose?"

"Well, yes'm and no'm. Hit did peer mighty funny fer dat stawm to come up on de very night she say. But I'd done make so much fun o' her, I jest natchly didn't dast to run off.

"De stawm hit died down bout de middle o' de night an de stars come out pretty as you please. You never see such a lot o' people in yore life as come stragglin back de next mawnin. I didn't have de heart to say nothin to 'em. Cose de cunjur woman she say she done tuk it up wid de man in Memphis an dey git de Lawd to put hit off, seein as evybody done run off anyhow."

Presently the jailer came in and said, "The officer has arrived who will take Mose to Collinsville." Mary started to turn away. "I think I'd better go now, Mose. Good-by. Remember I'm still looking out for you. I'll try to come down to see you in a few weeks. If you need anything, they will let you write me a letter. I'm going to write to the warden about you."

"Thank you, Miss Winsun. I'm goin to be all right. Don't you worry none."

Mary went out of the jail and returned to her office. In a little while she heard the train come into the station, then she heard its whistle as it left and she knew Mose was on his way.

She walked to the window, thinking of Mose and his suffering, and how the hands of all men had been shown empty before him. Far down the track the whistle sounded again, quick and faint, and it seemed to Mary to be the pulsing call of the endless movement of human misery.

XXVI

THURMAN had no peace. His friendship for Mose had been very real to him. Mose was the only person who had ever set off an upward-looking way of life in Thurman. The memory of that day in the courtroom with Mose sitting unresentful was an ever present torture.

He had tried several times since the trial to see Mary, but she had sent word each time by Uncle Moly, whom Thurman employed as his minister, that she did not want to see him because she did not trust him or anything he said.

Then one morning after Mose had been taken from the jail Uncle Moly came into her office. "Miss Winsun," he said, "you done ought to talk wid Thurman. Dis here de foth time he been here. He ain't rid neither. He done walk all de way to town to see you. He have de misery to see you."

"All right. Tell him to come on up here. I'll talk to him."

Thurman came meekly into her office.

"Thurman, I don't see how you have the nerve to come up here after what you've done. It was shameful. Why, they might have hanged Mose just because of what you said. And Mose was good to you. I know he was."

"Yes'm, I knows hit."

"Well, what do you want?"

Thurman sighed deeply. "I jest wanted to git right. I ain't been right wid mysef. I wouldn't want to die wid hit on my soul. I couldn't stand it."

"What do you propose to do about it?"

"I jest wanted you to know how hit was. I jest wanted to tell you bout it an all so's you'd unnerstan; I had to tell somebody. I'll do anything to make hit right. I shore will."

"I know about what happened, Thurman, already. You just want to tell me about it then?"

"Yes'm, I wants to tell you."

"Would you be willing for me to write it down and let you sign it? Would you swear to it? If you want to do that, it might help to get Mose a pardon. But it may get you into trouble with Mr. Birney if you do it. I want you to understand that clearly. If you make a statement, I will want you to tell everything just as it was, even about Mr. Birney. You know Mr. Birney would be mad with you."

"Yes'm. I don't keer no more. I jest wants to help Mose."

"All right then. You tell it to me. Talk slowly and I'll write it down. Then we can get a man to see you sign it. I'll read it all over to you before you sign it. Is that what you want to do?"

"That's all right."

Mary was unable to reproduce Thurman's story exactly but she tried in so far as possible to do so. She did not wish to give it any color by adding her own thoughts in any way. Finally she read it all aloud to Thurman to see if he wanted to change it in any detail.

"I testified for the State of Mississippi in the case of Mose Southwick, when he was tried for killing Willie Stubs. The case was tried at Clarksville, Mississippi, in —— of 193–.

"Before the trial I talked with Miss Mary Winston about what I knew about this killing and I talked with Mr. Birney and Mr. Durden and I talked it over with Mr. Waldran,

when he was at the plantation examining the house where the killing took place. On each of these occasions I told the same story, which is this:

"That I was sitting on my front porch on the night when the killing took place and that the first thing I knew about any trouble was when I heard a heavy report of a shotgun fired from the front porch of Mose Southwick's house and that it was followed by three pistol shots and then there were no more shots. That I waited a few minutes where I was and I saw Mose go by in the direction of Mr. Birney's, the manager's, house. I called to Mose and asked him what was the trouble up at his house and he told me there had been a shooting.

"I asked him did he kill Willie Stubs and he told me he did not know but he thought he had hit him. He went on off then toward Mr. Birney's house. This story states the true facts of what happened.

"The story I told on the witness stand was false. I did not hear any words at all that night of the killing. Mr. Birney, Mr. Orvil Rutherford, Mr. Lonnie Rutherford and Mr. Durden caused me to tell the falsehoods I told on the stand. When Mr. Orvil Rutherford found out I had talked to Miss Winston, he talked to me alone and asked me what I had told her. I told him how it was. He then told me what I must say on the stand about Mose firing the first shot and the quarreling and that I must say that I heard Mose dare Willie to come out on the porch and that I heard the shotgun shot after the pistol shots. I did testify to all of this, but it was false.

"Mr. Orvil Rutherford told me that if I did not testify to these things for him, he would have me put in the peniten-

tiary. He told me that he was very influential and powerful in Clarksville, that he stood in with Mr. Watson, the sheriff, that he was a deputy-sheriff himself, and the sheriff would do anything for him. He also told me that he was very close to Mr. Durden, the District Attorney, and to the County Attorney, and that they would put any negro in the penitentiary that he wanted there, and that they would protect any negro from going there that he did not want convicted of a crime. He told me that if I did not want to go to the penitentiary, I must testify as he told me, for he wanted to see Mose go up; that Mose was not guilty of murdering Willie Stubs, for he shot Willie in self-defense, but that Mose had refused to take a whipping when Mr. Birney tried to whip him shortly before the killing and that any negro at Lisbon who refused to take a whipping from a white man who wanted to whip him had to serve time if Orvil Rutherford had anything to do with it. He said he could put me in jail and would, if I did not do as he said, and Mr. Durden would do it for him. I agreed to do as he said and to testify as he told me.

"Mr. Birney talked to me several times about testifying as Mr. Rutherford told me. He said if I did not do it, I would very likely be beaten to death and that he would help to do it. Mr. Durden and Mr. Rutherford both told me at different times that I would be paid money if I would testify as they told me and that I wouldn't get a cent if I testified for Mose. Several times they went over with me what I was to testify to. But they have not paid me any money either then or since.

"Mr. Rutherford found out from me that I knew some of the talk about Mr. Birney living with the wife of Mose

Southwick and with other colored women on the plantation. He told me I must deny all of this if I were questioned about it and I promised to. He told me I must deny knowing anything about Mr. Birney wanting Mose killed and knowing Mr. Birney gave his own gun to Willie to kill Mose with and telling Willie to pick a fuss with Mose and kill him and that he, Mr. Birney, would get him out of it. I promised not to tell any of it.

"I told Mr. Durden I had told Miss Winston a different story and she had written it down and I had also talked to Mr. Waldran and I was afraid they might do something to me if I storied about it. He told me they could not do anything to me because they could only prosecute through his office and he would not prosecute me.

"Mr. Lonnie Rutherford said in my presence several times before the case was over that the jury was going to be a fixed jury and that Miss Winston thought she was sure to clear Mose and that all the time she did not even have a chance. That the jury would give Mose life because the jury was fixed by him and Mr. Orvil Rutherford, that he had friends on the jury that he could depend on and that they would carry the others for him, that he had attended to it all himself, that he could not leave it to Mr. Birney, for Mr. Birney did not have brains enough to fix a jury.

"Just before the lawyers' arguments in the case were finished, I was sitting in Mr. Durden's office at the courthouse with Mr. Birney and Lizzie Stubs and Mr. Orvil and Mr. Lonnie Rutherford and, I think, Mr. Morrison. Mr. Orvil Rutherford sat down at Mr. Durden's desk and wrote a note. His brother watched over his shoulder as he wrote and at one time told Mr. Orvil Rutherford to correct something that

he had written, which Mr. Orvil did correct. Before Mr. Rutherford wrote this note and as he wrote it and after he had finished writing it, he stated aloud to us all that he was writing this note to the jury, that the jury was fixed and was sure to convict Mose but that he was doing this one more thing which would make everything certain, that he was writing a note to the jury telling them something that would make them convict Mose. Mr. Birney asked him what the note said but Mr. Rutherford did not tell him in my presence. He said he would deliver the note to one of the bailiffs in charge of the jury and that this bailiff would see that the jury got it and that everything would be all right. He finished the note, writing in pencil, folded it up, and went out. He came back in about five minutes and said to Mr. Birney that the jury got the message and that it would be all up for Mose. He did not say to which bailiff he gave the note."

Mary said, "Do you want to take it and read it over to yourself, Thurman?"

"No, ma'am, I can't read."

At Mary's request, the notary whom she called in read the paper to Thurman. Thurman said he understood it and did not wish to change anything. The notary acknowledged his signature.

"I jest want you to tell Mose I didn't mean him no harm."

"Mose knows that. He told me so himself."

"I kind a felt Mose would know. But I didn't want him to hold no hard feelins."

"I don't think he does. I'm sure he doesn't."

"You reckon maybe Mose goin to haf to stay in de pen a long time?"

"I can't tell. We will have to wait a while and then we

can try to get him a pardon. I don't know how long it may take."

"You don't hold no hard feelins on me no more, do you, Miss Winsun?"

"Well, I feel you did very wrong, but I guess I couldn't blame you. You've done the best you knew."

"Yes'm, I has. I guess I is jest triflin anyhow. I guess I ought to go on back down on de Yazoo. Git on way frum here. I ain't seed nothin but misery since I left my mammy."

"Maybe things will get better. If Mr. Birney tries to bother you, let me know. I hope things will work out better for you than they have been."

"De Lawd bless you. I shore would like to git away."

"And you be sure to go down and see Mose. He'd like to know you thought that much of him."

"I shore will do hit. I'll jest have Luella make him a mess o' victuals fer me to carry. Mose did like Luella's victuals."

XXVII

THE prison farm is west of Collinsville and runs for several miles along the river. It is beautiful. The land is black and fertile; the roads and drainage ditches are well cared for. But one does not enter its confines without feeling depressed and melancholy, for here and there in the fields one sees groups of uniformed men working. Perhaps they are singing monotonously of their labor; and sometimes they look off beyond the horizon and become silent; but the pause is only momentary, for following behind them are other men carrying rifles. These men are prisoners also; they are ever vigilant. To kill an escaping prisoner usually means a reward which is measured in so many years of sentence returned, as it were, to the faithful guardian.

Sergeants or overseers direct the work. They are unarmed. They seldom speak to the men, only when it is necessary to give instructions.

The prisoners working do not resent the vigilance of the men with rifles. They know it would be the same with them. They look forward to the time when they too may be made trusties. There will be no hard work to do then, only a rifle to carry. Perhaps a man will try to run away; a clean shot might mean immediate release. Then there would be nothing to hold one back, to keep one from going straight down the middle of the road, back to the Free World, as the prisoners call it, back to children's laughter and freedom from the endless enforced routine, an hour to do every little thing, a certain way to walk in line, to sit at table and eat, always the same day after day, until the days make weeks, months, years, many of them. Even if one is sentenced to prison for life, that does not prevent his thinking of the Free World; he will not be in prison forever. "No, no," he finds himself shouting, tears running down his face. But then he remembers; he becomes silent, working, trying to stem the flooding ache and misery.

The camp building is a two-story brick structure, a long rectangle, rising abruptly and in contrast to the monotonous extension of fields; the upper floor is divided by a wide hallway into two rooms. The walls of each room are whitewashed and along the floors are two rows of twenty-five closely placed cots. These are the cages. The prisoners come here after the evening meal and do not leave until morning. There are bars across the windows.

The faces of the men are sometimes deformed in brutality; more often they are dull and almost expressionless, but in each there is a deep subdued sadness. Sadness is the all-pervading atmosphere of their lives and mingled with it is enforced toil. Every action, though it may superficially show curiosity, fear or hatred, is but a transmutation of sadness. It is so limitless that it thrusts itself out into the sound of an occasional note of laughter, making it fall dead and hollow against the walls.

No one who has brought fruit from the earth has failed to observe the earth's pain as it lies hard and black and broken while the roots grasp it, sucking out its vitality. The earth is conscious; it swells and groans in the spring to bring forth, and in the early winter its hoary flanks are deeply written with destruction and retribution. How all things have their awakening, their flower and their decomposition in the earth. Yonder lie the forest's fringes, the fields of broken clods and over all the smoky haze from off the river, the earth's own ancient exhalation. Powerful, but weary, and crying in unhappiness.

And looking out through the barred windows across this expanse the prisoners find no relief. Their sadness is re-echoed until it goes mounting and ringing off against the clouded boundaries of heaven itself.

In spite of what he may have said, Mose never really believed that he would be sent to prison. It took some time for the fact of imprisonment to enter his mind. And beating against his dogged unspoken cry to stop while he might reorganize himself was the procession of activities of this new life, giving him no time to perceive rationally what had taken place, to find how he might adjust himself. For many days he moved automatically, terrified, cheerless. He hated the very earth beneath his feet and loathed its dark resentful taunt. He remembered that he had loved the peace of order. Here everything was ordered. But there was a vast difference. Perhaps a day here might be the same as a day in his cabin as far as the movement was concerned. It was that the horizon lights had somehow been changed, deadened, so that they no longer cast anywhere any hue of brilliance. It was a colorless purgatory of physical toil. The soul of man had been extracted and extinguished.

It seemed as if all the evil and corrupted decay of a more than evil world had been visited mountain high upon his tortured frame. Mose no longer loved. This was death.

He had never known before how deep a man may walk and yet retain breath. The very life-giving sun brought only a tormenting heat. The food within him was negative and leprous, prolonging useless activity, a rope that tied him into a pattern he no longer cherished.

The sight of a lash rising and falling against the form of a man provoked only a casual ache. And when the same lash fell against his shoulders, he found it was not the physical pain that impressed him so much as it was wondering how long a man's strength would permit him to beat another without pause.

Many times Mose thought of dropping his work and running across the fields toward the woods. There was the probability of death and the possibility of freedom. Rather it was almost a certainty of death. As he thought about it, there seemed nothing else to do. Death, unknown as it might be, held no feared ways more awesome than this present. But he could not do it. Something in him held him fast.

And upon this seed that Mose could not name or identify life began to grow.

He passed into resignation wherein he toiled and slept and cared not. The intense weariness he had experienced on first being put to work after so many months in close confinement was gone. His strength was returning and he began to feel again his own physical superiority and bodily grace.

He found himself singing in his work and pushing hard upon the heels of the man in front of him. He broke the earth with merciless exertion, grinding his own consciousness against this resisting medium. He was watching the plants, literally daring them to refuse to grow under his severe hands.

Then one day as he came down the rows, he noticed here and there tender green squares lying wilted and parched on the hot earth. He dropped to his knees and examined them in fiery anger. These were the young bolls from which the cotton must come; without them the luxuriant plants were a fruitless mockery.

With the squares in his hand he went to the sergeant.

"Them boll weevils has been a cuttin at my cotton. You goin haf to do sumthin bout dis. Dis fiel goin be ruint in no time. Ain't no use to wuk de lan to feed no boll weevils wid."

The man took the squares in his hand and examined them, looking curiously at Mose at the same time.

"That's right, Mose," he said. "We're going to have to look after your cotton better than this. I'll go straight to the manager and see what can be done about it."

Mose turned away, muttering to himself, began turning back the leaves of the plants, seeking out this pest to destroy it.

He remembered what he had said to the man, was amazed. "My cotton," he had said. He looked off across the field. "My cotton"; he repeated it.

It was several days later when the sergeant called Mose to him one evening after supper. "They tell me, Mose, you're a preacher."

"Well, yes sir. I done preach some. I ain't never been ordained."

"Then maybe you could use this. Maybe you'd like to read it of an evening before you go to bed. It used to belong to one of my boys and he most wore it out, but I guess you can still read it all right." He held in his hand a small Bible.

"You goin give hit to me?"

"Yes, you take it."

Mose took it slowly. He did not open it then but placed it reverently inside his jacket. He wanted to thank the man but at the moment was unable to. He bowed slightly, turned and hurried up to the cage.

Mose was happy. Here was an occupation for his few leisure hours. He was deeply touched by this simple act of kindness. No friendship had been offered him. That was not possible, he knew. He did not ask for it. But the gift was significant; it was recognition; it set a mark and an obligation upon him that he could not reject.

Not long after the sergeant stopped Mose again. "There wouldn't be anything to prevent your doing a little preaching around here on Sundays if you wanted to and anybody wanted to listen to you," he said. "You could use the side porch on Sunday evening. It would be all right. Only you'd maybe want to be careful what you said, that's all."

Mose was very serious now.

"I'd shore like to, indeed I would. I can talk to my people so dey unnerstans me. I knows how dey feels. I does fer shore."

The other prisoners were doubtful and suspicious. A preaching might be only the warden's voice coming through his spokesman. Sunday was their only rest day, not to be lightly wasted on foolish enterprises.

But Mose did not show his bitter disappointment when the gathering on the porch was pathetically small. A few came to lounge on the floor and sit along the railing. They were not too attentive at first, but gradually they became quiet and only Mose's voice was heard. It was no longer the voice that had echoed in the meeting house. It was quieter now and more forceful, beating insistently in even modulation, proceeding from deeper sources of experience. No pulpit now, no setting to lend dignity; only a man in prison stripes standing talking to a group of fellow prisoners.

"My brethren, where de Lawd's word am spoke, am de Lawd's temple. Yestiddy dis was de porch long side de cage. Now we is in de Lawd's holy church."

He walked back and forth across the porch, making gestures.

"You see, here is de Lawd's altar all laid out wid silk an gold. An here am de mourners' bench. Long side here over dis way am de Amen Corner, where de old mens sets to lay dey voices on to de Lawd's word.

"You all is a settin out dere in de great church. De windows done retch up so high you can't see where dey ends way up dere in de loft. You looks up dere an thinks maybe you sees angels flyin back an foth while de Lawd peers down over dey shoulders to where you is a settin all wrapped up in fine clothes. De sun am a settin an where hit shine through de windows, de shadders falls cross yore haids an you can't tell but maybe hit's de Lawd Jesus walkin long by de river in de evenin, lettin his shadder fall cross his people.

"Now you all is a settin dere an de music done stop but you hears hit fer a minute or two, rollin on round de church an ruslin out de windows an doors. Den de preacher, he step up an you commences to ask, whisperin roun, Now wonder what's he goin to talk bout dis evenin.

"An de preacher he say:

"My brethren, I'm goin to talk to you dis evenin bout de Free Worl.

"Man done been bawn a prisoner, done been a settin all

he days in a jail house, wailin in de misery an de pain. He done have burdens to tote roun wherever he go an hit done gall de flesh an make wounds in de body. An hit seem like he ain't no better'n things dat has to crawl roun on de groun thout never bein able to lift deysefs up to de light.

"Man don't have no joy, don't have nothin to laugh fer, nothin to sing glad bout. He jest mourn, an de soun of he voice am dark an he don't know how hit all goin to end.

"He don't know where all de misery come from. He don't see no reason fer hit. He beat he fistes on de groun an curse he own name an wish he hadn't never been bawn.

"An all de time he look away off crost de edge o' nowhere to where folks say dey am de Free Worl. Folks say fine things bout de Free Worl an evybody want to git dere. But dey is in a prison an dey can't git away. Dey burdens is chained to 'em.

"But one night in de dark, man am a settin by hissef thinkin an studyin an hit seem he can't bear de burden no longer. He riz up an bust he chains off an set out runnin cross de fiels.

"Pretty soon he hears de houns snufflin an a bayin on he tracks an he know dey is after him to fotch him back. An he run all de harder. By an by he come to de swamp he got to cross, an de water am black an full o' snakes, an de mud pull at he feet to hold him back. But he fight on twell he am wore down to nothin. He know dat maybe he am goin to die tryin to git away but he don't keer none, he keep on goin.

"But dis man am very strong. He git on past de swamp where de dawgs can't follow de trail no longer. An after a long time he come to de Free Worl.

"He shout fer joy an sing twell de tears run down he face,

an he am so happy hit most kill him. An he jest go roun all day shoutin how free he am. But pretty soon he git plumb wore out wid shoutin an singin. People don't pay him no mind an he commence to feel like a man what didn't have but only one arm or one laig.

"Folks commences to axe him don't he never do nothin an hit worry him. He don't want people to think he ain't right. Folks says, How come you sings? You ain't got nothin to sing fer. You don't never do nothin. You ain't no count nohow. An den de man he open he eyes a little more wider an he see all de other people is totin burdens jest like he done tote befo he come to de Free Worl. An dey swings dey burdens roun right sprightly an seem to like hit too. An he set an study bout dat a long time.

"Den he go to somebody an he say, How come you don't let me tote dat long wid you? An de man let him tote a little of hit an dey tote hit all de day. At night after he been totin all day, he tired but when he see how fur dey got, he pleased wid hissef an' smile all over.

"An in de early mawnin o' de next day he go off by hissef where won't nobody see him an he commence to pray. He say, Lawd Jesus, I wants my load back. I done been in misery. I wants to carry my load long wid de others, so's I can be happy like dey is.

"An he look an he see de Lawd Jesus standin dere smilin at him so he fall down on de groun, but Jesus he say, You git up an walk long side o' me. So he gits up an he see den dat de Lawd Jesus am carryin de cross on he shoulders. It am mos heavy an Jesus he jest kin stumble long under hit. So he say to Jesus, I is stronger'n you is. You lef me carry hit. An he take de cross on he own shoulders an dey walk long side o' each other all day twell dey comes in de evenin down by de river side. Den Jesus he say, You can't come no further. You is got to go back. I done give you my cross fer yore burden.

"You is been wantin to git to de Free Worl. Can't no man git to de Free Worl thout he have he cross wid him. Don't make no difference what kind of a cross, jest so's he have one. An one more thing. Git love in yore heart. You love yore brethren an love me an you is in de Free Worl. De Free Worl ain't nowhere. It ain't no place. You can't tetch hit. Hit am in a man's heart. An den Jesus say agin, Love me.

"Den he step out on de water an walk cross to de other side. De man look up den an he sees a whole jubilee o' angels a playin on dey harps an in de middle am Jesus an he done took up another an a bigger cross dan what he give de man to carry.

"Den de sun commence to git lower an hit git dark so's de man can't see de Lawd Jesus no more. An he turn roun an go back wid he cross."

XXVIII

IT WAS a summer afternoon before Mary was able to go to Collinsville to see Mose. Although she would be unable to give him any definite encouragement about the pardon, she felt that the visit would show him she was still interested in him and that he would be cheered by this thought.

The day was clear and hot. Along the top of the levee in the distance the air danced in vibrant waves. In the broad fields that surrounded the squat prison buildings the convicts were working the cotton.

The warden had Mose called from the field and told Mary she could talk to him there in the prison yard. He assured Mary that Mose had been an excellent prisoner and that just as soon as the rules permitted him to do so, he would see that Mose was made a trusty, which would give him more freedom.

Mary stood at the gate and watched Mose striding across the fields and then up the dusty road. There was no defeat in this man, surely. His head was held firm and his body swung easily. He seemed healthier than when she had last seen him.

"How are you, Mose?"

He wiped the sweat from his face with the sleeve of his jacket. "Jest doin fine. We shore goin have a fine crop dis year. Done hear de warden say so hissef."

"Do they treat you well, Mose?"

"Yes'm, can't complain none."

"They don't beat you?"

"Well, no'm they don't. Jest give me six strokes."

"Six strokes? What do you mean?"

"I didn't count off. You see, when we comes in of a evenin, we has to count off, an I fergit to cause I was new, an effn you don't count off, hit's six strokes. I don't think dey shore nough wanted to beat me. Jest think dey wanted me to git de taste o' de leather so's I would be good. An I ain't fergit no more.

"I wants you to take a look roun here befo you goes. I likes hit here by de river. I likes cuttin bresh on de levee so's I can watch de river."

"Mose."

"Yes'm."

"I haven't forgotten that I was going to try to get a pardon for you, but we will have to wait a while yet. I am going to do the very best I can. It may take a long time. But I don't want you to lose hope."

"No'm, you needn't worry none bout me. De sergeant done lets me preach on Sunday evenins on de gallery an I goes to de hospital too an talks wid de boys what's sick. I wouldn't be sprised none if I gits de job regular. De warden done tole me on de side like, he say, 'Don't you say nothin bout hit but I'm countin on you to do good mongst de boys here.' Hit's done got to where dey likes to come to preachin. Cause I'm no different from what dey is. I ain't uppity none."

"That's just fine, Mose. I don't want you to feel badly about my not coming down sooner. But it's a long drive down here and I just haven't been able to get away."

"Dat's all right, Miss Winsun. I ain't tole you bout de airplanes, is I?"

"I don't think so, no."

"De govvermint done got airplanes what flies over de fiels an blows out a pizen smoke to kill de bugs an de boll weevils. Hit shore do kill 'em too. You kin walk long an see 'em layin on de groun."

"Mose, aren't you even interested in what I was trying to tell you about the pardon?"

"Yes'm, cose I is. But I done know we is did our best. Can't nobody blame you none.

"Ef you jest step a little more to de side, over by de gate here, you kin see out better. Now you answer me de truf. You ain't see a prettier fiel o' cotton nowhere, now is you?"

"It is fine, Mose. You ought to be proud of it."

"Hit's what I been tryin to tell you. I done been shore nough proud. I done feels like hit was mine."

Mary did not say anything more about the pardon. Mose took her on a tour of the prison buildings, through the hospital ward, the great kitchens and bakery and the quarters of the convicts.

At dusk the guards began to come in with groups of eight or ten prisoners each. Mose stood with Mary watching the men line up, count off and go to the cages.

"Dat's what I fergit. To count off. I don't fergit no more."

There was nothing Mary could say. Mose was beyond her now.

They stood there a few moments longer. Then she turned to him. "I must be going on, Mose. It's getting late. It will be dark soon."

"I hates fer you to have to drive back through de dark by yosef."

"Oh, I don't mind."

When the car reached the turn in the road, Mary looked back. In the twilight Mose was standing just inside the gate, his arm lifted in a gesture of farewell. Mary waved in return and Mose was lost from view.

Mose turned back to the building and walked up on the porch looking out to the river. It was growing dark. The moon lay deep in the top of the distant forest blackness, casting a warm glow across the heavy-scented air.

In his heart was the crying of many unexpressed emotions. He was wondering what victory really was and how this land about him could sometimes be so beautiful and sympathetic.

He looked out across those fields of toil, across the wide ridge of the levee and the black mud flats, to where lay the river, silent, majestic, silver in the moonlight. On the other side was dimly seen the sweep of other fields and over all the limitless night, holy, touched by the hands of peace.

THE END

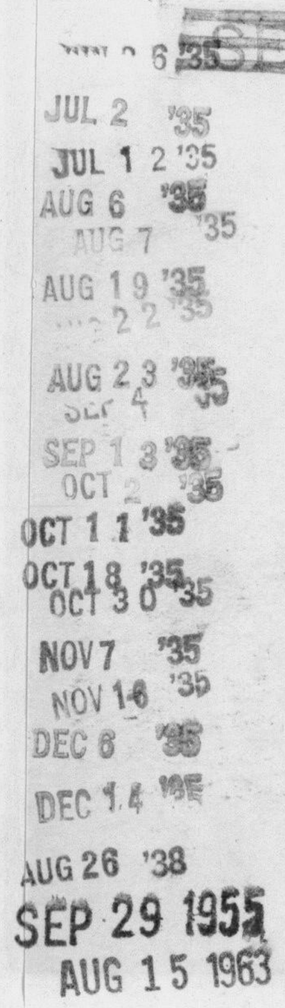
JUL 2 '35
JUL 12 '35
AUG 6 '35
AUG 7 '35
AUG 19 '35
AUG 23 '35
SEP 13 '35
OCT 2 '35
OCT 11 '35
OCT 18 '35
OCT 30 '35
NOV 7 '35
NOV 16 '35
DEC 6 '35
DEC 14 '35
AUG 26 '38
SEP 29 1955
AUG 15 1963